# THE LION KILLER

## THE DARK CONTINENT SERIES BOOK I

# JAMES GARDNER

D1595386

# PENNINGTON PUBLISHERS

# THE LION KILLER

PENNINGTON PUBLISHERS

PENNINGTON PUBLISHERS

ISBN 978-0-9760898-1-0

Trade Paperback
© Copyright 2009 James Gardner
All Rights Reserved


Requests for information should be addressed to:
Pennington Publishers, Inc.
PO Box 740020
Boynton Beach, FL  33474
sales@thelionkiller.net
www.TheLionKiller.net
www.PenningtonPublishers.com

Pennington Publishers and the Pennington logo
are imprints of Pennington Publishers, Inc.

Cover Redesign: Donald Brennan / YakRider Media
Interior Redesign: Donald Brennan / YakRider Media

Printed in U.S.A.

FOR BARBARA

# ACKNOWLEDGMENTS

I would like to thank my editors: Barbara Gardner, Michael Takiff, Tad Knutsen, John Jolley, Mary Cole and Lisa Burns. Special thanks to my agent, Marianne Strong. I'm grateful to some great raconteurs who must remain anonymous because of political uncertainties in Zimbabwe. I owe special gratitude to some good friends who were very supportive: Bill Flaherty, Bob Barrett and Eileen and Joe Cornacchia.

# PART ONE

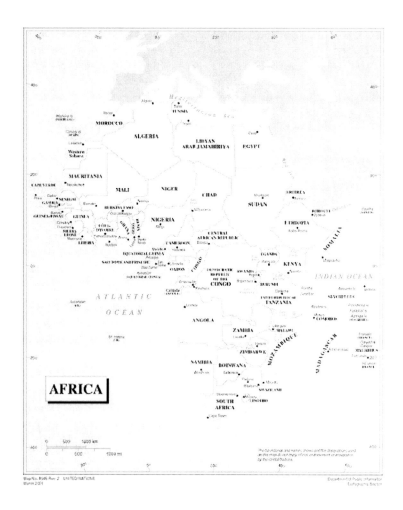

AFRICA

Department of Public Information
Cartographic Section

# 1

# BWINDI, UGANDA

## Africa

A blowfly clung to the underside of a leaf on a red-hot poker tree. The weaverbird perching on one of the tree's orange flowers, cocked its head to identify the insect. The bird tried to dislodge the insect by pecking, but the blowfly held fast.

It was time for the blowfly to seek out the carrion that would sustain its maggots. If the female started its search too early, it would have to fly through hungry jungle birds. If the fly waited for darkness, it risked being eaten by white-bellied bats. The weaverbird gave up on the blowfly, hopped off the flower and onto an adjacent twig where it caught a purple butterfly in its beak. After smacking the butterfly on the twig, the bird swallowed it and flew away.

A gentle wind from the Congolese mountains carried an odor. Sensory cells on the blowfly's antennae detected decaying flesh. The blowflies spiraled up through the canopy of mahogany and ironwood trees. The insect's harmonic hum hushed the rainforest. The silence spooked a colobus monkey; she tucked her baby under her belly and climbed higher in an ebony tree. A bongo antelope stopped browsing to investigate the stillness. The only sound was the hiss of a waterfall. Below the swarming insects there were pink orchids and yellow flowered creepers suffocating thorny fruit trees and fig palms. Flocks of brown honey guides and yellow-throated bee-eaters took to the air. For the birds, the smell of death meant a meal of blowflies.

Some flowers secrete a scent of rotting carrion to attract insects for pollination. This time the blowflies would not be fooled into pollinating tropical flowers. Nor would they stop to feed on chimpanzee or mountain gorilla dung. The flies swarmed over the top of the crab-wood trees and stands of bamboo. Red-breasted starlings and wattle-eyes picked them off by the thousands, but their numbers were overwhelming.

The insects followed the scent to a clearing. There were eight gas-bloated human corpses. The female blowfly landed on a man's eyeball, crawled across his face and disappeared into his ear. After depositing her eggs, the insect exited the man's ear canal and landed on the woman's face lying next to him.

A man wearing a white smock leaned down and pulled back a tarpaulin covering a woman's body. Her pink toenails indicated a recent pedicure. Her trimmed pubic hair was fringed in razor stubble. He uncovered the rest of her body. The nipple of her left breast was missing; it showed evidence of a human bite. The bullet that ended her life had entered her left temple, damaging the optic nerve, leaving one eye open and one closed. The man trapped the blowfly in a test-tube as the insect crawled out of the woman's nose. He sighed and corked the glass tube, labeled "Calliphoridae—from female cadaver number 5."

Graham Connelly jumped out of his mud-spattered Land Cruiser and ran into the undergrowth, where he vomited. He emerged from the bushes embarrassed. Ian Laycock handed him a surgeon's mask that had been soaked in camphor. "I say, old boy, not feeling well today, are we?"

"What the hell's going on here? Why haven't these bodies been taken someplace where they can be cooled down?" Graham asked, wiping his mouth.

"Don't blame me. The Ugandan military has taken control of the situation, which means nobody's in control. This should put a crimp in Uganda's eco-tourism. Here's a list of the dead ones." Ian handed the list to Graham. "We're having trouble identifying the bodies. I've rounded up the victims' passports, but we can't match them up. The hyenas have been busy. Why do they always chew off the faces? It looks like all of the women were raped. Bloody savages. Here's my report. Any questions, before I head back to Kampala?" Laycock asked, handing him the report.

"Who's the geek collecting the bugs?" Graham asked, blowing into his cupped hand.

"Dr. Malcolm Rutherford. He's a forensic entomologist from

Nairobi. Very well informed, our doctor. Did you know that these bug doctors can identify cadavers' DNA taken from the digestive tracks of maggots? You're not going to be sick again, are you?" Laycock asked, grinning. Graham nodded no, but was unconvincing.

Lycock retrieved a pinch of ostrich biltong from the breast pocket of his khaki jacket and stuffed the dried meat into his mouth. He chewed and rolled it from one cheek to the other, and then gulped down the gristle like a pill. He walked over, twisted a thorn off of an acacia bush and used it to pick his teeth.

"Jesus, bon appétit. How can you eat?" Graham asked, nodding at the bodies. "I wonder if there's anything in this world that could ruin your appetite. Give me your report. There's nothing I can do here. Embassy Security Chief was supposed to be an adventure. I never thought it would be like this."

"My friend, you missed Rwanda," Ian began. "This is a garden party compared to what the Hutus did to the Tutsi population. Eight hundred thousand Afros killed in one-hundred days. The bodies were so thick on the roads that we had to drive over them. They made the most dreadful popping noises. And let's not forget what's going on in the Darfur. That's what I call proper family planning."

"Ian, you're a wonderful humanitarian, a real credit to our Queen. What about the missing American?"

"Nothing as of yet," Laycock answered. "The dead ones include six Americans and two Brits. A French woman, the safari guide, and his Ugandan tracker are all being treated at the clinic in Kasese. The Afro's name is Peter Gono. He took one hell of a beating, but it looks like he'll make it."

"We need to make sure the proper authorities notify the families before the BBC gets on to this. The American woman who survived, what's become of her?"

"She's been taken to the American Embassy in Kampala. They tell me she's related to some VIP in the States."

"You're sure her husband is missing?"

"Yes, but what do I know? I work for British intelligence."

"British intelligence! There's a lovely oxymoron." Graham smiled at his own joke.

When Laycock spoke it was around another mouthful of biltong.

"Very funny. You should try your comedy on the telly. See you back in Kampala. Don't lose the report, it's my only copy. Are we still on for Sunday?"

"Wouldn't want a minor international tragedy to get in the way of our golf match, now would we? See you on the first tee at nine bells. I need two more shots," Connelly insisted.

"You're a thief. I'll give you the strokes, but you're buying lunch."

"Done. See you Sunday."

Laycock didn't answer. Instead, he raised his hand in acceptance and waved goodbye.

Connelly studied his friend in the rearview mirror. Ian Laycock had worked in Africa for almost thirty years. The military coups, the famines and the genocidal lunacy had changed him. Britain's influence on the continent had dwindled to little more than pomp and ceremony, which meant Africa, had become a cemetery for Foreign Service careers.

Connelly found his friend's disparaging remarks about Africans odd, given the fact he was living with a Ugandan woman. Laycock's wife, like many Europeans, had not liked Africa. She returned to England, and as her visits became less frequent her husband took a black mistress. When his wife stopped visiting all together, Laycock's arrangement became permanent. It was a common but frowned-upon indiscretion.

Connelly drove down the mountain road away from the carnage. Halfway down, he passed a line of military vehicles heading in the opposite direction. Christ, now you show up, he thought. Closing the window didn't lessen the stench. He pulled over and picked up Laycock's report.

### The Bwindi Massacre

This is the eyewitness account of safari guide Robert Neff as collaborated by his Ugandan tracker, Peter Gono. Both men are fluent in Swahili as were the perpetrators.

The following is a list of the deceased and my interpretation as to how they died. It should be noted that the bodies were attacked so brutally that any speculation as to the actual cause of death is highly suspect. Dr. Malcolm Rutherford was on scene, and accordingly, his report should be available within a few days.

### Victims:

**British subjects:** William Smyth and Barbara Smyth.
**American citizens:** Roland Collins. Debbie Collins.
James Cole. Jeffery Cole. Ralph
Courtney. Margaret Courtney.

A French woman, Marie Camondona, was released, as was the safari guide, Robert Neff and the Ugandan, Peter Gono.

Two Americans escaped. Last names: Turner. Mr. Turner is still unaccounted for as of 2100 hours, 15 September. After being treated at the medical clinic in Kasese, Mrs. Turner was taken to the American Embassy in Kampala where she remains in seclusion. The American ambassador has blocked any attempt to question Mrs. Turner. It is my understanding that a private aircraft has been sent to Uganda to fly Mrs. Turner back to the United States.

On the morning of the Bwindi Incident, safari guide Neff reported hearing small-arms fire coming from the direction of one of the outer camp chalets. He believed the shots were being fired by the Ugandan military involved in an anti-poaching operation. Within minutes, the camp was surrounded. Ten men armed with AK-47s and machetes swarmed into the camp. Intelligence indicates they are part of the Interahamwe, an extremist group partially responsible for the 1994 ethnic genocide that slaughtered eight hundred thousand. A top Interahamwe commander operating inside of the Democratic Republic of the Congo, has taken credit for the "Bwindi massacre."

His faction, the RPF (Rwandan Patriotic Front) claim the attack was in retaliation for the United Nation's Security Council's recognition of the present Rwandan government.

The rebels led their victims on a twenty-kilometer march that was intended to take them into the Congo. Because they were unfamiliar with the terrain they forcibly used a local Ugandan, camp tracker, Peter Gono, to guide them. Gono, disregarding his own safety, led them in a circle hoping to be intercepted by the Ugandan military. The rebel leader, who is still unidentified, became suspicious and had Gono beaten until he confessed his deception. Neff stated, "That was when the discipline within the group started to breakdown." According to Peter Gono, the Courtneys, who were in their late fifties, became fatigued and refused to go on. Mrs. Courtney was raped by four of the rebels. Both Courtneys were executed with head shots. The Collin's woman and Barbara Smyth were also raped and brutally killed in front of their respective husbands, who were also killed. During the confusion, Arthur Turner and his wife slipped away into the heavy underbrush. They floated down a river emptying into Lake Albert. Mrs. Turner was found wandering by a Ugandan military patrol. She was incoherent and was taken to a local clinic. Mr. Turner was not found. In my opinion, his survival is unlikely.

It is also my opinion that the rebels have escaped back into the Congo. They are now under the full protection of the Congolese president.

The Ugandan military has assembled an incursion force of approximately six hundred soldiers. Intelligence sources believe they are headed north to the Kivu provinces of the DRC. With as many as 25,000 Rwandan rebels operating in that region, it is doubtful that any of the perpetrators will ever be brought to justice. A more detailed report will be available in forty-eight hours.

Laycock


Graham Connelly rolled up the report and used it to swat a blowfly on his windshield.

# 2

# SPANISH CAY, BAHAMA ISLANDS

## One year later

Rigby Croxford treaded water thirty feet above a coral ledge where the Nassau grouper he'd speared had wedged itself into a crevice. A cloud of blood seeped from the ledge. When he heard the grouper's distress grunts, he lifted his diving mask and looked for his wife. He scanned the beach until he found her. Good, you're safe, he thought. He filled his lungs, turned upside down and started for the bottom. He grabbed a purple sea fan and pulled himself under the ledge. The mixture of blood and stirred-up sand ruined his visibility. When he stretched his arm into the crevice, the grouper grunted and wedged itself deeper into the reef. He squeezed his gloved hand into the fish's mouth and latched on to its lower lip. The grouper struggled, but Rigby slipped his other hand under its gill plate and started for the surface.

When he popped up, he saw the dinghy bobbing on the horizon. Damn wind must have blown it, he thought. He swam slowly at first, but realized he wasn't gaining on the skiff. A movement caught his attention. It was a large black-tipped shark circling beneath him. He picked up his pace, but dragging the fish hampered him. I've got to quit smoking, he thought. It was only a few yards to the skiff. The black-tip reversed its direction and swam at him. At the last second, he flung the grouper up into the skiff and spun around, but the shark was gone. "Oh, no you don't. I worked too hard to give it up to the likes of you," he thought.

\*     \*     \*

The Croxfords were citizens of Zimbabwe. Rigby's ancestors had immigrated to Africa from Britain in the early nineteen hundreds. His wife, Helen was born in Connecticut. When Helen's brother offered to let them use his yacht, they turned him down. When he mailed them airline tickets, they buried their pride and accepted.

Helen was a doctor. She felt guilty about leaving her patients, but she needed a break from African politics. Despite worldwide condemnation, their president, Robert Mugabe, continued his confiscation of the white-owned farms. It was only a matter of time before Mugabe tried to seize their farm. Helen knew her husband would not go quietly.

Earlier that day, they anchored in a lagoon on the leeward side of Spanish Cay. Their captain, Bonefish Foley secured the boat's stern to a coconut tree and then set the yacht's anchor under a brain-coral dome. The old Hatteras lay captive to her moorings in the crystalline waters of Turtle Bay.

Captain Foley scanned the horizon. When he saw Rigby pop to the surface and fling the grouper in the skiff, he relaxed. The weather had treated them fairly, and with only a few minor mechanical problems, the cruise was running as smoothly as an island schooner sailing downwind. In two weeks, thought Captain Foley, the Croxfords will go back to Africa and I can go back home to Bimini. He picked up his knife and continued skinning a conch.

Something caught the corner of his eye. It was a yacht clearing the outer reef passage. The sun reflected off the yacht's bridge windows. Squinting, Foley watched men scurrying about on deck. The Bahamian looked at the shoreline to check the tide. Oh Lord, he thought, its high tide. Damn, Mr. Rigby's gonna be pitching a fit. I gotta find us another island.

A crewmember standing on the bowsprit directed the captain with hand gestures to help him avoid the coral-heads. The captain pivoted the yacht into the wind. The sound of rattling anchor chain echoed across the lagoon. Sulfur-smelling exhaust smoke covered Turtle Bay. The crew went to work putting inflatable tenders and wave-runners over the side. When the yacht swung into the wind, her name and homeport came into view: *The Liti-Gator*, Palm Beach, Florida.

Foley heard the whine of an outboard engine. Damn, Mr. Rigby's gonna be raisin' some hell, he uttered to himself. Foley watched the skiff idle towards him. "Goddamn it Foley, there's hundreds of islands in the Bahamas," Rigby yelled. "Why does this son-of-a-bitch have to pick our island? He could see we were already anchored up. Inconsiderate bastard." He stuck his thumb in one of the grouper's eye sockets and his pointing finger in the other. He hoisted the fish up and waded ashore.

Rigby's wife, Helen, left the shade of a coconut tree and walked down the beach to inspect the fish. She closed her book and sighed. "Check out the name. *The Liti-Gator*! Give me a break! As if we don't have enough lawyers."

"Yaaa, vell, I guess I must find us another island," said Foley. Like all Bahamians, he reversed V and W in his speech. "I don't expect people should be so unruly." He shook his head.

Helen pushed her sunglasses up, securing them in her hair. She grinned at her husband before speaking. "Are you sure you don't feel emasculated by this man's boat?"

"At least my middle-aged wife looks decent in a swimming-costume."

"Did you just say 'decent'?" Helen kicked sand at her husband. Rigby grabbed his wife and pulled her into the water. She screamed, handed her book to Foley, and tried to push her husband's head under.

They held hands watching Foley filet the grouper. "It's not the end of the world," said Rigby. "Tomorrow we'll pull anchor and find ourselves another lagoon. Whoever he is, he just violated a rule of common decency, that's all I'm saying." Rigby took a few steps closer to Foley. "Anyway, we've got more important issues," he continued, putting his hand on Foley's shoulder. "I believe it's time for our daily spear-fishing competition."

"Not today, Mr. Rigby, I've got work that needs doin'," Foley said, picking up the fish. "Besides, there are too many sharks round 'des island. You go ahead."

"Suit yourself. Helen, what about you?" She ignored him and walked up the beach. Guess I'm on my own, Rigby thought.

Foley helped him push the dinghy into deeper water. Rigby hopped in and Foley threw him the anchor line. Before he could start the engine, one of the *Liti-Gator*'s wave-runners idled up behind him. The young Bahamian sitting on the wave-runner was as black as an eight ball. Rigby started to voice his displeasure, but something stopped him.

"Ahoy, Captain. Say, my boss sent me to find some lobsters. Vould you know vhere I could find 'dem?" the young man inquired. "My name's Kewin," he said, extending his hand. "Mr. Rigby has been findin some nice lobsters on dem coral-heads," Foley indicated, pointing.

"Be careful. I've seen sharks," added Rigby.

Kevin looked fearful. "My boss will fire me if I don't bring back some lobsters. Could you take me with you?" he asked.

"I could use some company. Jump in. Captain Foley chickened out of our daily spear-fishing contest. I'm Rigby Croxford. This is Bonefish Foley, who happens to be the second-best spear fisherman in the Bahamas. I hate to blow my horn, but you're about to witness something special—a great diver in action. Isn't that right, Foley?"

"Mr. Rigby, you're a special one, all right. Lord, you can tell some big fibs," said Foley.

"Thanks," said Kevin. He shook each man's hand with the customary Bahamian limp handshake.

*     *     *

Rigby ran his skiff offshore. When he located a coral-head he turned the helm over to Kevin and leaned over the gunwale to look through a glass-bottom bucket.

"Do you see lobster?" Kevin asked.

"As Foley would say, 'Dey is as thick as grains of san' on the beach.'"

"You sound like an Englishman," commented Kevin.

"I'm from Zimbabwe. You could say, I'm an African."

"You're an African?" Kevin scratched his head.

"I'll explain later. Hand me those gloves."

Rigby pulled his diving mask over his face, grabbed his Hawaiian sling and fell over the side of the *Whaler,* backwards. He turned upside down and disappeared. When he resurfaced, he had three lobsters skewered on his spear. On his last dive, he speared a hog snapper. They headed back to the lagoon.

As they nudged up on the beach, Helen walked down to greet them. "Any luck? I wish you wouldn't dive alone."

"I wasn't diving alone. Kevin was with me," Rigby said, holding up the spiny lobsters.

"Kevin, I'm Helen Croxford."

"It's nice to meet you. Say, I almost forgot. My boss wants both of you to have dinner with him tonight."

"Tell your boss we appreciate his hospitality, but we've already got something planned," Rigby answered.

Kevin looked disappointed and said, "Now I know he'll fire me."

"Young man," said Helen, "you tell your boss we'd love to join him for dinner. The head chef and bottle washer needs a break. Besides, I'm dying to see his yacht."

"You take the lobster," Rigby demanded.

"Are you sure?"

"Of course I'm sure. Now that my admiral has spoken, what time do you want us? What's your boss's name?"

"Cocktails are at seven. His name is Mr. Maxwell Turner."

*     *     *

Using binoculars, Rigby watched a seaplane land southeast of the entrance to the lagoon. Three passengers departed the plane and boarded a skiff. The launch deposited them at the *Liti-Gator*'s stern. A man wearing a blue blazer and white pants met them as they disembarked. He offered his hand to the woman struggling for balance.

"How was the flight?" Max Turner asked.

"It was breathtaking," replied the woman.

"Molly dear, why don't you go below," said Max. "It'll give you a chance to freshen up before dinner. I need to borrow your husband. Tucker let's go topside. You can fill me in on our friend." Max motioned to a steward. "Make Mr. Dodge a scotch and soda." Max waited for Tucker Dodge to light his pipe and take the first sip. "What did you find out?" Turner asked.

"Let's start with Croxford's brother-in-law. He's the one with the deep pockets. Croxford transferred the title to his Zimbabwean farm to him for the time being, Mugabe has been reluctant to confiscate the foreign-owned farms. Max, this could pose a problem. Money may not motivate this guy."

"You feel Croxford's my best shot at rescuing Arthur? Assuming, he's still alive."

"Croxford's a legend in southern Africa. He was a decorated Selous Scout in the Rhodesian Bush War. A Selous Scout is like a Navy Seal on steroids. He fought as a mercenary in the Congo and Angola. And he's hunted in the Central African Republic and the Sudan. If your son's alive, Croxford's the man to bring him out," answered Tucker.

"That's what you said about the last guy. After I paid him, I never heard a word," Max said, looking through a porthole at the setting sun. Turner stuck his nose in the wine glass and sniffed before tasting it. He placed his glass on the bar and turned to Dodge. "Well, if Croxford's our man, you let me worry about hiring him. No man likes another man paying his way. I need to put this nightmare behind me." He patted Dodge on the back. "Thanks, Tucker. Nice job. Let's go below. Our guests should be arriving. I'm curious to meet Croxford."

The *Liti-Gator* looked like a lit-up New York skyscraper floating on its side. Her underwater lights illuminated the lagoon. Turner met the Croxfords at the top of the stairs on the fantail.

Maxwell Turner had spent a lifetime trying to enhance his masculinity. He was five foot six. His posture indicated he was trying to elongate himself. A facelift gave his eyes that slanted Hollywood actor look. He wore an expensive toupee, but the salt spray made it look like something women wrapped around their shoulders in the thirties. Turner was one hundred and seventy pounds of solid muscle. He shaved his arms to enhance the rippled effect. When he shook your hand, you could feel the calluses of a weightlifter. When he spoke, his accent sounded generic, but his tone was like the rhythmic notes of a bass saxophone.

"Good evening," Max said, extending his hand. "Croxfords, meet the Dodges. This is Tucker, or Tucky, and his better half, Molly. What can I have my steward get you to drink?" Turner latched on to Helen's hand and refused to let go. It was his way of testing the waters. Rigby was oblivious to Max's flirtation. Helen pulled away gracefully.

The group gave drink orders to an Asian-looking steward. Max ushered them into a salon that would have made a Saudi prince jealous. Fearful of soiling the expensive upholstery, Rigby sat on the edge of his chair.

"Before I forget, the lobster hors d'oeuvres are courtesy of Mr. Croxford. I'm afraid I had to give up diving. It's my ears." Max pointed at his ear and mocked pain. Something made Rigby think that he had fabricated the excuse.

"I can't tell you how happy this makes me. I mean, your accepting my invitation. Right up front, I want to apologize for barging in on your lagoon. Now, where do you folks call home?"

"We live in Africa. Although Helen's a Yank by birth," answered Rigby. "Helen guessed you were a solicitor."

"She's right. What's your business in Africa, Rigby?"

"I'm a farmer and a professional hunter."

"Mrs. Croxford, what did you do before this extremely lucky man shanghaied you to the Dark Continent?"

"I'm a doctor."

"And where did you go to medical school?"

"Yale."

"Do you have any children?"

"One daughter. She's also a doctor."

"My God, beauty and intelligence. Like I said, Mr. Croxford, you're a lucky man. I'm afraid my academic credentials aren't as impressive." Helen blushed as Max's visual frisk lingered on her a second too long. Turner walked over and stood next to the spiral stairway to the bridge. "If you're interested, I'll give you the grand tour after dinner," he said, indicating he was speaking about his yacht with an expansive wave.

"We look forward to it," Helen said, hooking her arm through her husband's elbow.

Turner always reverted to using his wealth to attract women and belittle men. Rigby and his wife's display of affection for each other irritated him. He attempted to hide his annoyance, but couldn't. "Of course, it's just another boat. You people look like real boaters. I wish I had the time."

"It's not our boat. It's on loan from her brother," said Rigby.

"Max, you seem to be doing okay," Helen added, offering an olive branch to lessen the awkwardness.

"I'm doing all right. One step ahead of my creditors, as they say. Helen, I'm curious about your brother's boat. Those classic fifty-threes are hard to come by nowadays. Do you think he might have an interest in selling the old girl?" It was obvious his interest was disingenuous. Before Helen could answer, he turned away.

"Excuse me. Yes, Bob." Turner turned to receive a message from a large bald man. Bob had a twisted nose. The folds of accordion skin on the back of his neck gave him the look of a Shar-Pei dog. His piggish eyes were not as repulsive as the way he enunciated his words with his lips extended like a goldfish. The steward handed a wine list to Rigby.

"Folks, I need to take an overseas call. Why don't you choose your wine? I won't be a minute. You all can get acquainted."

Rigby waited until Max disappeared into the wheelhouse. "Christ, a wine list. I reckon we need to improve the service on our *classic* boat." He used the wine list to block the sound. "What's with Bob? His head looks like a penis."

"Do you have to be so gross?" Helen whispered to Rigby, trying not to smile. "Give me that wine list. You don't know anything about wine."

"The amount of wine I've consumed makes me an expert. Although I must admit, Zimbabwean wine is probably better suited as a cleaning agent."

Helen was uneasy about exposing her husband to the Dodges. She had gone to college with hundreds of men like Tucker Dodge. He's probably a stockbroker, or maybe a mergers-and-acquisitions lawyer on Wall Street, she thought. He had undoubtedly gone to a fancy prep school and would have followed in his father's footsteps by attending Yale or Harvard. His enunciation was too punctilious not to be Ivy League.

His wife came from a wealthy family, Helen figured. People like the Dodges don't get married, instead, they merge. She was Connecticut frumpy with thick ankles and heavy arms. She wore her hair in a bun. Her chinless face was blemished. Helen sized her up and realized that the Dodges' marriage wasn't a merger; it was an acquisition. Mrs. Dodge is the one with the money, she concluded.

Molly rummaged through her Chanel handbag. When she located the cigarette-holder she handed it to her husband without looking at him. He secured the cigarette, lit the end and handed it back to her. She accepted it without thanking him.

I knew it, Helen thought, congratulating herself.

Helen had gone to Yale on a scholarship. She looked at Rigby, and a warm contentment washed over her. God, I'm glad I married you, she thought. She glanced at Tucker and then at his wife. Helen, you're too damn cynical. At least give these people a chance, she continued thinking. What she heard next would confirm her first impression.

"It must be exciting living in Africa," Molly directed at Helen.

"Yes, we like it very much."

"A couple of years ago we went on a photographic safari in Kenya. We loved it. Didn't we, dear?" Tucker said, looking at his wife for confirmation. She nodded her approval. "It was absolutely marvelous," Molly added.

"Mr. Croxford, I understand you're a professional hunter. I've never liked hunting. The cruelty seems so senseless," Tucker said.

"I'm only working as a professional hunter until I can get back into farming."

"Mr. Croxford, what's your take on Mugabe reclaiming the farms and giving them back to the rightful owners?" Tucker inquired, sucking on his cigar until it ignited. He blew out the match and held up his empty glass, looking for a refill.

"Rhodesia was the bread basket of Africa. Now the people are starving."

"You don't look like you're starving," Tucker stated.

"Actually, we were starving. That's why we've come to the Bahamas. It's a brilliant spot to fatten up," Rigby said with a smile.

Tucker continued. "And you feel no guilt for what the white man's done to the Africans." Tucker's face narrowed in contempt.

"Africa's complicated. You must live there to understand it."

"Come now, Croxford, I find that hard to believe."

Rigby's brow narrowed. He looked squarely at Tucker. "Ducky, I have no regrets about trying to maintain order in Africa. I lost a lot of my best mates in something called the Rhodesian Bush War. I fought next to some very brave men—it might interest you to know, some of them were black. I'm sorry, but I'm not interested in your opinions." His acid tone had them squirming.

"The name's Tucker. Look, I apologize if I've said something to offend you. I'm just trying to understand your thinking." He turned away from Rigby's glare and stood up. "I wonder what's keeping Max," he mumbled, trying to quicken the clock-ticking silence.

Turner looked over the shoulder of his secretary. He read the following email to himself.

> To: Maxwell Turner
> From: Rutherford, London School of Medicine—
>        Forensic Science Department.
> RE: Post-mortem pathology

Dear Mr. Turner: DNA samples taken from the human body parts retrieved from the stomach of a crocodile killed on Lake Albert, Uganda, inconclusive because of the high level of corrosive digestive acids. More tests are required. Sorry to put you through this ordeal.

Kindest regards,
Dr. Malcolm Rutherford

"Is everyone getting to know each other?" Turner asked, walking back into the salon. "If you folks will follow me, I think they're ready to serve us dinner."

As soon as everyone was seated, Max Turner insisted they hold hands and bow their heads. "Let us pray," he started. "These six things the Lord hates. Yes, my friends, they are an abomination to Him: a proud look, a lying tongue, hands that shed innocent blood, a heart that devises wicked plans, feet that are swift in running to evil, and a false witness who speaks lies." They thought Max had finished his sermon, but he was just getting warmed up. Just when the atmosphere seemed almost suicidal, the Amen came. Relieved, they all smiled, except Helen, who frowned at her husband who had been fidgeting like a school-boy in church. Max caught them winking at each other.

They dined on rack of lamb. Helen deferred to Max's wine selection, a 1998 Chateau Petrus. The dinner chit-chat was limited to Max's grilling the Croxfords about Africa. Tucker and his wife were still licking the verbal wounds inflicted by Rigby and seemed unwilling to participate in the conversation.

After dinner, the group retired to the back deck. The men smoked Cuban cigars and sipped cognac. When the wind lulled—the clouds dissipated leaving a star studded sky. Occasionally, a distant streak of heat lighting gave form to the coconut trees on the shoreline.

"Mr. Dodge, what's your line of work?" Rigby asked, trying to repair his earlier damage.

"I'm an attorney. I represent Max."

"I'm confused. Max, I thought you were a lawyer."

"You can never have enough attorneys around," answered Max.

"Says who?"

"Rigby, for God's sake," his wife interjected.

"It's all right, Dr. Croxford. Rigby, did my prayer make you nervous?"

"I wouldn't say it made me nervous."

"Oh really? Don't you think Voltaire said it best when he wrote, 'I die adoring God, loving my friends and not hating my enemies'?" Max asked, looking at Rigby.

The wine had thickened his recollection of clever answers. He glanced at his wife, looking for help. Helen countered with, "Let's not forget Lucretius, who wrote, 'How many evils have flowed from religion?'"

"Folks," said Max, "I think I may have gotten in over my head. It's not often you meet such *au courant* people in the Bahamas." Turner continued his cross-examination. "Rigby, are you a religious man?"

"I'd say I'm more of a spiritual man. I've seen so much injustice in my life. And I'm embarrassed to admit I've been a participant, although an unwilling participant, in so much violence, I guess I'm afraid to think about Godly matters. Turning to less lofty subjects, I must tell you, Max, you're an absolutely brilliant host. I reckon that wine was the best I ever tasted," Rigby slurred.

"At a thousand bucks, it ought to be."

"You're kidding. It's hard to imagine paying a thousand dollars for a case of wine. No wonder it was good. Say, how many bottles are in a case?"

"Rigby Croxford, you're a breath of fresh air." said Max.

"Thanks for a wonderful evening," Helen said, grabbing her husband's arm. "I better get him home." Max shook hands with Rigby. "Fair enough, but I need a promise from your husband."

"And what might that be?" asked Helen.

"I've always dreamed of hunting in Africa. Tonight, I met the only professional hunter I'd ever consider hiring. Dr. Croxford, that man is your husband."

"I'm flattered, but I'm booked for the next two hunting seasons." Rigby spoke so quickly his excuse sounded lame. "Max, I'd be happy to recommend another PH."

Turner acted like he didn't hear. "Let's talk about this tomorrow. We're going to pull anchor in the afternoon. It's time we returned your lagoon."

They turned and stared at a woman standing in the companionway. She wore a silky nightgown outlining the sensual curve of her hips and accentuating the line of her breasts. She was the type of woman who could tongue-tie men and pucker the noses of older women. "I'm sorry. I didn't know we had guests," she said, folding her arms over her chest. Her voice sounded weak.

"Sweetheart, you shouldn't have gotten out of bed. Ashlyn, I'd like you to meet the Croxfords. You know the Dodges. Ashlyn's my daughter-in-law."

"I'm pleased to meet y'all. I haven't been feeling well. I think it's motion sickness. I'm worn thin as summer cotton. I think I better go back below. Goodnight." She turned and disappeared down the hallway. The smell of her perfume lingered for a few seconds. The way Turner looked at his daughter-in-law puzzled Helen, but she dismissed her thought. When Turner realized Helen was watching him, he looked uncomfortable. Turner should have offered more information about his daughter-in-law, but he didn't.

"Folks, this has been the highlight of our cruise. I can't tell you when I've had a more enjoyable evening."

"It was wonderful," concurred Helen.

"Rigby, I need a favor."

"After that, how could I say no?"

"How about coming onboard for lunch tomorrow? I'd like to pick your brain. I was serious when I said I wanted to do an African hunt. Let's say we make it around noon." Max knew his compliments would make his invitation unavoidable.

"See you tomorrow," Rigby answered.

\*   \*   \*

Later that night, in the privacy of their stateroom, Helen quizzed her husband. "Did you find that woman attractive?"

"You mean Molly?"

"Don't play games with me. You know which woman I mean. I think I've read about Turner. He's a personal-injury lawyer."

"That Tucker was a wanker." He used curled hand movements to illustrate the remark. "Was it me or did I see Turner drooling over his daughter-in-law?" he asked.

"You have a dirty mind. Don't you dare let him talk you into taking him on safari."

"My dear, it'll never happen. He might bring the Dodges. Helen, he had to be lying about that wine costing a thousand dollars a bottle. There's no way."

"Come here, my sweet African naive," she whispered, snuggling next to him.

\*     \*     \*

At noon the next day, Rigby tossed a line to Kevin, who secured it to the *Liti-Gator's* stern. Max was waiting for him at the top of the stairs. He was wearing sweat pants and a sleeveless tee shirt. The fantail of the yacht had been turned into an outdoor gymnasium. Exercise machines with pulleys and counter weights lined the walls. A blue wrestling mat had been rolled out.

Max wiped his forehead with a towel and handed it to a steward. "You're just in time to watch our martial-arts exhibition. Bob's a master of karate and tae kwon do. He was a ranked boxer, before I bailed him out of a problem he had with the Miami police. Kevin warms him up before he works me over." Max nodded at Bob, who was busy stretching.

Turner's staged bravado was therapy for his small-man complex. Croxford on the other hand, reeked of masculinity. His jet-black hair and honest blue eyes irritated Turner. Turner considered using his wealth to knock him down a few pegs, but sensed it would be a waste of time.

"Kevin doesn't look very enthusiastic," said Rigby, moving to get a better look.

"He's fine. You look like a weightlifter. How much do you weigh?"

"I reckon about a hundred kilograms. As far as lifting barbells, I got my muscles the old-fashioned way—manual labor."

"Rigby, my father died at fifty. My two younger brothers are dead, both from heart attacks. When you talked about waiting until next year to go hunting, I may not have a next year."

"There are lots of great professional hunters in Africa."

"You're the best PH in the business. I always insist on the best."

"I'm not the best professional hunter in southern Africa."

"Modesty becomes you. I've been doing my homework. I know your father was a professional hunter as was his father. He named his four sons after gun companies. One brother was named Smith, another one's Wesson and another Browning. I guess your preferred weapon has to be a

.416 Rigby. I know you were a Selous Scout in the Rhodesian military. And that you led clandestine operations into Mozambique and Botswana. You're fluent in Swahili as well as Afrikaans, and you speak four or five other African dialects." Max smiled at Rigby and continued. "The Internet's a marvelous invention."

Rigby heard a thump. He turned around and saw Kevin on his knees. He seemed dazed as Bob danced around him. "Are you sure Kevin's all right?"

"He's fine," Max said, without looking. Max stood up and blocked Rigby's view. I've tried pity and flattery. Now let's try greed, he thought. "You know, my friends say I have a Napoleonic complex. I hate to think what my enemies say about me. I know one thing they can't say. They can't say I'm cheap. How much does a lion hunt go for these days?"

"You've got a minimum of twenty-one days at two thousand per day, plus hunting permits, taxidermy and miscellaneous costs. We're talking about seventy thousand, give or take."

"Fine, I'll make it one hundred and twenty thousand."

Rigby stood up and walked over to the railing. The amount of money Max had just offered was staggering. He didn't want Max to see his enthusiasm. Helen will kill me, he thought. "As I told you, I'm booked for two years. When I get home I've got two weeks to get ready for my first hunt. On top of that, all the lion permits in Zimbabwe are taken."

"You said that after you arrive in Zimbabwe, you've got two weeks open? Zimbabwe's not the only country in Africa that allows hunting. I'm perfectly willing to pay for three weeks and only stay for two."

"There's always Mozambique. The living conditions will be raw."

"How so?" Max asked, sensing he had softened Croxford's resolve.

"Mozambique is lawless. Bloody country's been embroiled in a civil war for thirty years."

When Rigby heard another thump he looked over Max's shoulder and saw Bob back-kick Kevin in the chest. He could see Kevin's nose was bleeding. "Max, did you say this Bob was a professional fighter?"

"That's right. Now he works for me," said Max, trying to refocus Rigby's concentration. "Let's do this. I'll pay you one hundred and twenty thousand. I'll only stay for two weeks and I'll pay you a bonus of another fifty thousand if I get my lion. That way, I won't be interfering with your first safari."

Rigby didn't answer. He got up and walked over to Kevin who was still on his back. Blood dripped from Kevin's nose. His upper lip was puffy. "Mate, are you hurt?" Rigby asked. Kevin's eyes were vacant. Bob continued shadowboxing.

Rigby approached Bob on the mat. "Bob, I went to school with someone who used to move his lips like you do. It was like he was sucking on something. Do you think you could give me a few pointers in this martial-arts business?"

Bob motioned Rigby onto the mat. Both men started circling each other. "I heard what you said last night," Bob said. "Come a little closer. I won't bite you." An evil smile crossed his lips.

"This isn't gonna be a tango lesson, is it?" Rigby asked.

"Let's make sure nobody gets hurt," Max yelled. "If either man raises his hand and gives up, it's over, or as they say in French, *hors de combat*."

When Rigby turned to acknowledge Turner, Bob used the distraction to duck under and go for his legs. The big man's speed surprised him. They crashed to the mat, but Rigby took the brunt of it. He felt the air forced out of his lungs. Before he could gather himself, Bob got one leg pinned over his neck and his other tucked under his armpit. He started to bend Rigby's arm, using his twisted elbow as a lever. Rigby felt the ligaments in his shoulder starting to give way. The circulation in his hand was cutoff. He felt incredible pain flowing from his shoulder into his neck. Turner jumped down and pounded the mat, "Rigby, give up before he breaks your arm. He's got you in an arm-bar. Give up before you get hurt. Please, I'm begging you!"

Kevin dropped to his knees and also pleaded. "Mr. Rigby, don't let him break your arm. It's my job to fight him."

Members of the crew screamed to stop the fight. Above the noise, Rigby heard Tucker Dodge encouraging Bob. When he glanced into the man's eyes trying to break his arm it gave him a burst of energy. Bob's grip started to slip. Rigby ran his free hand inside of Bob's thigh and grabbed a fistful of the man's testicles. Driven by rage, he crushed his balls like walnuts. The veins in his forearm gorged with blood. Bob's screaming sounded like a wounded animal. He tried to unlock Rigby's grip, but it was useless. Rigby rolled on top of him and used his free hand to trap his windpipe.

"Stand up!" When Bob refused, Rigby squeezed until he jumped up on his tiptoes. As they approached the railing, he rocked him back on his heels and pushed him over. He missed the launch by inches. The crew cheered as Bob hit the water.

"Max, is there a place where I could wash my hands? By the way, the move I used on him is known in South Africa as the 'dreaded nut press.' We use it in rugby matches," he said, fabricating the story for Kevin.

"I'll do your safari under one condition. I want the hundred and seventy thousand in advance."

"I thought I agreed to pay you the last fifty after I get my lion."

"You'll get your lion. I'm afraid it's nonnegotiable."

"Consider it done. Now, I have a request. I never fly commercial. I own my own airplane. I'd like for you and your wife to fly with me to Africa. There's no sense wasting time."

"It's eight thousand miles to Africa. That must be some plane," replied Rigby.

"It's big enough to go transatlantic. Comes with a dining room and sleeping quarters. Even has a workout room."

"I hope to hell it doesn't have a wrestling mat," said Rigby, drying his hands. "Thanks, Max, but I'm afraid I'll have to pass. Helen's staying in the States for another two weeks. If we're gonna do this thing, I've got loose-ends to take care of."

"For instance?"

"For one thing, I need to arrange visas."

Rigby and Max began walking back to the fantail. Max spoke. "Your captain mentioned you're headed to Bimini. We thought we might spend a few days in Bimini before we head back to Palm Beach. Maybe we'll run in to each other."

"I almost forgot. There's one more condition," said Rigby.

"And that one is?"

"You retire Kevin. If Bob ever lays a hand on Kevin again, I'll make it my business to find him and put a large bullet hole in the front of his bald head."

"You're kidding, of course. I mean about shooting Bob."

Rigby didn't answer. Turner shivered inwardly when he saw Rigby's expression. The man's incapable of idle threats, he thought. "Anything you say, my friend."

The woman Rigby had seen before appeared at the top of the stairs.

She was wearing a string bikini. She held her unfastened bikini top with a free hand, but her breasts spilled out of the sides. Her bronzed body looked long and lean. She took off her sunglasses and shook her hair to clear it from her face. Her auburn hair glistened from the sun and rolled like incoming waves against a beach. Rigby glanced at Max. When he looked back, she was gone.

"Sorry that I can't stay for lunch. I'll give Kevin the wiring instructions for the money. I'll be in touch. Goodbye Max."

Kevin helped Rigby fend his skiff off the yacht's stern. "Kevin, be sure to thank Bob for the martial-arts lesson," he said, winking. Kevin started to speak, but stopped when he saw Max looking at him.

Max spoke without turning to face Tucker Dodge. "You were right. Croxford's our man."

Rigby took his time idling back across the lagoon. He readied himself for the argument. As soon as the skiff touched the yacht's stern, Helen opened the salon door. She moved into the sunlight to get a look at her husband. Rigby kept his back to her, but she turned him around. "What in God's name happened to you?" Before he could answer, she asked another question. "Did you fall? Hold still. Let me have a look at your face. You turned him down, didn't you?"

"So many questions—so little time. Which one do you want me to answer first?" He walked over and inspected his reflection in the salon window. He wet the bottom of his shirt with saliva and used it to wipe the abrasion on his chin.

"Tell me you're not taking that yucky man on a hunt."

"Max was persuasive. He's paying me more money than I make in four hunting seasons. And listen to this—he's only staying in Africa for two weeks. I can put up with anything for two weeks."

"I knew you'd do this. Of course he's persuasive; he's a lawyer." Helen held up her hands in exasperation and looked at Foley for support. "Where did you fall?" she asked.

"I didn't fall."

Helen grabbed his arm and turned him to inspect his face. He pulled away and massaged his shoulder. "I got in a fight. It really wasn't a fight. I guess you could call it more of an exhibition. I planned on telling you that woman attacked me, but I can see you're in no mood for humor."

"Living with you for thirty years is about all the humor I can stand.

Did you see his daughter-in-law?" She placed her hand under her chin as she waited for his response.

"I saw her, but only for a second."

Bonefish Foley stopped wet-sanding the teak deck. There was something about Max Turner that troubled him, something he couldn't put into words. He considered speaking up, but decided to keep his thoughts to himself.

Helen continued her tirade. "I don't like this. There's something strange about this man."

"The idea of returning one hundred and seventy thousand dollars makes me nauseous." Helen's eyes widened. "You heard me, one hundred and seventy thousand. I'm beginning to feel like a kept woman with your brother paying our bills. It's time I started pulling my own plow."

The *Liti-Gator* left the lagoon on the high tide. The next three days onboard the *Hatteras* ran wonderfully together. Helen continued to press her husband about his pending safari with Max Turner. She was anxious to reach Bimini where she hoped they would run into Turner, giving her husband the opportunity to cancel Max's lion hunt. Unbeknownst to her, Rigby was driving a brand new Land Cruiser in his dreams, and it was bought with Max's money.

*       *       *

They anchored behind Wood Cay waiting for the weather to improve. After waiting for three days, Foley decided the seas had laid down enough to make the sixty-mile crossing to Bimini. At first, the ocean treated them kindly, but gradually a freshening northeast wind furrowed whitecaps. The old Hatteras smashed headlong into mountainous waves that had rolled down unimpeded from the North Atlantic. She would ride over a flat-faced swell and then dig her nose into the next wave jettisoning sheets of foamy blue water. Angry wind blew salt spray in their faces so hard they had to cock their heads to breathe. It felt like the ocean had spawned needles. And then, as suddenly as the ocean had turned ugly, it relented. The water color changed from deep purple to turquoise as the ocean climbed from a thousand fathoms to less than three. The gin clear water on the Bahama Bank was oily calm. They watched torpedo-shaped barracudas and cero mackerel skirt away from the bow. Off the stern, they saw purple sea fans and orange coral whips bending in the current like windblown grasses.

Rigby watched his wife standing at the yacht's helm. For a split second they were lost in each other's gaze. Helen was experiencing that moment of bliss most people find elusive. She wondered if her husband felt the same way. As Rigby scanned the horizon, he remembered the first time he met his wife. *It was at a New Year's Eve party on Willie's farm in South Africa. I was on leave from the Rhodesian Army. She was on holiday from her Peace Corp duties. I was becoming disillusioned about the war. She had bubbling enthusiasm for her work. I was trying to kill Africans. She was trying to teach them to read. I remember she asked me a harmless question about the progress of the war. "Miss O'Neil, I'd like to remind you, I'm fighting for my country's survival. We're standing up to the communists. Rhodesians are dying for something your country failed to do in Southeast Asia. You thank us by boycotting my country. You bloody liberals are so wonderfully full of yourselves. You'll forgive me if I'm not overly impressed by your work here in Africa."*

*"So, you're killing Africans to prevent them from becoming communists. I'm afraid your logic escapes me."*

*"No, Miss O'Neil, we're trying to kill them before they kill us. You see, that's the way it works in a war. I guess you'd spit on us just like you spit on the soldiers returning from Viet Nam."*

*"Willie dear, please excuse us. I need to speak with Mr. Croxford in private." As soon as we were alone, she lit into me. "How dare you label me. You don't know me or anything about me. Teaching poor African children doesn't make me the enemy. Why if I didn't feel so sorry for you, I would have slapped you silly in there."*

*"I don't believe you're capable of slapping anyone," I said.*

*"Believe what you want." Her eyes darted as she spoke. Her cheeks were flushed. Helen was the most beautiful woman I had ever seen. I remember a feeling of serenity wash through me. Whatever it was, it made me shudder.*

*"Miss O'Neil, I know you're going to think I'm crazy, but I have something I need to say."*

*"Let's hear it. Leaving the table like that was impolite. Not that you'd know what's considered bad manners."*

*"I...I think I've just fallen in love with you." I stood up and turned my back to her.*

*"What? Why that's the silliest thing I've ever heard. I think you've had*

*too much to drink or you're suffering from some type of battle fatigue. Poor man, I think we need to get you some medical help."*

*"Wait, there's more. Someday, we're going to be married. I've never been surer about anything in my life. And yes, I have had too much to drink, but I know exactly what I'm saying."*

*"I see. I'll say one thing. You are, without a doubt, the strangest man I've ever known. We better go back inside before they think we've both lost our minds."* Rigby suspended his daydreaming to point at a speck on the horizon; it was North Bimini Island. The sighting of land reassured them, but for some reason, Helen felt uneasy.

As soon as they anchored, she started in on her husband. "If you're serious about canceling with Max, do it now. I've got a bad feeling about this safari." Rigby yes-honeyed her, but he was searching for a way to accommodate Max.

He took his time running the launch across the bay. The *Liti-Gator* was docked on the northern tip of the island. Rigby headed for the south end. He needed time to think. He tossed the bowline to a Bahamian standing on the dock. The man was stoop-shouldered. He wore a tattered business suit and a woolen sky-cap. His eyes had lost any hint of whiteness. "The name's Cornbread," he said, securing the dinghy's line. "Captain, are you in need of a guide? I know everything about Bimini."

"Do you know Captain Foley?"

"Foley's my step-husband? Yaah, ve go vay bock."

"Friend, I'm unfamiliar with the term, 'step-husband.'"

"I'm married to Foley's ex-vife."

"Interesting. Cornbread, I do need a guide. Why don't you show me where the *Liti-Gator*'s tied up?"

"Yaah, you must be a big-shot if you know Mr. Turner."

"So, you know Max Turner?"

"Vell, I couldn't say I know him personally."

As they walked down the potholed road to the marina, Cornbread gave him a Cook's tour. As Rigby listened, he remembered reading that Bimini was one of Hemingway's favorite haunts, and that he affectionately referred to the island's inhabitants as what was left after God was given an enema. He looked at Cornbread and smiled. They met a man on the road. The man gave Cornbread a smelly barracuda covered in flies. "Are you gonna eat that thing?" Rigby asked, after the man walked away.

"Damn right I'm gonna eat it. I'm gonna make me some fish-head stew. If you vant, I could bring you some."

"Thanks, but I'm not much of a fish eater."

The road dissected sagging shacks and unpainted buildings. A giant mound of discarded conch shells provided the foundation for a rickety dock. A half-sunken sloop lay at anchor in the harbor. Some rotting dinghies bobbed against the shoreline. There was a freighter, the *Fascinating Bitch*, moored to a wharf. A mangy dog stopped licking himself and growled halfheartedly at the men.

They met a fat woman standing in the middle of the road. She wore a tee shirt with the words "Jesus is coming and he's pissed off" printed across the front. Cornbread stopped to introduce her, but when he turned his back, she sucker-punched him. The blow knocked him flat on his ass. "Cornbread, you good for nuttin' bum. If I catch you messin with 'dat woman again, I'm gonna beat you shitless," the woman hissed.

"Are you hurt?" Rigby offered, helping Cornbread up.

"I'm not hurt. My feelings are hurt."

"Who was the woman?"

"Her? She's my vife, I'm sorry to say. That gal's mostly too rough for me."

"You should fight people your own size."

"Yaah, she's a big one all right. Bahamian men like the fat ladies. But Lord, 'dat girl is so unruly."

Rigby reached out and straightened Cornbread's lapels. "Cornbread, it's been fun. Here's a little something for you," he said, handing him some wrinkled bills.

"God bless you." The old Bahamian stuffed the money in his pocket and saluted.

\*     \*     \*

Max Turner watched Rigby Croxford walk towards him. He knew Rigby would try to worm his way out of the lion hunt. Everything was riding on hiring Croxford. Max had devised a plan that would deliver Rigby back into the fold. "Well, well, I figured you'd turn up," Max yelled down to Rigby. "How do you like Bimini? It's always reminded me of a rotten tooth in a woman's smile," Max said, with an expansive wave.

"Oh, I don't know. I guess I like Bimini because it reminds me of Africa."

Max ignored his rebut and continued, "Praise the Lord. My prayers have been answered. Rigby, I owe you more than you'll ever know," Max stammered, stepping down on the dock.

"Max, we need to talk."

"I know, I know. But first, I've got a confession to make. Rigby, you said you have a daughter."

"She lives in Cape Town." Rigby was about to explain why he couldn't take him to Africa, but Max was one step ahead of him. Max held up his hand to stop Rigby from speaking. His face was pinched in sadness and there were tears in his eyes as he spoke. "I have a confession. I wasn't totally honest with you about my reasons for wanting to go to Africa. A little over a year ago, I lost my son in Uganda. It was a senseless terrorist attack. I'm sure you read about it. Life for me has been meaningless, ever since. I felt something when I met you. I need to go to Africa to bring closure to the worst thing that can happen to a parent, the loss of a child. I apologize for not telling you the truth." Max wiped a tear from his eye and looked up at Rigby. His face was flushed with emotion as he continued. "You said you had something you wanted to say."

"It really wasn't that important."

"Let's never talk about this again."

"I understand. I guess I should. The next time we see each other, it'll be in Africa," Rigby said, shaking hands.

Max watched him disappear behind some weathered shacks. There was never a doubt, he thought, smiling. Max entered the salon and used the spiral stairs to the staterooms. He tried to open his daughter-in-law's door, but it was locked. "Sweetheart, are you all right?" he asked with his ear against the door.

"I'm a little better."

"Can I get you something to eat?"

"I don't think I could keep it down," Ashlyn said, taking a bite of her sandwich.

*     *     *

# 3
# WEST PALM BEACH

Dan Gillespie gargled with mint flavored mouthwash, swallowed and then grimaced. He exhaled into his hand to check his breath, satisfied he extinguished a cigarette and waved his hand to disperse the smoke. He closed his eyes and rocked back in his chair. Why would someone like Lynn Allison or Lynn Turner or whatever she calls herself, hire me? He used a dime to rub off a lottery ticket. "As usual, fucked again," he said to himself, tossing the crumpled ticket in a file cabinet. If I can talk her into paying me a retainer, I could pay my dockage.

The knock on the door startled him. Before he could answer it, Lynn Allison stepped into his office. He had seen her picture in the society section of the local newspaper, but nothing prepared him for seeing her in person. He felt his heart race. Women like Lynn Allison oozed sexuality like a flower secretes scent. Danny boy, control yourself, he thought.

Scanning the society columns was one of Gillespie's hustles. He looked for a younger woman married to a wealthy older man or the reverse. In Palm Beach, both sexes were fair game in the divorce business. Set up a tight surveillance schedule, and *voila*, that little old indiscretion seemed to always rear its ugly head. A photo with his card attached and bang he had a client. Gillespie knew it was a dirty business, but he had bills to pay.

"Won't you sit down? Would you like something to drink?" he asked, guessing she would refuse given the condition of the glass sitting on his desk.

"No thank you," she said.

"It is Mrs. Allison or Mrs. Turner?" he asked.

"I use Lynn Allison."

"I was wondering how you got my name."

"The sign out front confused me. Colonic hydrotherapy. Body massages. Private detective. What *is* the nature of your work?"

"I'm the detective, all right. We like to think of it as one-stop shopping. Sorry, it was a bad joke. Who did you say recommended me?"

"I didn't say, Mr. Gillespie. We haven't discussed the work I have in mind. Perhaps you'll understand more after I explain a few things," she said in a low rolling southern twang.

"I'm all ears, Ms. Allison." He couldn't stop staring at her. He knew he had to edit his words carefully or he would say something asinine. Beautiful women made him say stupid things.

"What do you know about Maxwell Turner?"

"Well, let me see. I know you were married to him. I know he's loaded. He's the biggest ambulance chaser in the state, if not the country. Sorry, maybe I should have used 'attorney.'"

"There's nothing you could say about my ex-husband that would offend me. People know him as a philanthropist. I'm afraid I've seen a somewhat darker side of Mr. Turner."

"Exactly what's your problem with Turner? I mean, above and beyond the obvious problems of an ex-wife."

"Did you know my sister's married to Max's son, Arthur? Arthur was Max's only child. Arthur was from Max's third marriage. I'm sorry to say, I was his fifth wife."

"I'm confused. You said your sister's married to Turner's son and you were Max's fifth wife," he said, rubbing his forehead.

"Puzzling, isn't it?"

"Well, yes, but then again, it is Palm Beach." God damn it, you just had to say something to piss her off.

"Arthur disappeared in Africa a little over a year ago. My sister was one of the survivors. It was that terrorist attack in Uganda. It was in all the newspapers."

"I don't read gossip columns," he said, without thinking. There you go again.

"I'd hardly call this gossip," Lynn snapped. "You *are* a private investigator, aren't you?"

"That's what it says on my county occupational license. Please continue."

"Terrorists killed eight tourists. It was barbaric. Since that nightmare, Max has kept my sister in total seclusion. I've called his office, but I keep getting the same old runaround—'We're sorry, your sister's not ready to see anyone.' I know my sister. This is not like her. There's something not right about this."

"So you want me to make contact with your sister. That should be easy enough."

"I wouldn't be so sure. People say Max is grief stricken, I'm not buying it. I just need to make sure that my sister's safe. Is that too much to expect?"

"I'm not following you. Why wouldn't your ex-husband be grief stricken by the death of his only son? And why wouldn't your sister be safe?"

"Did I say that? I didn't mean it that way. This thing has been very upsetting," Lynn quickly replied back at Gillespie. She stood up and walked over to the window. Gillespie felt his pulse quicken as he visualized her naked. She took a cigarette out of a golden case and placed it between her lips. After lighting it, she ran her hand along the windowsill and didn't seem surprised by what she found.

"You already tried hiring some of the other detective agencies in town and they all turned you down, because they all do business with your ex-husband's law firm. Now it makes sense. I mean, why you finally got around to hiring me."

"I hired Richard Langley two months ago," she said, blowing the windowsill dust from her fingertips.

"Two weeks ago, the police found Langley in a motel room," Dan said, interrupting her. "He'd been sodomized and damn near beaten to death. Poor guy's still in a coma. Police report said it was a gay thing. Not that there's anything wrong with being gay. It just surprised me. He was always a puss-man. Sorry, I was thinking out loud. We frequented the same watering holes in town and chased the same...." Embarrassed, he retreated back to his desk.

"This is a copy of Mr. Langley's report," Lynn said after a pause. "Once you've had a chance to read it, you'll understand why I'm concerned about my sister."

"Are you using Miss or Mrs. Allison? Have you remarried?" He brushed back his hair and straightened his tie.

"Allison's my maiden name. I haven't remarried, nor do I have any intention of ever doing so. Why do you ask?"

"I just thought it might be more convenient if we discuss our business over dinner." He looked at her and smiled suggestively. Oh shit! Now she's really pissed off. You just had to say more stupid shit, didn't you? He tried his forgive-me-for-being-an-asshole look, but she wasn't buying it.

"I see. Mr. Gillespie, do I detect a Yankee accent?"

"I'm New York born and bred."

"I have no interest in having dinner with you. Puss-man, isn't that the vulgar term you used? I'd like to keep our arrangement on a purely professional level. Be sure to think about how much you're going to charge me. As you know my ex-husband's very rich—unfortunately, I'm on somewhat of a tighter budget. Now, if you'll excuse me." She looked Dan right in the eye.

"Anything you say, Miss Allison. After all, you're paying the freight. Sorry about the comment. The last thing I wanna do is fight the Civil War."

"I don't care for the term, Civil War. I prefer to call it the Great Unpleasantness. Goodbye, Mr. Gillespie. Call me when you have something."

Bingo! She hates me, but I just made last month's alimony payment. He watched her cross the street from his office window. That, my friend, is a world class ass, he said to himself.


By midnight that evening, Gillespie had consumed the better part of a fifth of Bullet bourbon and smoked all but his last cigarette. He fanned the pages of Langley's report across his desk. He washed his face with his hands. Was there a connection between Langley's beating and Max Turner? No way, couldn't be. What about these fucking cases? Turner would shit if he knew someone was examining his private files. He reread the note Langley had sent to Lynn Allison.

Dear Ms. Allison:
    Your suspicion may be justified. The lawsuit of Willie Jamal Rolle v. Golden Tobacco Inc. did show a similar pattern

to five other cases. There was a multimillion-dollar judgment in favor of the plaintiff, who was found to be mentally incompetent. The late Mr. Rolle died six months after receiving his settlement. Rolle's estate was left to the church in question, as were the other settlements. All plaintiffs died within one year after receiving their final settlement checks. All of the estates were never contested. There were no heirs. Max Turner holds the mortgages on the church and the surrounding twenty-two-thousand-acre ranch. I should have more information next week.

> Sincerely,
> Richard Langley

Langley, you stupid son-of-a-bitch, of course they all died. They died of fucking lung cancer. He extinguished his cigarette in an overflowing ashtray. Gillespie tipped up the bottle to take another swig. Over the top of the bottle he looked at a man who had slipped into his office. He was a large, bald man.

"You have the wrong office," Gillespie said, thumping his chest to ease the heartburn.

"I have the right office. Smoking is such a filthy habit. I hate the smell of cigarettes on a man," the big man said, licking his lips.

# 4
# ZIMBABWE

## One month later

Rigby Croxford flew back to Africa alone. He had mixed emotions about leaving his wife in the States. In the end, she decided to attend her previously scheduled medical seminars and stay behind.

\*　　\*　　\*

Rigby had been driving for two days to Mozambique and a rendezvous with Max Turner. Zimbabwe's cantankerous roads slowed them down. His men were either fixing tire punctures or nursing their geriatric vehicles.

At the same time, Turner's private jet landed in Johannesburg. Rigby's long-time hunting partner, Hansel Martin, met Turner at Jan Smuts International Airport. Turner chartered a King Air to fly to the private airstrip at the Sabu Safari Lodge on the border between Mozambique and the Kruger National Park in South Africa.

\*　　\*　　\*

Sam Mabota, Rigby's African tracker, slept in the backseat. Sam emerged from under a woolen blanket and yelled to Rigby over the wind noise. "*Baba*, we traveled this road during the war." Sam always called Rigby *Baba*, the respectful equivalent for father in his native language. "We were being chased by the Mozambican Army. Do you remember?"

"Of course I bloody well remember," Rigby yelled back. "Let's hope the Mozambicans have forgotten. Sam, look there." He pointed at a demolished bridge. "Isn't that the bridge we blew up?"

"It is the same bridge." What was left of the concrete bridge had been abandoned like most broken things in Africa. The rusting remains of two army trucks lay like overturned tortoises at the bottom of the dried-up riverbed. A skinny boy tended some goats at one end of the bridge. The boy waved to them as they drove past on the newly constructed bridge.

"I miss the war. Hey Sam, it was some good times, wasn't it?"

"*Yebo*. Some days were good, but other days were not so good."

"I suppose you're right. Christ, I'd love to give it another go. Sam, do you remember the operation into the Ngorima Lands?"

"That was a good day," replied Sam, smiling.

"I should have never let you tie me up." When he thought about their feeble attempt at counterterrorism, he laughed. He let Sam march him into a suspected terrorist village at gunpoint. Sam told the headsman he wanted to turn Rigby over to the local communist bigwig. His daydream ended, and he glanced back at Sam.

"I can't believe you just left me. I reckon women can be the most vicious things God ever created. Those Shona women beat the shit out of me. Not often you get to beat a white man. I'm screaming for you to save me, but you're busy talking with some *umfazi* you wanted as your fifth wife. Look at you, you think it's funny," Rigby said, looking at Sam in the rearview mirror. Sam tried to mask his amusement, but couldn't. "If I had rescued you too early, they would have become suspicious."

"I remember the chief sent his sons to help you guard me. As soon as we were out of sight, I got myself untied. His sons wanted me to kill you. Said they were waiting for the right time to jump you and let me go. There's no word for loyalty in Shona. I think they ended up fighting on our side."

"It is true, *Baba*. But mostly, they were hiding."

He downshifted to allow a troop of baboons to cross the road. "We should be at Dutchy's place anytime now. That's if these bloody tires last. His mother must have been a rhino. I reckon no man that strong can be human. He shoots a .570 nitro express, which is almost an artillery piece. Anyway, he's a damn fine professional hunter, and he knows Mozambique. More importantly, he gets on with the Renamo bandits."

Sam closed his eyes. I forgot about the bandits, he thought. The lion hunt was the cause of a fight with his youngest wife. He remembered her lecturing him: "Mozambique is the home of devils. Bad things will happen if you go on this safari."

"Woman, you're trying my patience."

"I have dreamed about these things," she said. "Tell Rigby you're too old to go. I love him as much as you do, but he wants to fight another war. I won't watch him get my husband killed. Don't tell me you're doing this for the little money he pays you."

Twenty years ago, he would have beaten his wife for such insolence. A man becomes tolerant of a woman's words when he gets old. And he liked the feel of her smooth skin against him at night. His older wives would have been happy if he had beaten her. Men and women are not the same, he reflected, smiling.

"*Baba*, *ugifuna* a smoke?"

"I thought you quit smoking, Sam."

"I'll stop again after we finish this hunt."

The landscape bottomed out into a savanna or a *bosveld*, as the Afrikaners call it. The Lebombo Mountains appeared out of the afternoon haze. Rigby turned onto a washboard road and then crossed a wooden bridge spanning the Limpopo River. The other trucks followed him in a serpentine conga-line procession, zigzagging around the fallen mahogany trees crisscrossing the road. Elephants had pushed the trees over to feed on the succulent seed pods.

They drove into a meadow or *vlei* populated by umbrella acacias. The land sloped gently down to a narrow tree-lined river. They heard the chuckle of moving water coming from the river. A thatch-roofed sandstone house lay nestled under a large silver terminalia tree in the center of the clearing. There were racks of spiral and sickle shaped antelope horns over the windows. Two bleached elephant skulls marked the walkway to the house. The trucks scattered some clucking chickens. The man who walked around from behind the house was almost a giant. A cape of black hair covered his shoulders and chest. His bare feet were the size of boat paddles. Jan Bosshart or Dutchy looked fiendish without incisors. His wife looked like his twin. She suckled a child riding her hip. Two more children hid behind her. Her rump could have hidden more children. Her smile was also in need of dentures. Their African house-servant covered her mouth to hide her smile as is the custom in that part of Africa. She was also barefooted. Dutchy's wife barked at the woman in

Afrikaans. The woman chased, caught and rung the necks of four scrawny guinea fowl and three even skinnier chickens.

"*Hoe gaan dit met jou?*" Jan Bosshart greeted Rigby in Afrikaans.

"I am good. And your wife and children?"

"*Goed, dankie.* Come, my friend, we wash up before we eat. Christ man, it's *goed* to see you," he thundered, putting his hand on Rigby's shoulder.

Rigby's men got out of their truck to stretch. Before they could light their cigarettes, a Jack Russell terrier exploded out of the house. The black-and-brown-spotted dog made a beeline for one man and latched on to his pant leg. Two other mongrel dogs yapped and barked, but didn't bite the terrified African. He managed to free himself and climb up on the truck's roof. The enraged terrier raced around the truck trying to find a way up onto the roof.

"*Nee,* Jocko, you little shit. Leave him," Dutchy yelled, grabbing the growling terrier by the scruff of his neck. "My friend, when was the last time you wore those pants? Don't tell me. I will tell you. You wore them on a hunt. Was it a leopard or a lion hunt?"

"It was a leopard hunt," the man answered.

"One of you, get him another pair of britches before my Jocko kills him." The man changed his pants from the safety of the roof. When he tossed the old pants on the ground, Jocko cocked his leg and urinated on the pants. Contented, he jumped up on the same man he had harassed demanding his affection.

"I reckon Jocko is the best hunting dog in all of Zimbabwe. The fact that he hasn't been eaten proves it. If hyenas come around at night, he hides under my bed. If it's a lion or a leopard, he won't stop barking until I let him hide under my covers. Isn't that right, Jocko, my lion killer?" Dutchy said to his dog.

"What took Jocko's ear?" Rigby asked.

"A bloody puff adder bit him. I think maybe he's learned his lesson about snakes. Jocko, tell them you've had your fill with snakes."

The dog barked and nipped at Dutchy's heels. He motioned to his wife. "Come, woman, make us something to eat. We must make our plans for the lion hunt."

Twin campfires illuminated the Bosshart homestead that night. The Africans tended a fire down by the river. A large, black iron pot of mealy-meal simmered on an open fire. Bats swooped down to feed on the insects attracted to the light. The men were tired from the long drive, but the palm wine lifted their spirits. Soon, singing and bouts of laughter erupted. Jocko lay next to the man he had attacked. Nightfall brought out the hyenas. Their giggling carried across the river. The cackling sent Jocko scampering to his master's side.

The mood around the other campfire was more somber as Dutchy outlined his plan for the hunt. "My friend, the lion hunting in Mozambique has changed. The old way of hanging meat from a tree to bait them no longer works."

"What's happened to the lions?" Rigby asked.

"In Mozambique, we must use more effective methods." Dutchy drew a map in the sand with a stick. "This is the Kruger National Game Park. It extends four hundred kilometers along the Mozambican border. For the last five years, Mozambican refugees have been crossing into South Africa. Some are cannabis smugglers, but most of them are looking for work." He scratched lines in the sand showing the refugee border crossings, and then stuck his stick in the sand. "This is where we will find our lion. We do have a problem—these Mozambican lions have developed funny appetites."

"What kind of funny appetites?" Rigby inquired.

"Renamo bandits poached out the buffalo and wildebeest. There was nothing left for the lions to feed on, so they started eating the refugees. In the old days, we used a tape recording of hyenas at a kill or the roars of a big male to bring them into shooting range. These lions have grown too clever to fall for our old tricks." Dutchy sucked a chicken bone clean and handed it to Jocko. The little dog stood over it and growled at the mongrels.

"We only have two weeks to get Turner's lion. Do you think two weeks is enough time?" Rigby asked.

"*Ja*, two weeks is plenty. I scouted the river last week. The lions are as thick as flies on buffalo shit. Your client will take his lion. The trick is to avoid being eaten," Dutchy answered and then laughed.

"Mother, show Rigby how we attract the lions," Dutchy said, turning to his wife.

Dutchy's wife turned on a tape recorder. It was a recording of a woman and a young child screaming. The sound quieted the men. Jocko started to whimper.

"It's horrible. Is that you?" Rigby asked, addressing Dutchy's wife.

"*Ja*, she's a fine actor, no? The lions cannot resist it. We must be very cautious, my friend."

"I'll certainly drink to that." Rigby clicked his beer bottle with Dutchy's. "Helen will skin me alive if I get myself eaten."

\*       \*       \*

They broke camp early the next morning. Dutchy couldn't squeeze into the cab of Rigby's truck; he grabbed Jocko and climbed into its bed. Both were sleeping by the time they reached the border. The Zimbabwean border guards demanded bribes, which Rigby refused to pay. In the end, the guards relented and waved them through.

Rigby remarked that the roads in Mozambique made the roads in Zimbabwe look like a German autobahn. Five hours after crossing the border, they came to a barricade. Four raggedly dressed Africans with AK-47s draped over their shoulders walked out of the bushes. One man was missing a hand. Dutchy jumped out of the lead truck and walked forward to greet them. As he walked by, he whispered to Rigby, "Renamo *banditos*. I know this bunch. All they want is some of our food."

Rigby continued to smile, but eased his rifle into his lap. "Sam, if the shit starts—remember to duck."

"The devil with one hand is their leader. Shoot him first." Sam whispered back.

"Precisely my thoughts. Just be ready." His voice faded so that only Sam could hear him. "And how are you today, you sneaky-looking bastards?" he said, smiling.

Their leader greeted Dutchy in his native language. "*Avuxen ku njihani?*" he inquired politely. Dutchy answered him in Portuguese. "*Ola, bom dia.*"

The bandits laughed and touched Dutchy's massive arms. Dutchy nodded to reassure Rigby. Their one-handed leader swung his weapon down and stuck his head in the window. "Hello. How are you today?" he asked, trying his best English.

"Do we have some food for them?" Dutchy yelled. "They say they have not eaten in two days."

"Dutchy, ask them about the lions."

"*Ja*, they say there are lions at the bottom of the valley. They can hear them roaring at night. They have been sleeping in the trees like baboons. This one says we should sleep in our trucks." Dutchy put his hand on the man's shoulder. "My friend, I think he gives us good advice."

"Come, Dutchy, let us leave this place before they turn my Matabele warriors into screaming women," Rigby yelled, glancing back at his men, who were all grinning. When he opened the door, he made sure the bandits saw his .416. They moved closer to get a better look. "Such a fine weapon—you waste it on lions. Have you killed many with it?" one man asked. Another man walked behind the truck, but jumped back when Jocko tried to bite him.

"I've killed many things with this rifle."

*     *     *

They made their camp on the Luvuvhu River. After the men collected hook-thorn bushes, they interlocked the scrub into a protective circle, known as a *boma*. At the end of the day, Rigby and Sam Mabota inspected the thorny barrier for gaps. Satisfied, they closed the entrance from the inside.

At first the night was peaceful, but then it started. A distant male called his females with a few resonating snorts. Dominant males warned other males. Females called their pride sisters to fresh kills. The bellowing got so loud it sounded like the lions had penetrated their *boma*.

Jocko was not amused. The dog whimpered and sought comfort from Dutchy, who pushed him away. The terrier nipped his hand. "Jocko, these men will think you're a sissy." Dutchy reached down, picked the dog up and kissed him. He pushed Jocko under his blanket.

Croxford was exhausted, but he couldn't sleep. He shared a tent with Dutchy, whose whiskey-induced snoring was louder than the lions. Just before dawn, Rigby found refuge under a truck where Sam and the other men had slept. The tyranny of the night abated at first light. The mournful cooing of doves replaced the night sounds.

"Sam, could you find sleep?" Rigby asked, yawning.

"*Awa*. Only death could bring sleep with the Dutchman's snoring. Let's look outside the *boma* for lion spoor."

When Dutchy walked up behind Sam and Rigby, they were inspecting some pugmarks. Sam picked at a pile of bloodied lion feces with a stick. The foul smelling heap contained hair and human teeth. The stench overloaded Jocko's olfactory system. The dog raced around marking the area with urine squirts. As he leaned in to check the scent under a mopani bush, Dutchy tossed a stick into the bush and snorted. The dog vaulted into his master's arms. When he laughed, Jocko growled.

"My brother, are there any males?" Rigby asked Sam, urinating with one hand while picking an errant piece of tobacco from his teeth with the other.

"*Yebo, Baba, kubili.*"

"How big?"

"Very big," answered Sam.

"I reckon we should make our thorn-walls higher," Rigby said, stooping down. He tried to span the lion track with his hand; the pug-mark was bigger. Normal lions shun humans, but these lions are different, Rigby reasoned.

\*   \*   \*

At midday, Rigby and Sam left the compound to pick up Max Turner. The road was so rutted even wallowing in four-wheel drive couldn't stop the truck from heading off in directions contrary to Rigby's efforts. After struggling for hours, they drove up behind two women and a skinny young girl walking on the road. They had knapsacks slung over their shoulders. The women started to run, but when they realized it was too late, they froze.

"My sisters, do not fear us," Sam yelled in Afrikaans. The young girl looked scared and refused eye contact. She had a clubfoot and walked with the aid of a stick.

"Ladies, come ride with us," said Rigby. "We need protection from the Renamo bandits. Although I must say, if you let our noisy truck sneak up on you, I doubt you can offer us much protection." The two women laughed and the young girl giggled. They climbed into the back of the truck. Within seconds, the crippled girl was sleeping.

Sam learned they had walked from Maputo, a coastal town in Mozambique. They had been with a group of thirty refugees, but had split up into smaller groups hoping to sneak across the South African border. The women had endured bandits and wild animals, but what they feared the most was getting caught by the South African police.

They parked under an ebony tree. The men shared their lunch with the women. When Rigby saw how quickly they devoured the food, he insisted that he wasn't hungry. Sam cut and whittled a better walking stick for the crippled girl. When it was time to go, the women declined to ride with them. They explained they were afraid the truck might attract the attention of the border police. As the truck pulled away, the women yelled something, but their words were consumed by the straining engine.

"Walk with God, my sisters," Sam yelled. One hour later, they arrived at the South African border crossing.

"*Pra't jai enals?*" the border guard asked Rigby.

"Yes, I speak English."

"Did you see any kaffirs?" the guard inquired, looking at Sam. Sam stared back defiantly.

"We were stopped by bandits yesterday," said Rigby.

"What about refugees?"

"We've seen no refugees. We're collecting our client at Sabu. We should be back here in two hours."

"You're out of luck. This border crossing closes in one hour. There's no way you'll catch me out here after dark. Too many lions to suit me. See you bright and early. We open at 0600."

"Right you are. See you at first light," Rigby yelled.

"That white hyena turd is too foul for lions to eat," Mabota said, as they drove away.

*     *     *

Sabu Safari Lodge was one of those luxury safari camps only the grotesquely rich could afford. Rigby set out to find Max Turner. Waiters wearing formal attire and red fezzes scurried along the walkways carrying silver trays of drinks and food.

Max Turner walked out of his chalet wearing a safari outfit complete with knee socks and desert boots. His Indiana Jones style hat was banded in zebra hide. He wore elephant hair bracelets on both wrists. Croxford bit his lip to keep from laughing. "Welcome to Africa, Max. You might be slightly overdressed for Mozambique." Before Max could answer, Rigby's partner, Hansel Martin, walked up behind him.

"We have a problem. Mr. Turner has brought two guests," Martin said.

Rigby saw Max's daughter-in-law standing in the doorway. "Max, this isn't what we agreed to. Mozambique is no place for a woman or your fucking buddy. No pun intended. This isn't gonna fly."

"I didn't think there would be a problem. You wouldn't object to them staying here?"

"Of course not."

"That's settled. Anything else?" Max sounded irritated.

"That covers it. We'll pick you up one hour before dawn. Tell your friends you'll see them in ten days."

"I thought we agreed to two weeks."

"The agreement was to get you a lion. Where we're going is crawling with lions. Getting you a lion in ten days won't be a problem."

"Great. Sorry about the mix-up. What about dinner tonight?" Max asked.

"I'm afraid that's quite impossible. I pitched my tent down the road. These bloody hotel rates would force me to sell my farm. Remember, I need you ready to go at first light. We're in for a hell of a drive. Cheers, Max, see you in the morning." As they walked away, Rigby remarked to Martin, "I'd rather eat hyena shit than have dinner with that asshole. I'm gonna need you to keep an eye on his friends. Turner's a snake. I'd like to get this safari over as quickly as possible."

"Turner's woman is something else. I can't remember seeing a better-looking bird."

"That woman's not his, she's—let's just say it's complicated. Do yourself a favor, stay the hell away from her."

"Christ, Rigby, no need to get so huffy. I've never seen you so edgy."

"I haven't slept a wink since I agreed to do this hunt. I wish I'd listened to my wife." Rigby said goodnight to Martin and retreated to his tent.

*        *        *

Dawn peeked over the Lebombo Mountains as they arrived at the border post. There were two South African army trucks parked next to the Customs and Immigration building. One was a flatbed. Rigby saw what appeared to be bodies covered by a dark green tarp. "What's going on here?" he asked the border guard.

"Poor devils, three women raped and killed by bandits. Say, the kaffirs who stopped you. Was one missing a hand? Are you all right?"

Rigby felt dizzy. He paused before speaking. "Sorry. Yes, one was missing a hand. Are you sure it's the same bunch?" Rigby asked, handing him passports and papers.

"Quite. Preying on refugees is their pleasure. Wicked devils. Be careful, my friend," the guard said.

"Cheers. Thanks for the warning," Rigby replied.

Rigby walked over to the truck and lifted the edge of the tarp. When he saw the clubfoot, he gently re-covered it. Turner questioned him. Rigby mumbled something about a dead animal, but Sam knew otherwise. Rigby dried his eyes, but when he realized Sam was staring at him he regained his composure.

The six-hour drive to camp was done in almost total silence. They stopped once to give way to a herd of elephants lumbering across the road. Rigby refused help with the driving and seemed to take out his hostility on the bumpy road. Max's endless questions were answered with terse responses. Rigby stopped at the same place they stopped the day before. Instead of eating, he walked down by the river.

When they pulled into camp, Dutchy greeted them with Jocko tucked under his arm. "Did you miss me?" Rigby light heartedly asked Dutchy.

"I missed you. Jocko missed you. You should have heard them last night. In the morning, we followed the sticks. It was a young male and his three lionesses." Dutchy turned to Max and extended his hand. "You must be Turner."

"Max, the men place sticks in the direction of the last roars they hear," Rigby explained. "It helps us find them in the morning. Lions don't venture far in the heat of the day. It'll all be clearer tomorrow. You might want to sleep with earplugs. The sound's quite deafening."

"Don't worry about me," Max scoffed.

"Suit yourself. Just remember, I warned you. Now, let's make sure that fancy rifle of yours is zeroed in. We've put some targets up at a hundred meters."

Both Dutchy and Croxford were surprised by Turner's marksmanship. He had obviously been practicing.

"A charging lion is not a paper target," Dutchy said to Rigby with his back turned to Max. "We'll see how well he shoots when the time comes."

*   *   *

Max wasn't sleeping. After the second night, he demanded that Rigby place an armed guard outside of his tent. The next morning Max complained. "The night guard's useless. I heard him snoring."

To calm Turner down, Dutchy and Rigby took over the guard-duty detail. Two nights later, Turner caught Rigby napping. The third time Turner woke Rigby up, the reception he received shocked him. "Max, if you wake me up one more time, I'll put a bullet right between your bloodshot eyes. Do we understand each other?"

In the morning, he handed Turner his first mug of coffee. "Sorry about last night. Sleeping with these lions is enough to drive any man insane."

"All's forgiven, as long as I get my lion."

"Lion hunting is never easy. The dumb ones have already been shot."

"I hope I get a chance to redeem myself," Max said.

At dusk, Max shot a zebra stallion. It was a head shot at over two hundred meters. The men used parts of the zebra carcass to bait three blinds. That night, they had no takers except for two large lionesses and a male so young he still had the camouflage spots on his flanks. On the fourth night, Rigby tried a tape recording of a male roaring, but it silenced the younger males. Even the recording of hyenas on a kill would not bring them into shooting range. On the fifth day the lion hunting improved, but it was the worst day of Rigby Croxford's life.

*       *       *

Dutchy and Sam returned from their morning scouting expedition. They had seen white-backed vultures circling above a baobab tree. It was enough to get Rigby and Turner scrambling into the back of the truck.

"Max, I know you're getting tired of hearing it, but this could be the day. Just remember what we've gone over. A male lion broadside is three meters long. You need to shoot him here." Rigby indicated a place under his armpit. "That way, you take out a lung and maybe his heart. If he charges your target size is reduced to the size of a man's fist. A lion's skull is shaped like an arrowhead. Let him get close before you pull the trigger or you may get a ricochet. When I say close, I mean so close you can smell his breath. We'll wait for you to fire the first shot, but after that one, we'll all be firing. I know I've said this before, but you can't run. If any of us bolt, it'll turn a mock charge into the real thing. A good shot is what we need from you. Any questions?"

"Don't worry about me. I won't run, and I won't miss." Turner's boasting caused Rigby and Dutchy to glance at each other.

It took them an hour to drive to the circling vultures. They got out of the truck and started to move up. Sam made sure they were downwind. The baobab was at the edge of a died-up pan. The tree was covered in vultures and marabou storks. Underneath its twisted branches there was a tan-colored form. Sam led them into the heavy "adrenalin" grass. The area around the pan was thicketed in mopani scrub and hookthorn underbrush.

During the night, two black-maned lions had fought over a woman's carcass. One lion rested under the baobab guarding what was left of her. His belly was swollen with human flesh and organs. He flicked his tail to ward off blowflies and he lapped blood off of his paws. His brother waited nearby for his turn to feed. He licked at a deep gash inflicted by his brother. Instantly, both lions stood up to investigate a noise.

Dutchy increased the volume on his tape recorder. The sound of a child screaming carried on the wind. They saw the lion under the tree, but no one saw the second lion circling in behind them. Dutchy had left Jocko in the truck. When the dog saw the second lion crawling towards his master, he went wild. Dutchy turned and motioned to silence him. The lion was now only fifty meters behind him. Jocko tried to squeeze through the cracked window.

"Take him, Max," Rigby whispered. "No wait! Wait!" He hooked Turner's elbow and pulled him forward. "Watch his tail. As long as he's flicking it, we're safe. If he straightens his tail for balance, he's coming." The hunters fanned out with Dutchy on the flank. Rigby and Turner stayed in the middle. Sam put his fingers in his ears and squatted.

The lion charge started in slow motion. The male under the baobab came at them slowly at first. The cat extended his massive forelegs to build speed. His arrow-shaped head stayed level. His yellow eyes locked on his prey. As he closed the distance, the big male extended his razor-sharp claws, opened his jaws and spewed deep resonating snorts.

"Take him, Max! Shoot him, for Christ's sake. Shoot him!" Rigby screamed. Mentally thickened by fatigue and the chaos of the moment, Max had forgotten to release the safety. When he pulled the trigger, he got no response. When he turned to run he hit Rigby in the face with his rifle butt, knocking him to the ground. Sam Mabota took the full charge of the five-hundred-pound lion. The sound was one of bones breaking. Rigby and Dutchy swung their weapons inward, but realized they would shoot each other in the crossfire.

The first lion's attack triggered his brother's charge. Dutchy turned around and found Jocko latched on the second lion's tail. The cat swatted Jocko. One quick bite crushed the terrier's skull. The lion dropped the dog and headed straight for Dutchy.

"Jocko! My baby," Dutchy cried. He fired his nitro express, but missed. His second shot blew a hole in the cat's thigh. The enraged lion pounced on Dutchy and tried to deliver a death bite, but Dutchy grabbed two fistfuls of the lion's mane and stiff-armed its jaws. Rigby discharged his .416 into the lion's ear. The big male collapsed on top of Dutchy. Frightened by the gunfire, the first lion bounded off into the elephant grass. The dust and gun smoke settled. The air was filled with the stench of cordite.

"Is anyone hurt?" asked Rigby, his voice shaking. "Where in Christ's name, did that second one come from? Max, why didn't you fire? What the bloody hell happened?" Rigby checked the lump on his forehead for blood.

"It was a defective cartridge," said Max. "I pulled the trigger and nothing happened."

"Nothing happened?" Rigby asked.

Dutchy sat next to the dead lion with Jocko in his arms. He was covered in blood and part of his scalp had fallen down over his face. He wasn't crying, but tears ran down his cheeks, mixing with his blood. "My poor Jocko, one of them finally got you. Rigby, I reckon Jocko's barking saved me. I never saw this one," he said, spitting on the dead lion.

"Jesus, Dutchy, you're hurt. Let me have a look at you. That lion worked you over." As Rigby surveyed the carnage, he realized Sam was still lying on the ground. One of Sam's legs had a bone protruding. "How bad is it?" he asked Sam, kneeling beside him.

"I have no feeling in my legs. I'd rather die than crawl like a worm. My youngest wife dreamed this would happen."

"Sam, you're talking rubbish. I'll get you fixed up proper. " Rigby lit two cigarettes and put one in Sam's mouth.

"We've had a good life together," said Sam, taking Rigby's hand. His face was contorted from pain. "I want to be buried in Zimbabwe. This country has always been cursed for me."

Rigby took Sam's hand and said, "My brother, we'll grow old and fat together."

Sam forced a smile and answered, "I'm already old."

Rigby had seen too many Africans die not to know that Sam was determined to end his life. He walked over to Max who was sitting on the ground. "Max, what's this bullshit about how you never miss and you never run?" Rigby had to be led away by Dutchy.

The Matabele trackers stayed behind to bury the woman's remains under the baobab tree. Next to her, they buried Jocko. They piled sandstones on the graves to prevent the hyenas from digging them up. When they arrived back in camp, they learned Sam Mabota had died in Rigby's arms. The men wrapped Sam's body in a tent and placed it in the back of Rigby's truck.

A somber Max Turner stood over Sam's body. "I will pray for his soul tonight. I wish he was a Christian. 'The Lord instructed one prophet to say to another, strike me, but the man refused to strike the prophet. Then the prophet told him. Because you have not obeyed the Lord, a lion will kill you. He was attacked and killed by a lion.' Kings 20:35.'"

"You can take your religious hocus-pocus and stuff it," Rigby said. "One of my men will drive you over the border. I'll refund your money, less our expenses. I've got one hell of a long drive ahead of me. Let's say goodbye, and leave it at that."

"I know you're mad, but there was nothing I could have done differently. It was a defective bullet. I don't care about the refund. As a matter of fact, I'd feel better if I could send some money to Sam's family," said Max.

"Max, I'm mad at the world. Sam Mabota was like a brother. If you could help his family, I know they could use it. I need to get on the road. Goodbye, Max." He waited until the truck carrying Max was out of sight before turning to Dutchy, "It took a lot for me not to kill that son-of-a-bitch. Don't think for a minute, I didn't consider it."

Rigby stood next to Sam's body. "You didn't deserve to die like this. I should never have let you come on this cocked-up safari. This is as much my fault as Turner's. I wish it was me and not you."

Dutchy put his arm around Rigby and spoke. "Don't punish yourself. Sam knew the risks."

"Bullshit, Dutchy, Sam was too old to do this hunt."

"*Ja*, but how many of our friends have been killed in this hunting business? We know the dangers, but we must feed our families."

Rigby turned and looked at Dutchy. "Let me have a look at you. I think a career in the movies is definitely out of the question. It doesn't look too bad, mostly blood, but nothing too deep. We'll get you to a doctor on the way out. You're in for a fair amount of stitching and antibiotics. I reckon a lion's claws are the filthiest things on God's earth."

"I don't trust quacks. You've got needle and string. You stitch me up. You need to get him in the ground. Sam was a *goed* one. I'll miss him."

"You won't miss him as much as I will. You there, bring me some whiskey," Rigby yelled at one of his men. "The doctor needs to steady his sewing hand."

Dutchy didn't flinch as Rigby reattached his scalp. They consumed a liter of whiskey between them. As Rigby tied off the last suture, he thought about how much he hated Max Turner.

After Rigby finished his doctoring; he drove out of camp with Sam Mabota's body in the back of his truck. A few minutes into the ride, he pulled a bottle of whiskey from under the seat and placed it between his legs.

His first stop was at the baobab tree where his men buried the African woman and Jocko. He took a swig of whiskey before getting out of the truck. Turner said he ejected that defective cartridge near the graves. If I don't have a look, I'll never know, he thought.

He stood over the graves and looked at a spot under the baobab tree. The brass bullet glistened in the sunshine. Before loading the round, he held it up. Just as I expected, the cap isn't dented. The gunshot echoed down the valley. Rigby stuck the spent shell in his pocket and walked back to the truck.

As he drove, he thought about what he would say to Sam's wives. The thought depressed him. At the last second, he turned around and headed back to the place where they had encountered the bandits. God, I hope I find you, he said to himself. He opened the breach to make sure a round was engaged. He downshifted and started up a gentle rise. When he reached the top, he recognized the barricade. As soon as he stopped, they walked out of the underbrush. So, you haven't left, he thought.

"*Hoe gaan dit met jou?*" the man missing a hand asked.

"*Goed dankie*," Rigby answered.

"How did you find the lion hunting?"

"*Goed*."

"Where's your friend, Dutchy? Haven't you heard, there are many bandits in Mozambique?" The other men found their leader's words side-splitting. Rigby never took his eyes off of the man talking.

"I think you should give us some food."

"Quite right. I have a nice side of impala wrapped up in the back. Take what you want," Rigby said, throwing his hunting knife in the back of the truck. Two of them leaned their AK-47s against the side of the truck and jumped up into the bed. They cut the bindings and started to unroll Sam Mabota's corpse.

"Be sure to leave some for me," Rigby yelled as they uncovered Sam's face. They screamed and jumped back. The others ran to help their friends, but when they saw Sam's face, they also started screaming. Rigby struck the leader on the bridge of his nose with his rifle butt knocking him to the ground. He hit him again. A blood geyser erupted from the man's face. He hit the next one in the temple. He caught the third one flush in the mouth. The last man kneeled down and begged for mercy. One bandit tried to run, but his legs appeared boneless and wouldn't support him.

"*Wat doen jy?*" the one-handed leader asked.

"For starters, take off your clothes. Be quick about it, or I'll shoot all of you."

"What are you going to do with us?" another man asked.

"I'm gonna watch the lions eat you," he slurred. "No self-respecting lion would feed on gutless scum like you." He fired his rifle at their feet. "Start running."

"*Asseblief*, you cannot take our weapons. Only a demon would leave men out here to die." The man with one hand tried to standup, but he wobbled and fell to his knees.

"What about the women? What chance did you give them? You remember the girl with the crippled foot? I'm giving you better than you gave them." He threw the men's clothes in the back of his truck. He kept firing until they were out of sight.

After taking a swig of whiskey he glanced back at Sam's body and smiled. Sam, you should have seen their faces when I told them I wanted to feed them to the lions. I do believe they shit themselves. Only good thing to come out of this cocked-up safari.

# 5
# HIGHLANDS, ZIMBABWE

Exhaustion and whiskey beat him into submission. Just before sundown, Rigby pulled off the road and crawled under his truck to sleep. He covered himself with Sam's woolen blanket and dozed off. He closed his eyes and remembered the day he met Sam. It was at the Selous Scout Regimental recruiting headquarters in Salisbury. *An officer sitting behind a desk addressed Sam. I was next in line. "So, Mr. Mabota, you want to join the Selous Scouts? You do know only one man in ten finishes the course. Yet you still wish to volunteer?"*

*"Yes, sah, very much so, sah," Sam answered, clicking his heels together.*

*The officer circled around Sam, examining him. "Africans never show their age like the rest of us mortals. It says here you think you're about forty. A bit old for this kind of duty, wouldn't you agree?"*

*"Sah, does it say there I finished number one in my class?"*

*"Yes, quite right, Mr. Mabota," he said, twirling a tip of his mustache. "Because of your basic training record, I'm inclined to approve your selection. Your application is accepted. Next," the officer said.*

*"Mr. Croxford, is it?"*

*"Yes, sir."*

*"Well now, Croxford, I must say there's nothing stunning about your basic-training record. Your late father had a brilliant military career. But you see, unlike you, he was a disciplined soldier. Because of your father, I'm inclined to approve your application. I'd be surprised if you make it through the first week. Good luck Mr. Croxford, you'll certainly need it."*

Rigby needed to urinate, but he resisted leaving the warm hollow under his truck. He forgot where he was and banged his head. "Shit," he uttered. What caused the goose flesh on my arms, he asked himself. He thought he heard something. He strained to hear, but it was quiet. Get a grip, he thought, chiding himself. The sound of leaves rustling made his heart race. He heard an animal sniffing and when he looked out from underneath the truck he saw hairy legs and shadows. The lions started excavating him from his burrow. He tunneled deeper, but the lions were better diggers. When he felt the truck move he knew they were in the bed. You're not lions. You're bloody hyenas and you're after Sam. He crawled out, climbed in his truck and switched on the headlamps. His truck was surrounded by glowing eyes. The canvas tarp wrapping Sam's corpse had been shredded. "Get you filthy buggers," Rigby screamed, firing his rifle. The cackling hyenas loped off.

Rigby was driving before sunrise. The hillsides were dotted with umbrella acacias budding in anticipation of the rainy season. He passed a cart pulled by four miserable looking donkeys; it was stacked with firewood and Africans. As he waved back, he wondered why Africans appear happy. Maybe it's because death in Africa isn't abstract, it permeates your soul. Life is tolerable when you know death intimately, he reflected. As he drove, he daydreamed about his wife. Early in their marriage, he tried to shelter his wife from the brutality of Africa. *"Rigby, tell me what you did in Mozambique? The London Times is calling it a massacre. It says the Rhodesians killed over a thousand freedom fighters."*

*"Helen, I wouldn't believe anything in the Times. We had been getting intelligence about a terrorist camp operating in Mozambique. The insurgents have been sneaking over our border and laying landmines. Those landmines are killing children. Someone finally decided to do something. That's all."*

*"Please tell me you didn't kill anyone?"*

*"Me? I was part of a demolition team."*

*"Thank God. Will this lunacy ever end?" She daubed her eyes. "I'm glad you're not like the others."*

*"For me, this war ends in two months," I told her. But my tour of duty didn't end and as the war turned against us; I became one of the 'others.' She never asked me about the war again. Men do God awful things in war. Grisly things we keep hidden. Sam was right, some days were not good.*

Lupano was a village on the road. Rigby pulled up to the lone petrol pump and got out of his truck. He was surprised by the lack of children. The petrol attendant explained that the story of his journey had preceded him. Africans were wary of a man transporting a corpse. Rigby told him that he felt like Livingstone's trusted servant Susi, who carried the doctor's salt-cured corpse a thousand kilometers to Zanzibar to be shipped back to England for a proper burial. The man said he never heard of Livingstone or Susi. He politely asked Rigby to leave.

*     *     *

Sam Mabota's funeral turned into a theatrical extravaganza. People came from every corner of the country. The attendees pitched tents on the Croxford farm. At night, smoke from their campfires cast a halo around the moon. African music struggled against monotonous native rap. Rigby had a truckload of *chibuku* delivered to his farm. Mounds of empties scarred the landscape. Some men slept where they fell, too drunk to find their way back to their tents. The drunken celebration of Sam's life lasted for three days.

On the fourth day, the time came to put Sam in the ground. To the consternation of some, Sam was to be laid to rest in the Croxford family plot. Each attendee carried a small stick to the funeral. A black iron pot sat next to Sam's grave. If they had been treated fairly by Sam during his life, they deposited their stick in the pot. If Sam had wronged them, they would retrieve a stick. The length of the eulogy praising Sam's life would be directly proportional to the number of sticks in the pot. Not one stick was taken from the funeral pot that day.

Sam's five wives and thirteen children wailed and threw themselves on the ground. After his brother's death, Sam had married his sister-in-law for her protection as well as her children's. This was the African custom.

The honor of giving the eulogy was given to Rigby. He delivered the first part in Isindebele. He concluded by quoting Scott Holland's famous sermon in English. "It does not count. I have only slipped away into the next room. Nothing has happened. Everything remains exactly as it was, I am I and you are you and the old life we lived so fondly together is untouched, unchanged." After the service ended, the mourners waited in line to shake Rigby's hand.

After the ceremony, Mabota's wives buried him under a flame tree in a sitting position facing the setting sun. The approach of the rainy season had only teased the farmers, but it rained that day. People said it was Sam looking out for friends. Whatever or whoever brought the rain, it caused a bursting forth of new life. Green grass shoots and wild flowers escaped hibernation. The scarred landscape was replenished as Sam's journey was concluded.

A sad silence lay on the rolling green hills of the Croxford farm. Three months after the funeral, Rigby continued to visit Sam's grave. He would sit quietly under the flame tree sipping his whiskey. From time to time, his mind would cast off in an unavoidable direction. His daydreaming returned to Max Turner. When he thought about Max, he fondled the spent cartridge he carried in his pocket. It was the bullet that should have killed the lion.

# 6

# PALM BEACH

Max Turner enjoyed using his mansion in Palm Beach to interview prospective attorneys. He loved seeing his guests swoon over his art collection. He especially enjoyed showing them a painting some unscrupulous art dealer had sold him at a horribly inflated price. Their jaw-dropping gasps were almost orgasmic for Max. If they weren't connoisseurs of art, he would take his guests down to his wine cellar where he would give them a lesson in the cost of rare French Burgundies.

Today, he would conduct the interview in the privacy of his den. The black walnut-paneled room was decorated with glassy-eyed animal heads and African art. Pictures of his jet and the *Liti-Gator* were mixed in photographs of Turner shaking hands with politicians.

He reviewed the prospect's résumé: Jesse Spooner graduated in the middle of his law-school class. Played football; all SEC cornerback. Considered turning pro, but opted for law school. Mother still works in the high-school cafeteria in Belle Glade. Father: unknown. Yes, Spooner would do. More importantly, he was black, which made him a perfect fit.

Max straightened himself as Jesse Spooner was led into his den by an English butler. He rose and a smile crept across his face. "Jesse, thanks for coming. I thought it would be fun to have our little chat here, rather than my office." He shook Jesse's hand with a tighter grip than necessary and sat back down. "Would you care for a glass of wine?"

"A beer would be great, Mr. Turner."

"See to it, Earl," Turner said, motioning to his butler.

"Right away, sir," Earl responded.

Spooner's eyes grew wide as he took in his surroundings. "Wow! This trophy room's bigger than my apartment. That lion is huge. They don't look that big on the Discovery channel. Did you shoot it, Mr. Turner?"

"I insist that you call me Max. That lion was a man-eater. And yes, I did shoot him. Unfortunately, not before it killed one of my trackers. May God rest his soul. We were hunting in Mozambique. It was a year ago, but it's still hard for me to talk about it. Anyway, enough about me, we're here to discuss your future. And I'd like that future to include Turner and Turner. Let's start with your questions. I know you must have questions."

"Only one. Why me? You've got over fifty attorneys working for your firm. Most of them attended the best law schools in the country. My mother says you want to hire me because I'm black."

"Your mother's a damn smart woman. I won't sit here and tell you color has nothing to do with our interest in you. Sometimes, black folks are more comfortable being represented by a black attorney. I think that's only natural. Jesse, the law business isn't for the faint-hearted. Anytime you can get a competitive edge, you take it. We're here to get justice for our clients. If we make a little money in the process, well, that's all right too. Don't get me wrong, there's nothing wrong with becoming a fifty-thousand-dollar-a-year crusader working over at the county courthouse. If that's what you want out of life, go for it. But if you aspire to something a little more, shall I say, comfortable," Turner said, opening his palms, "Jesse, we think you'd be perfect for us."

"I could ask you a bunch of questions about your firm, but I might say something stupid. If you're sure you want me, I have only one question—when do I start?"

"What about tomorrow?"

"Tomorrow works for me."

"Good. Earl, bring up a bottle of 1996 Cristal," he said, activating the intercom on his antique desk.

"Jesse, I do believe the good Lord's brought us together. Make no mistake about it—we're going to do great things together. Working for Turner and Turner will be the smartest decision you've ever made. You're destined for great things, my friend."

They finished the interview with small talk. Jesse sensed Turner wanted to get rid of him. After saying goodbye, the butler showed Jesse to the door.

Max looked across his manicured lawn at Jesse Spooner's worn-out

Chevy pulling out of his driveway. As he shuffled through his mail a hand-addressed envelope caught his attention. The lettering on the envelope was his son's handwriting. Turner's pulse pounded in his ears. It had been posted from Kampala, Uganda on December 11, which was after his son disappeared. Maybe Arthur wrote the letter before he died. Or it could be another extortion attempt. He had difficulty breathing. As he read, his expression turned dark. He reread the last page, crumbled the letter into a ball and threw his champagne glass at the mounted lion. When he screamed, it was bloodcurdling.

"Mr. Turner—is anything wrong?" his butler asked. Turner didn't answer.

"Can I get you something?"

"What? No. I'm fine. What do you want?"

"Sir, Bob is waiting to see you."

"Show him in. Have the maid clean that up." He pointed at the broken glass.

Turner peeled back a section of carpet behind his desk. He spun the tumbler in opposite directions. The safe made a clicking sound. He pulled the door open and extracted four twenty-five thousand dollar packets. He closed the safe before Bob was led into the room.

"Sit down," Turner demanded. After a pause, he began. "I want you to bug Spooner's apartment. Use the detective we just hired. I'm inviting Spooner to a cocktail party onboard the *Liti-Gator* Friday night. That should give Gillespie time to break into his apartment. Let's put a tail on Spooner. Everything about this guy seems to be, as advertised. There's too much at stake to take chances. Stay close to him, but not too close."

"Is there anything else?"

"I want you to deliver this envelope to my ex-wife." Turner put the money in a large manila envelope and slid it across his desk. "Call me if you come across any startling bits of information about Spooner."

As soon as Bob closed the door, Max wrote the following wire instructions to his bank in Switzerland:

Dear Sirs:

This is your authorization to transfer one million dollars to Barclays Bank in Kampala, Uganda, Africa. Account number: 4344405T.

Maxwell Turner

Jesse Spooner checked his rearview mirror. His meeting with Max Turner had gone off without a hitch. It had been almost too easy. He punched the redial button on his cell phone. After he heard the dial tone, he entered his five-digit identifier. "It's Spooner. I'm in. Yes sir, every Friday at eighteen hundred. I understand. Goodbye."

*     *     *

A formally dressed string quartet played softly on the fantail of the *Liti-Gator*. The music muffled the bouts of counterfeit laughter. Max met his guests at the top of the gangway. There were handshakes for the men and cheek-kissing for the ladies. The young wives of the junior partners flirted with Max. The older wives of the senior partners whispered to each other about the flirtations. Over the years, some of them had been intimate with Max in an effort to propel their husband's careers, but the passage of time played tricks on their memories.

Jesse Spooner straightened the lapels on his new Armani suit. Max said something to a man that produced disingenuous laughing. Finally, Max motioned him up the gangway.

"Jesse, I've got someone I'd like you to meet," he said, putting his hand under Jesse's elbow. He walked him over to the railing where a woman stood looking out at the nightlights. When she turned around, Jesse felt his pulse quicken.

"Savanna, I'd like you to meet our newest addition, Mr. Jesse Spooner. Jesse, I must warn you, Miss Williams is one of the brightest legal minds we've ever hired at Turner and Turner. If you'll excuse me, I should get back to my other guests. Why don't you two get acquainted?" Max waved to a couple, indicating he would be with them momentarily. "What's wrong, Jesse, cat got your tongue? Lawyers should never be without words, it's our stock-in-trade. We'll visit later. Savanna, be a dear and look after Jesse."

Spooner waited until Max was out of hearing range. His nervousness made the words slippery in his mouth. When he spoke, she started to speak at the same time. "Sorry, you were saying?" he said.

"I was going to ask you why you decided on personal-injury law. There are more lofty legal careers. Remember, I never said that," Savanna said, smiling at Spooner.

"I could ask you the same question. As for me, I turned down the

NFL for law-school. I need to take care of my mother before she works herself to death. We were so, as they say in the South, 'po,' we couldn't afford the 'or.' When Savanna laughed at his joke, Jesse seemed more self-assured as he continued. "As you know, Max's lifestyle can be very seductive. You sound like you're not happy working for Turner."

"I'm happy enough." Savanna was smiling when she answered him. "I have college loans to pay back. As far as working for Turner, well, let me see. I've been working for the firm for two years, so I guess I've become a regular. Most of the new attorneys don't make it through the first year. I guess it all boils down to if you don't mind being despised by just about everyone in the world, personal injury law is great." Savanna stopped suddenly. "Jesse, what is it about you? You've got me telling you all kinds of personal stuff."

Savanna's skin was black-satin smooth and her eyes were almond-shaped. She wore her hair pulled back in a professional bun, but it didn't detract from her good looks. "You stay put. I'll be right back." He couldn't take his eyes off of her spherical bottom as she walked away in a self-confident glide.

Jesse lived with one underlying fear: The fear of losing his mother. As the man-child of the house, he would sneak into her bedroom at night to check on her. This is not the time to get involved, he thought. You've got a job to do.

"Have you seen enough of the sideshow?" Savanna asked Jesse.

"Will Max get pissed if we split?"

"Not really. His show-and-tell is over. You'll get used to these affairs. Say, why don't we have dinner? It'll be my treat. I'd like to do my part in helping your mother."

"I'd love to have dinner, but I'm buying. You pick the restaurant. Better make it a cheap one. The new suit cleaned me out."

"Where did you grow up, Jesse?"

"Fifty miles west of here in a town called Belle Glade. I'm afraid I've still got Okeechobee muck between my toes. When I was in high school I drove to Palm Beach with some friends. The cops pulled us over the minute they saw us."

"Probably arrested you for having dirty feet," she said, grinning.

* * *

Despite the tragedy in Mozambique, Helen Croxford remained in United States. She had good reasons. Her prearranged speaking engagements were intended to help her raise funds for her medical clinic. The other was to solicit pharmaceutical companies for drug samples. To save money, she opted to stay on her brother's yacht. The yacht was docked at a marina in West Palm Beach.

She was watching the evening news when she heard someone yell her name. She walked out into the cockpit and glanced up at the woman looking down at her. A light of recognition flickered, but she lost the thought when the woman spoke. "Sorry to be a bother. I'm looking for a Dr. Croxford." The woman spoke with a silky southern drawl.

"I'm Helen Croxford. How can I help you?" She stretched to shake the woman's hand.

"Dr. Croxford, we have a mutual friend. I was wondering if you'd have time to answer a couple of questions about Africa. I promise—it won't take five minutes. If this isn't a good time, I could come back."

"Now's as good as any. Watch your step. Let me help you," Helen said, offering the woman her hand.

"Do I detect a southern accent?" asked Helen.

"I grew up in New Orleans. Listening to Florida Yankees has worn me as thin as summer cotton. I'm Lynn Allison. I'm delighted to meet you." She accepted Helen's hand and stepped on the yacht's covering-board. "It must be wonderful living on the water."

"The accommodations are courtesy of my brother," she said, indicating she was speaking about the yacht. "Why don't we go inside?"

Helen had heard the words "worn as thin as summer cotton" before, but she couldn't remember where. Lynn Allison was a beautiful woman. She was positive she had seen her before, but she drew a blank.

"I was only kidding about the Yankee thing. You did say you were from the South."

"I was born in Connecticut."

"Now I've done it."

"Nonsense. You mentioned something about a mutual friend?"

"I apologize for popping in on you like this. I'm afraid I'm a little frantic at this point."

"Can I offer you a drink?" Helen asked.

"You're very kind. If that's white wine, I'll have the same. If it's not too much trouble."

"Don't be silly. Now then, about our mutual friend," said Helen, pouring the Chablis.

"How well do you know Maxwell Turner?"

"Max Turner? I'm afraid Mr. Turner is currently at the top of my shit list. Pardon my French."

"I know things about Max that would even lower your opinion of him. He's done some pretty rotten things to me. I wouldn't be offended by anything you could say about Max."

"Now I recognize you! You're related to the woman I met on Max Turner's yacht."

"She's my sister, Ashlyn. She is—or rather was—married to Turner's son, Arthur. Do you remember that terrorist attack in Uganda? I'm talking about the one where eight tourists were killed."

"Of course I remember. I live in Africa."

"My sister survived that attack. Her husband, Arthur, was reported killed, although his body was never recovered."

"Let me get this straight. Was your brother-in-law killed or not? I apologize for my insensitivity."

"The Ugandan military says he's dead. So does the American ambassador to Uganda. I'm not so sure." Lynn lowered her eyes. "Helen, Arthur's nothing like his father. My sister was devoted to him. I know your next question. What does my sister have to say about this? Unfortunately, I haven't been allowed to talk to my sister. Max has brainwashed her. I mean, about me. I'm at my wits' end."

"You just lost me. Why would Max stop you from seeing your sister? Did I miss something?"

Lynn finished her wine. When Helen tried to refill her glass, she placed her hand on top of the glass. Instead of answering Helen, she asked her own question. "What happened between your husband and Max in Mozambique?"

"Max hired my husband, Rigby to take him hunting. There was an accident. A man was killed. Rigby believes Max was responsible for that man's death." Neither woman spoke. Helen chose her words and began, "When I saw your sister in the Bahamas, she acted normal. That is, she acted like she was there of her own free will. I don't know how to say this. Our captain said some of Turner's employees told him they believe

Turner's living with your sister."

"Do you mean...?" Her expression showed she knew what Helen was implying.

"I'm afraid I do."

Lynn got up and walked over to the salon window. She bit her lower lip and shook her head in disbelief. "It's not true, I know my sister. Max might push it, but Ashlyn, no way. My God, this is a new low, even for Max."

"Maybe it was disgruntled gossip," said Helen.

"Nobody knows Max Turner better than I do. I ought to, I was married to him. I know what you're thinking: Two sisters married to a father and son is weird. Of course, you're right. I was Max's fifth wife. I'm afraid his four other wives didn't fare too well. The first ended up in a mental hospital. His third wife fell off of Max's yacht on a trip back from the Bahamas. Her death was ruled an accidental drowning. Arthur was her son and Max's only child."

Helen maintained a passive facial expression to show she had no such thoughts, but the idea of being married to Max made her skin crawl. *I can't wait to talk to Rigby,* she thought.

"Helen, my family was poorer than church mice. We ran away from home when we were teenagers—when I say we, I mean my sister and me. We ran away because, well, let's just say we had a damn good reason. We needed a roof over our heads and Max provided it. Looking back, Max may have had his motives, but we were desperate. I see I've shocked you. I apologize. I'm afraid I'm babbling. I've taken enough of your time. I should be leaving."

Helen shrugged indicating she wasn't shocked, but, in fact, she was so shocked she had trouble swallowing a mouthful of wine. Lynn's honesty turned Helen's revulsion into empathy. She reached forward and touched Lynn to reassure her. "Lynn, why don't you stay for dinner? I warn you, it won't be fancy."

"You've been very gracious. I know I must sound like one of those dreadful people on the Jerry Springer show. Some crazy divorced woman ranting and raving about her ex-husband. I can assure you, I'm neither. If I had my way, I'd never see Max Turner again. I've always taken care of my sister. To cut me off like this is not like her."

Lynn's eyes welled up with tears at the thought of her sister. Her face turned angry as she began to speak again. "Don't believe for a sec-

ond that running into Max in the Bahamas was an accident. I'm convinced the hunting safari was a smokescreen. Max's real purpose was to
hire your husband to help him find out about his son. This is the first I've
heard about the hunting accident. It must have prevented him from carrying out his plan. I can assure you he'll try again. He needs certain assur-
ances, or he's——." She stopped, as if conflicted by her thoughts.

"What were you going to say?" Helen asked.

"It's nothing. If I told you what I'm thinking, you'd think I'm crazy.
You probably already think I'm nuts. Being around Max tends to do that
to a person."

"Is there something you're not telling me?"

"I shouldn't have told you this much. The people around Max have
a habit of getting hurt. The hunting accident, the accidental drowning
of his third wife—there's much more, you know. I'm convinced there's
a good chance Arthur may still be alive. I think my sister believes he's
alive. That's the only reason she's staying close to Max. Now I hear he's
trying to—God, I hope it isn't true. Max will pull out all the stops to get
to his son. I know what you're thinking—this sounds like a distraught
father and a vindictive ex-wife."

"I have to admit, it did cross my mind," Helen confessed. "Why is
Max obsessed with hiring my husband?"

"Max has heard rumors about his son being alive. The last information he received was that Arthur was being held in the Congo. I'm told
that getting into the Congo is easy. Finding Arthur is the problem. For
some reason, Max is convinced your husband's the only man in Africa
that can give him what he wants."

*     *     *

Lynn Allison left Helen Croxford around midnight. She decided to
take the coastal highway to her seaside condo in Boca Raton. She lowered the window, hoping the sea breeze would clear her mind. The salty
smell triggered memories of growing up in Louisiana. She flashbacked to
her mother's funeral: The embalmer had done his best to re-sculpture her
mother's facial bones. Her mother's boyfriend had broken her nose so
many times it no longer looked like it belonged on a human face. A beau-
tician had puffed her hair into a fuzzy pompadour. Her wrinkles were
packed with makeup to hide the harsh reality of a life gone wrong. What

was left in that yellow-pine coffin was pitiful. Lynn was conflicted by her mother's death. She remembered telling her mother about the live-in boyfriend's molesting her, but her mother ignored her. Most of the time she could fend off the recollections, but when she was tired, she lacked the willpower to stop them. The irritating chimes of a cell-phone snapped her back to the moment. When she saw the incoming number was her ex-husband's, she felt sick.

"My dear, how did it go?" Max asked.

"I feel like a scumbag lying to that woman."

"Lynn, don't give me that shit."

"Helen Croxford told me about the hunting incident. Something you failed to mention."

"That, my dear, was unfortunate. What did she say when you told her I wanted to hire her husband?"

"It won't be easy. She didn't have anything nice to say about you. I went away feeling her husband hates you more than I do. Why don't you find someone else?"

"I'm afraid Rigby Croxford is like all of us, even you. We all have our price. Some people can be bought cheaper than others, but there's always a price."

"Speaking of money, when do I get the hundred thousand?" Lynn asked.

"I'm having it hand delivered."

"Did you make the wire transfer to the bank in Uganda?"

"Of course I did. That's seven million. Even I can't continue paying at this rate. There's a limit." Max swirled the cabernet, letting the wine coat the inside of his glass. He stuck his nose in and inhaled. Picking at his ex-wife's vulnerabilities made him smile.

"Is there a price on how much you love Arthur?" she asked, trying to get even.

"I could ask you the same question. My generosity seems to get me nothing but ingratitude. I keep wondering if you're skimming for yourself."

"For God's sake, he's your only son."

"At this point, I'm not sure my son's alive. My money might be going to his murderer."

"Is that a chance you're willing to take? Answer my question. Why haven't you hired someone to find Arthur?"

"I've tried and I got ripped off. The Congo is run by crooks. You're never sure if you're bribing the right person. If Arthur's alive, I'm not about to take any chances with his rescue. I believe Croxford is the man to get me some answers. But then again, you don't give a shit about Arthur, do you?"

"It seems odd to hear you call someone a crook. What you said about me not caring about Arthur isn't fair. Hard to believe he's your own flesh and blood. I would do anything for him and you know it."

"I believe the Lord sent Croxford to me."

"Oh, please. Remember, I know you. When do I get to see my sister?"

"You haven't finished your assignment. Why don't you stop by on your way home?" He paused, but she didn't respond.

The thought of Max touching her was nauseating. She collected herself and asked the same question a different way. "You promised to let me see my sister. Why do you take such delight in torturing me?"

"Believe it or not, this isn't about you. Your job is to convince Croxford to help me. Offer him a half a million dollars. Hiring Croxford is a done deal. I'll bet everything I own on it. As you know, I own a lot." Max looked in an antique mirror and examined his toupee from different angles. Satisfied, he turned back to face the speaker-phone. "I was kidding when I asked you to stop by. Anyway, I found a woman who appreciates me. I can't tell you her name, at least not yet. Lynn, you and I were conjoined by animal lust, nothing more. Goodnight, love. Pleasant dreams."

\*     \*     \*

# 7
# PALM BEACH

Jesse Spooner's first week at Turner and Turner was overwhelming. He clung to Savanna Williams like she was his interpreter in a foreign country. The countless meetings with the senior law partners were a blur. There were incomplete memos and abbreviated emails. The secretaries spoke in legal shorthand. He had never felt more helpless in his life.

It was Friday, and Savanna was not in her office. Getting fired before he could do his job was unacceptable. The telephone on his desk rang. "Mr. Spooner, this is Dan Gillespie. I work for the investigative side of the firm. Mr. Turner thought it would be a good idea if we got together for lunch. I was thinking Brinkley's, say, around noon?"

"Noon works for me. How will I know you?"

"Don't worry. Something tells me I won't have trouble finding you."

\*   \*   \*

Jesse looked over the top of his menu at the red-faced man walking towards him. The man squinted to fend off a wisp of smoke from the cigarette dangling in the corner of his mouth. He stopped to speak to a barmaid. Jesse couldn't hear him, but he guessed what he said was off-color by the girl's reaction. It was apparent Gillespie was one of her regulars. He gave her a playful spank and waved to Jesse. "Mr. Spooner, I presume?"

"Mr. Gillespie, it's nice to meet you."

"Please, call me Dan. You're the attorney. I'm just part of the hired help. Say, it's Friday, which means I'm gonna have a martini. Care to join me?"

"It's a little early for me. For God's sake, don't call me mister."

"C'mon Spooner, don't be a pussy. I'm not gonna tell old Maxy boy. Besides, he's in the Bahamas on his fuckin' mega-yacht."

"I'll have a white wine," Jesse said, throwing up his hands.

"White wine, now there's a man's drink." Gillespie smoothed out the puffiness around his eyes and sighed.

"Rough night?" Jesse asked.

"No more than any other. So, how'd your first week go?"

"I have absolutely no idea what I'm doing. If it wasn't for Savanna Williams, I'd be completely lost."

"Savanna Williams is a ten with a capital T," he said, staring at a woman's ass who walked by their table. Williams has got too much class to work for Turner. He caught the same woman's attention and waved. She frowned and looked the other way. "Let's forget I said that. I've only had this job for two months—no sense getting fired before I get caught up on my alimony."

Jesse attempted to steer the conversation in a different direction. "You said Max thought it would be a good idea if you filled me in on what you do for the firm?"

"Turner doesn't know that I exist. I saw you play in the Sugar Bowl. Shit, you were good enough to play in the NFL. Hard to believe you gave up a career in professional football for chasing ambulances. But what the hell do I know?"

Jesse sniffed the wine and grimaced. "Even I know this wine stinks. I'm curious. How did you get the job working for Max?"

"I had a small detective agency in West Palm. By small, I mean like one person. I worked the divorce scene. Turner has every detective in south Florida on the take, except me. They funnel him information, like leads on possible cases and dirt on his competitors. You're in a dirty business, my friend. Or should I say, you've thrown your hat in the ring with a guy who likes to win and he doesn't give a crap how he does it." Gillespie took a sip of his martini and continued. "Turner's ex-wife approached me about doing some work for her. The next thing I know, some bald-headed goon shows up with an offer from Turner. Having absolutely no scruples, and about to do jail time for back alimony, I took it. End of story. This woman, I mean Turner's ex is some piece of ass. She'd give your friend Savanna a run for her money."

Both men turned their heads as their waitress sauntered up. The band of white skin on her wedding ring finger means she's on the make, Jesse guessed. She placed one hand on her hip and used a menu to fan her breasts. They were her best feature, and she knew it. "Danny, what's it gonna be?"

"Sweet Pea, a weekend in the Bahamas with you would be like winning the lottery."

"Danny, you're so full of shit. If I said yes, would you really take me?"

"Hey, would I lie to you?" He grinned. She smirked. After they ordered, she strutted away.

"I see you're wearing a wedding band," Jesse commented.

"Broads figure if I was dumb enough to get married once, hell, I might do it again." Jesse stared at him, not sure what to say next. Gillespie used the hesitation to ask a question. "What about you, Spooner? Why Turner and Turner? You look like a guy who should be running his own firm. You don't even sound like a black man. Not that there's anything wrong with talking like a rapper."

Spooner smirked at Gillespie. "Truth is—I wasn't much of a scholar. I spent four years shagging footballs for the Gators. Law school was hard for me. I failed the state bar exam twice before I passed it. Turner was my only offer. You know, going it alone isn't as easy as you think."

"No kidding. I'm sure it'll all work out. Unfortunately, I don't plan on staying around long enough to find out. No sir, soon as I get caught up on my alimony payments to the world's biggest bitch, I'm outta here. I live on a forty-two foot tub at the City Marina. She may look nasty, but she's paid for, and she purrs like a kitten." Gillespie finished his martini in one gulp, and then continued. "I got tired of giving houses to women I hated. I've been married three times. All of my marriages ended the same way. After we sobered up, we realized now much we despised each other. But fuck, she'd end up with the house and I'd end up with jack-shit. That's when I decided to live on a boat. Women love to spend a weekend on the water. The nice part is they don't see a boat as something permanent. Since my divorce from the latest dragon lady, I've spent my summers cruising in the Bahamas. You should stop by for a drink sometime. Meet some of my crazy boating neighbors."

"Is that a serious offer?"

"There's no law against having fun. My neighbors are about as colorful as you can get. They're derelict guitar-playing boozers. I'm not musically inclined, but I certainly pass the litmus test on drinking." Both men laughed. Spooner looked at his watch. Gillespie read his mind. "You need to get back to the office. I think I'll call it a day. It's party time, right sweetie?" Gillespie said, winking at the waitress.

\*     \*     \*

Helen Croxford's two weeks in the States extended into three. Lynn Allison visited Helen almost everyday. Practicing medicine in rural Africa meant Helen had few female friends. She looked forward to seeing Lynn. They forged a friendship. The experience was also cathartic for Lynn. It was never a question if Lynn would visit Helen in Africa; it was only a question of when.

The live-aboard boaters at the City Marina organized a farewell cocktail party for Helen. Lynn wasn't prepared to meet the last person in the world she wanted to see. Helen helped her down onto the back deck of the yacht. She looked over the top of her sunglasses at the man with his back to her. "What's he doing here? Or should I say what foul tide did he float in on?" Lynn asked.

Dan Gillespie was so surprised to see her; he spilled his tropical drink down the front of his flowered shirt. "Miss. Allison, I live here. Well, not exactly here. I live on the next dock over." Lynn's expression showed her exasperation.

"I'm sorry about what happened. I'd like a chance to explain." He brushed off his shirt.

"I can assure you that won't be necessary."

"I can't believe you two know each other," Helen said, trying to soften the atmosphere.

"I know him to be a spineless coward who would do anything for money. And he's a Yankee." Lynn expelled the words as if they were poisonous. She tucked her skirt between her legs as she prepared to climb up on the dock. At the last second, she turned and faced Helen. "What time does your flight leave?" She refused to look at Gillespie. "I won't spend another second with that man."

"Miss Allison, I'll go so that you can stay," he said.

"Helen, I'm asking you again. What time do you want me here in the morning?" she demanded, as if she hadn't heard Gillespie's offer.

"What can I do to make you stay? What if I shoot Mr. Gillespie?" she said, trying to defuse the tension.

"He's not worth the bullet."

"Look, Miss Allison, I promise I'll leave, but not before you give me the opportunity to explain. Please, all I'm asking for is thirty lousy seconds. I should warn you, the Gillespie family has a long history of mental illness. I think it goes back to being persecuted by the British. If you don't hear my confession, my untimely death would be on your hands." Helen gave Lynn a nudge in his direction and left to mingle with the other guests.

"Untimely for whom, Mr. Gillespie?" continued Lynn.

"Touché. What about it? Will you step into my office?"

He opened the door. Lynn stepped into the salon. She stood there with her hands on her hips, shaking her head. She looked over the top of her tortoise-shell shades. "Mr. Gillespie, this better be good."

"Miss Allison, could you please sit down? You look like you're about to slug me." She sat down on the corner of the sofa. Gillespie spoke right to the point. "Now, the reason I went to work for your ex-husband was simple enough—I found out my ex-wife convinced some judge to issue a warrant to have me arrested. Knowing her, she was probably shacked up with the judge. She sued me once for a bumper sticker I had made up for my car that read, 'Honk your horn if you haven't slept with my wife.' Anyway, I needed to get caught up on my alimony or I'd be wearing prison blues. Remember, I did return your retainer."

"Did you really get sued over that bumper sticker?"

"Would I lie to you? Forget I said that. I can accept most of what you said about me. I have been known to take liberties with the truth, on rare occasions. I have to admit I was born and bred in Brooklyn, but that coward tag is a little hard to swallow. Miss Allison, I'm a lot of things, but a coward's not one of them."

"Very well, Mr. Gillespie, I accept your apology. Just do me a favor. Never mention my ex-husband's name in my presence. I'm afraid you're going to have to learn about Max the hard way. Just remember that I warned you. How about getting me the same kind of a drink you're wearing on your shirt?"

"Your ex won't get a chance to screw me. My plan is to resign after I get my next paycheck. What I will do is find out as much as I can about your sister. Consider the information a peace offering."

*     *     *

Two weeks later, Dan Gillespie sat next to Jesse Spooner in Max

Turner's office foyer. At first, he thought he'd been summoned to be fired, but when he saw Jesse, he guessed Max had something else on his mind.

"Mr. Turner will see you," the receptionist said.

"Why do receptionists who work for wealthy men always act like they're doing you a favor?" Gillespie whispered to Jesse.

Neither of them had seen Turner's office. The parts of the wall not occupied by framed college degrees and complimentary newspaper articles about Turner and Turner were covered in a collage of paintings. Beneath a bay window there was a Bombay chest with models of his yacht and private jet on display. The side walls of the office were encased with reddish-mahogany shelves stuffed with gold-leafed law books.

Max stared at Jesse and Dan. "Men, it's time you paid a little of the rent around here." He pushed two manila folders across his desk. Max grabbed a cigar from the humidor on his desk. He circumcised the tip and rolled it between his lips as he lit it. He swiveled in his chair, stood up and walked over to the bay window.

Gillespie noticed a set of keys on the desk. He used the folder to hide his hand and brushed the keys off. The keys hit silently on the carpeted floor. Having gotten no reaction, he started to read the report.

The law firm of Turner and Turner arbitrated an out-of-court settlement in favor of our client, Willie Jamal Rolle. Golden Leaf Tobacco paid Mr. Rolle the sum of sixteen million dollars. Mr. Rolle, a mentally retarded man, died approximately one year after receiving the lump sum settlement. Since he had no known relatives, and in accordance with Mr. Rolle's wishes, the remainder of his estate was left to a charity. (Please review Exhibit Two: The last will and testament of Willie Jamal Rolle.)

It has come to the attention of certain contracted individuals working outside the confines of Turner and Turner that a Tampa law firm is preparing to file a case in which Turner and Turner will be named as the defendant in the alleged improper handling of the estate of the late Mr. Rolle. The plaintiff, Sally Mae Rolle, purports to be Mr. Rolle's half sister.

Outside legal council has reviewed all relevant legal documents pertaining to this case. The firm of Turner and Turner has done nothing wrong. Everything was done in accordance with the applicable Florida statues.

"I know what you're both thinking. Let her sue us. But you see— it's not that simple. Unfortunately, we are victims of our own success. The bad publicity could damage the reputation of Turner and Turner. Our competitors would rejoice in our misfortune. As the caretaker of this firm's future, I can't let that happen." Turner puffed on his cigar and continued. "I want you to contact Sally Mae Rolle. Find out how much money it'll take to get her to go away. And yes, it's like she's blackmailing us. It's happened before, and I have no doubt it'll happen again. At this point, I'm willing to settle with her for one million dollars.

"Jesse, I'm putting you in charge. It'll be a good learning experience for you. Let's see how you handle it. Gillespie, you're job is to help him. That's all of it. Keep me posted. Enjoy your weekend." Neither man moved. "Oh, there's one more thing. You know the old saying, 'No good deed goes unpunished.' Because of Mr. Rolle's condition, I took the case pro bono. We were entitled to forty per cent of the settlement, but we passed. Now this happens."

Gillespie's memory flashed back to the report Richard Langley prepared for Lynn Allison. Willie Jamal Rolle was a name on that list. Turner, you fucking crook, of course you passed on the fee. You passed because you ended up with the whole sixteen million, you crafty son-of-a-bitch. I'll bet you even avoided paying the estate taxes by running the money through that bogus church. A cold chill ran down his spine when he thought about the beating his friend, Langley had taken. Turner, your ex-wife was right about you.

Gillespie lingered. As he watched Jesse reach over the desk to shake hands, he reached down and stuck the keys between his sock and shoe. He tried to do it nonchalantly, but when he glanced up he knew Jesse had seen him. His mind raced through plausible denials, but Jesse never said a word.

Jesse and Dan walked out of Turner's office together. Savanna walked up behind them and slipped her arms through their elbows. "Boys it's Friday afternoon and you two are taking me out for a drink."

They walked three abreast, arm-in-arm from the Turner and Turner building to Taboo. Gillespie stopped suddenly and unhooked his arm. "I need to get a spare key made. There's a locksmith right around the corner on Brazilian. If you would be so kind as to order me a gin and tonic, I won't be a minute."

"Dan, let me take it. I need to see if my shoes are ready. The shoe-repair shop is next to the locksmith," Jesse said, holding out his hand.

"Not on your life. Savanna would never forgive me. That was a gin and tonic, squeeze of lime. Hold down the fort. I shall return."

He walked down Worth Avenue and ducked into a tropically land-scaped courtyard that opened onto the next street over. He slipped into the locksmith's shop unannounced.

Jimmy, also known as "The Clam," sat hunched over in his wheel-chair polishing a key on an electric grinder. He stopped momentarily and squinted through a jeweler's glass to inspect his work. Dan used Jimmy to copy keys. Duplicate keys were the tools of trade for a detective work-ing the divorce scene. The locksmith had gotten his nickname because everyone said his lips were sealed as tight as a clam. Gillespie sneaked up, tapped him on the right shoulder, stepped left, and roared, "Watch it!"

"You asshole, you coulda given me a fuckin' heart attack," Jimmy yelled, almost vaulting out of his wheelchair. "What kind of a prick would scare a handicapped person?"

"Pal, I need copies, pronto. Forget the car keys. Just do the house and office keys. How quick can I get 'em? Say, is there a shoe repair shop around here?"

"No 'Hello'? No 'How have you been, Jimmy?' Christ, I haven't seen you in six months. Fuck, I could have had open-heart surgery for all you know. Danny, you're cold-hearted."

"Open-heart surgery? You don't have a heart. So you can scratch the feel-sorry-for-me act. I've got a time problem with these," he said, hold-ing up the keys. "I need you to do a lookout for me so I can return the originals. It's a fifteen minute gig, tops. I've got a Benjamin Franklin with your name on it," Gillespie said, tossing him the keys.

"As to your questions. The nearest shoe store is over the bridge in West Palm. I can have the keys finished in thirty minutes. I'll do the lookout for the hundred bucks, but you gotta buy me dinner, and not some cheap joint. The restaurant has to use white table clothes."

"All right, you're on. Heart surgery, my ass. I'll pick you up at eight. And there'll be no dancing for you tonight," he said, grinning.

Walking back to the bar, Gillespie mulled over Jesse's motives. He knew Jesse lied about the shoes. Maybe he wants to be a hero and go straight to Turner. He checked his watch: It was already six. Better keep it to one drink, well, maybe two. Wonder what angle Spooner's playing, he thought. Anyway, I'll have the keys back in Turner's office in two hours.

*      *      *

It was eight-thirty by the time he picked up Jimmy. It took him another ten minutes to get him in the front seat and his wheelchair in the trunk. "Listen to me. All you gotta do is call me on my cell if anyone pulls up in front of Turner's building. I told you this was an easy gig. No questions? Good. Keep my seat warm. Don't you drive off and leave me."

"Very funny, you asshole. I hope these fuckin' keys don't belong to Max Turner. Something tells me this involves a woman. You better have your health insurance paid up if you're screwin' around with one of Turner's ex-wives. Don't leave me out here any longer than necessary," Jimmy said, looking up the vacant street.

"You worry too much." Gillespie got out of the car and hurried to the building's entrance. He opened the front door and re-locked it from the inside. On the second floor, he opened Turner's office door with the first key he tried. He slipped Turner's original set of keys under a sofa cushion. He put a flashlight in his mouth and started opening drawers. There was a thick manila folder in the top drawer. It was addressed to Nelson Chang. He replaced the folder and opened a lower drawer where he found a metal box. The box contained a bundle of letters. The letter on top had been postmarked from Africa three months earlier, on November the tenth. It was handwritten and hard to read in the diminished light. He redirected the beam of light on the signature line at the bottom of the last page which read: "Respectfully, your loving stepson, Arthur." It can't be you, thought Gillespie. You're dead. His cell phone vibrated, causing him to spit out the flashlight. "Danny, two men in a Bentley pulled into the parking lot. They're already in the building. One of them is Turner. The other guy's a big baldheaded creep. You need to get out of there."

Gillespie closed the metal box and replaced it. His hands trembled, which caused him to drop the keys. He found the key and locked the desk. The elevator bell rang as its door opened. He slipped behind the door to the bathroom. As his eyes adjusted to the darkness, he scanned the bathroom looking for a weapon. The only thing he could find was the porcelain toilet tank cover. Using the crack in the door he saw the office foyer lights come on. Two men emerged and took form in the dull light.

As they got closer, he could hear Turner talking. "Bobby, I must be going crazy. I know I left the keys on my desk. My secretary's searched every inch of this office."

Bob started with the bookcases and ended up on all fours checking the carpet. The last place he looked was the most obvious. "Are these yours, Mr. Turner?" he asked, holding up a set of keys.

"Where'd you find those?"

"Over there, under a sofa cushion."

"Impossible. I checked there myself. They must have gotten worked in between the layers of fabric. Thank God you found them." Max stood up abruptly and started for the bathroom, but he stopped in front of Bob. He placed his hands on the man's shoulders. "Now that we're here, let's talk. What's your read on the new guy?"

"Sir, Jesse Spooner hasn't got any skeletons in his closet, at least none that I'm aware of. Everything seems in order with this guy."

"What about the new security guy, Gillespie?"

"He's competent enough, but he's got money problems. And there's his drinking issue."

"I'm convinced we've got a snitch working for the firm. I don't think its Spooner or Gillespie. Spooner hasn't been with us long enough, and frankly, I don't think this Gillespie's smart enough to pull it off. It has to be someone else. Anyway, I've decided to put him to work under Spooner. Let's see how they handle the Rolle situation. Like I told you, I'd rather buy this woman off. If that doesn't fly, you're gonna need to get involved. Unfortunately, this old woman's digging up some stuff we need to keep buried."

"Sir, Gillespie's made contact with your ex-wife. It was at a boat party for Helen Croxford. Maybe it was an accident. Take a look at this," he said, flipping a snapshot of Dan Gillespie and Lynn Allison.

"I had you employ this guy to stop my ex-wife from hiring him. What do you recommend we do?" Unwilling to wait for Bob's response, Max answered his own question. "Once I give you the green light on my ex, I see no reason to keep Gillespie around."

"Any idea when that might be?"

Turner walked over to the window and stared out at the blackness. His voice dropped to a low whisper. Gillespie pushed his ear against the crack in the door and strained to hear, but he could only pick up intermittent words.

"I'm afraid my ex-wife's usefulness is almost over. Just remember how I told you I want it done. She has to disappear without a trace. I'm gonna be a suspect. Ex-spouses are always the prime suspects. That's why I'm taking the time to re-establish our relationship. Bob, I'm counting on you to take care of this. There can be no link to me." The volume of Max's voice was reduced to little more than a whisper.

"You give me the go-ahead, and I'll take it from there."

Max had one more job for his ex-wife. If Rigby Croxford refused to help him, he would have to use her to get to Croxford. She had become friends with Helen Croxford. Max had orchestrated the relationship. After he used her, he would give her to Bob. He had always prided himself on covering all the bases. The one loose end was to catch the informer in his firm.

"We can discuss my son on the way home. By the way, how's the new Mercedes?"

"It's wonderful. I can never thank you enough."

"You earned it. You know how much I depend on you. It's a pity Arthur wasn't more like you. We can do great things together, but we must strike down those who try to oppose us. It's just like it says in the Bible: 'Cursed be he who does the Lord's work remissly. Cursed him who holds back his sword from blood.' Jeremiah, 48:10."

Gillespie waited for them to turn off the lights. His breathing slowed down as the sound of their voices faded. Leaning over the bathroom sink, he splashed cold water on his face and sipped a handful to moisten his mouth. He sat down on the toilet and hit the return-call button on his cell phone. "Jimmy, did they leave?"

"Yes, they left. It's blacker out here than a whore's heart after a sailor's paycheck. Now get me the fuck outta here, Danny, you crazy bastard. I'm not about to get arrested as an accessory to a b-and-e for a lousy hundred bucks."

"Shut up, Jimmy. Give me five minutes." Gillespie sat down at Turner's desk, reached in the bottom drawer and pulled out the metal box. He took the letter from the top of the stack and stuffed it in his pocket. He replaced everything and scanned the desk to make sure he was leaving it the way he found it. He stared at the fancy humidor. He'll never miss them, he thought. He stuffed two handfuls of cigars in his front pockets. Gillespie, you're getting too old for this kind of work. I wonder what Max meant when he said he saw no reason to keep me around.

Jimmy was agitated by the time Dan walked out of the darkness and slipped into the driver's seat. "So tell me, what did you steal?" Jimmy asked.

"Not a God damned thing. What's your beef?"

"What's my beef? You leave me out here on the fuckin' street while you break in to Max Turner's office. You know I'm a three-time loser. If I get caught, I go away for the rest of my life. As shitty as my life is, it's all I got."

"Would I screw my best friend?"

"Don't give me that shit. You don't have any friends. I want half of whatever you stole in there. It's only fair."

Gillespie reached across and took a flask out of his glove compartment. He took a swig and handed it to Jimmy, who pushed it away.

"Oh, now I get it. You're pissed off, but you want half. As they say, 'The blind can see and the lame can walk.' Oops, sorry, that was shitty. Fine, I stole a four-page letter and a few cigars, for Christ's sake. Here, you keep the cigars. I'm not a thief. I'm a detective, you asshole. You're a locksmith who used to be a pretty fair thief and a half-assed safe cracker. The operative phrase is 'used to be.' If you'd known more about freaking explosives, you'd still be walking. Sorry, that was another low one. Now you've gone and done it, you've ruined my appetite. Jimmy, I'll have to owe you the dinner. I'm afraid some really bad shit's come up."

"You got a rain check. For the record, it wasn't my screw-up that caused me to blow myself up. It was a jealous cunt screwing with my explosives."

"You'd think we'd learn. Jimmy, be serious for a minute. How would you describe me?"

"I'm not following you."

"Do you consider me, let's say, intelligent? Do you think I'm trustworthy? You know what I mean."

Jimmy's face tightened into a mask of deep concentration. "You? Danny, you're a scumbag weasel. A drunken Irish scumbag weasel to be more precise. And you're no Stephen Hawking."

"Jesus Christ. Did you leave anything out?"

"Hey, you asked me."

"Yeah, but I didn't expect you to be honest."

Gillespie struggled to pull Jimmy in his wheelchair up the flight of stairs to his one-bedroom efficiency over the locksmith shop. He stopped halfway up to catch his breath. When he reached the top, he spun the chair around and pushed Jimmy to the edge.

"Ever hear of something called an elevator?"

"I pay a young guy to haul me up these stairs everyday. Danny boy, I think you're starting to show your age."

"I think this is far enough. Let's see if you can stay in this thing on the way down," he wheezed, pushing the wheelchair to the edge of the wooden stairs. The steps creaked a warning. "Take back what you said about me."

"Stop fuckin' around. You want a drink?"

"No, I've got crap to take care of. And don't look at me like that."

As he was leaving, Jimmy offered him some advice. "I guess there's no sense trying to convince you to let this thing go. Whoever she is, she's not worth it. I know she's paying you the square root of fuck-all, so you can't bullshit me. Just remember where you heard it."

"Jimmy, you missed your calling. You're a fucking clairvoyant. See you around, pal. And thanks for the kind words. I think I'll hang myself."

\*    \*    \*

He pulled over before he turned onto the Flagler Memorial Bridge. It would take him over the Intracoastal Waterway to the marina where he lived on his boat. Danny, you damned fool, Jimmy was right, you should go home and forget what you heard. Or what you thought you heard, he corrected himself. Every time you get involved with a divorced chick, you end up with your tit in a ringer. Christ, especially one who was married to a crazy cocksucker like Max Turner.

That's right, turn around, you stupid asshole. Call her, get involved. It can only go one way from here, and that's downhill. He checked his cell phone for Lynn Allison's telephone number and pushed the send button. Her phone rang before a recorded message clicked on, causing him to hang up. Better not leave a recording of your voice. At least you're not that stupid.

Before he could stop himself he was driving to Boca Raton. He reached for his flask. I'll just drive by and check out her apartment. He laughed at the lie. He almost turned around again, but the thought of Lynn Allison made him continue driving.

He drove past the gatehouse protecting the entrance to the condominium complex where Lynn Allison lived. He made a quick U-turn on A1A, doused the lights and idled in behind some landscaping. The security guard's either asleep or he's in the crapper, he thought.

Gillespie stopped in front of the barrier and dialed the telephone number listed for the gatehouse. The sign in the gatehouse window read: Thomas Casey on Duty. The guard stood up and indicated to Gillespie that he would be with him momentarily. He turned around and grabbed the telephone. "Say Tom, this is Mr. _____ in apartment ___," Gillespie mumbled, muffling the name and apartment number. "Look, I've got a friend stopping by. He drives a white Cadillac. How about letting him in. Why don't you drop by tomorrow afternoon for a cocktail, say around five o'clock? Thanks, Tom."

"Who'd you say this was?" The security guard yelled into the dead receiver just as Gillespie hung up his cell phone and smiled.

"I just got a call on you. What apartment number are you looking for?" the guard asked, opening the gate.

"I'm going to _____," Dan answered, finishing the sentence in mimed silence as his car window rolled up. The security guard scratched his head.

The downstairs lobby door was unlocked. So much for security, he thought. When he knocked a prehistoric-looking woman using an aluminum walker opened the door. She had a dark cheroot tipped with a smoldering ash hanging from the corner of her mouth. The apartment had that old people's smell about it. The volume on the television was turned up so high, the speakers buzzed.

"Good evening, Madam, I'm here to pick up Miss Allison."

"What's that you're saying?" she asked, cupping her hand around her ear. "Well, don't just stand there like a dummy. Harry, it's your podiatrist," she yelled over her shoulder to the old man standing behind her. He was also using a walker. There was a green tank fixed to his walker. The tank sprouted a clear plastic tube that formed a Y below the man's chin; a tube entered each of his nostrils.

"I'm looking for a Miss Allison."

"Why didn't you say so? She's on the top floor. Say, what the hell are you doing in our apartment? Harry, better call security, I don't like his looks."

The old woman shuffled closer. Her glasses were so magnified she appeared bug-eyed. After sniffing, she pinched her nose in disgust. "Is that booze I smell? You know we've had some rapes in this neighborhood. Harry, get my pepper spray. God damned drunken rapist," she hissed, waggling her arthritic finger in his face. Her hand was covered in purple liver spots and the end digit of her finger angled at a forty-five.

"Ruth, I'm not calling security. We know the security guard's an imbecile," the old man yelled. He cocked his head to inspect Gillespie. "Say, mister...." He stopped mid-sentence to clear the phlegm from his throat. "Say, mister, can I offer you a cocktail?"

"Thanks, maybe another time. I'll be leaving now."

"Suit yourself. God damn you, Ethel, I think you frightened the poor bastard off. Rape? Why hell, I've got a better chance of getting raped than you do."

"Shut up, Harry. Make me another Manhattan," the old woman barked from the corner of her mouth not occupied by the cheroot.

Gillespie stepped out of the elevator into the penthouse foyer. Looking down from the foyer window, he could see the security gatehouse. No movement meant the security guard had resumed his siesta. Lynn Allison cracked the door on the second knock, but she kept the safety chain fastened. "Mr. Gillespie, what an unpleasant surprise. Ever think of calling first? What brings you out at this time of night? How did you get into my building?"

"I landed on the roof in a stolen helicopter." He grimaced when she didn't smile. "Seriously, Miss Allison, I've got some information about your sister. I went out on a limb to get this stuff. Could you please open the door?"

Lynn Allison unhooked the chain. Her expression was one of skepticism waxed over exasperation. It was evident she had second thoughts about letting him in. She wore a terrycloth robe, which she tightened at the neck. Her message was clear: Don't even think about it. When she sat down on the sofa, she curled her legs under until all of her skin was covered, which reinforced the message.

"So, Mr. Gillespie, you said you had information about my sister?"

"The information I have is about your stepson, Arthur. I know this sounds crazy, but I believe your ex-husband intends to. Let's just say, he's not planning to throw you a surprise party."

"You're pathetic. Is this where I'm supposed to jump into your arms? I'm afraid I've already seen this movie."

He told her about breaking into Max's office. Gillespie admitted that he could only hear parts of Max's conversation.

"So that's it? That's all of it?" she said. "You know what I think? I think your coming here was Max's idea. You didn't break into his office. You must think I'm pretty stupid. I'm calling the police."

"I wouldn't do that. Not until you've read this," he said, handing her the envelope.

Lynn stood up and snatched it out of his hand. She sat down in a stuffed chair by a reading lamp. Her eyes darted along each line. When she finished she clutched the rumpled pages against her chest and turned around. She wiped her nose on her sleeve. "Have you read it?"

"I didn't have time. When I saw the signature and the date, I knew I needed to see you."

"This proves Arthur's alive. Max has known all along. Danny, you don't wanna get involved."

"I'm already involved."

"If I were you, I'd let this go."

"I can't do that. I've got some theories about your ex. That first detective you hired, Richard Langley, was a friend. He may never recover from the beating I believe your ex-husband arranged."

"Have it your way, but you've been warned. For starters, you better read this." She handed him the letter. He read the letter through and then reread parts of it again.

"I'm confused. This sounds like Turner's son wants to stay in Africa. Why all of the hush-hush about his son being alive? This letter proves Max knew his son was alive all along."

"It's complicated." She sniffled and looked away.

"I've pretty well figured out that Max stole some dough. I guess his son was an accomplice. The name of the firm is 'Turner and Turner.'"

"Max embezzled the money early in his career. His son didn't join the firm until later. Arthur's never done a dishonest thing in his life. I can't prove it, but I believe this is about Arthur's mother's death. Arthur was on Max's boat the night his mother supposedly fell overboard, or jumped over, or was pushed over. I know Max and his wife were on the verge of a divorce. There were rumors she was blackmailing him. You know something? There was never a suicide note. Max remarried six months later."

As he continued speaking, she let her legs slip out from underneath her robe. He noticed the change but was careful not to overplay his hand. "I gotta say, your story sounds fishy. None of this proves Max killed his wife. Fifty percent of the time, people who commit suicide don't leave notes."

"Arthur and I became very close. My sister may have been his wife, but there were things he needed to tell someone else. It was always the three of us against Max. Arthur always hinted he had reservations about what he'd been told about his mother's death. I wonder if the terrorist ordeal in Africa triggered some buried memories. Maybe I've seen too many mystery movies."

"I'm a detective working the divorce scene in Palm Beach. Super-rich people are capable of unimaginable acts when they think someone's after their dough. Nothing would surprise me," Gillespie responded.

"Unfortunately, I used to be part of that scene, even if it was only temporary."

"You seem like too good of a person to have been hitched to Turner."

His compliment dampened her apprehension. She dropped her hands and let the collar open naturally. "I ran into Max at a time when I needed help."

"One thing's for certain—I underestimated your ex-husband. Just to be on the safe side, we need to find you a safe place to crash for a few days. Have you got a friend you could bunk with?"

"I don't have any friends. Max never allowed me to have friends. Helen Croxford asked me to visit her in Africa, but we didn't set a date."

"If I suggest you stay on my boat, are you gonna think I'm trying to…you know what I mean. I know you're a lady. I would never—."

Yeah, right, she thought. "Someday, I'll tell you about my past. I've never been comfortable with this southern-belle crap. Max made the whole thing up. It was his way of trying to mold me into something socially acceptable. I've been playing the part for so long that I've come to despise it. What a joke! Let me throw some things together." Lynn's expression seemed relaxed, like she was finally able to play the part of herself.

"Does the name Nelson Chang mean anything to you?" Gillespie asked.

"Why do you ask?" Without thinking, she closed her robe and pulled her legs under. It was as if mentioning Chang opened a mental door she needed to shut.

"When I was rummaging through Max's desk, I found a folder with his name on it. I almost grabbed it, but I was afraid Max would miss it."

"Nelson Chang is Max's biggest client. Chang's an arms dealer among other things. He's super rich. I met him a couple of times on Max's yacht. He gave me the creeps. Max always treated him like he was God."

"Let's get out of here," he said, standing up.

The security guard smiled at Gillespie as he opened the gate. He wrote down the license plate number and picked up the telephone. "Mr. Turner, this is Tom Casey. Yes, sir, Tom Casey. C-A-S-E-Y. I'm the night-guard at your ex-wife's condo. You told me if I should ever see anything suspicious, I should call you right away. You said there would be a little something in it for me. So you do remember me. Your ex just left here with a man driving a white Caddy convertible. He's a red-faced fella. Kind of a wise guy. Thought he fooled me when he snuck past me earlier, but I was onto him from the get-go... Yes, sir. That's mighty nice of you. Say, I got the first two letters of his license plate. They were FL— Mr. Turner, are you still there?" He listened to the dial tone for a few seconds and hung up.

*    *    *

Gillespie glanced at Lynn as they drove along the beach road to the marina in West Palm. Her face was puffy. From time to time, she dabbed her nose with a hanky. There was a childlike quality about Lynn Allison that was fueling his infatuation. Everything told him his association with Lynn would end badly. Gillespie, why in God's name are you getting involved with this woman? I know why. It's because I'm an idiot. Seems like I've already been there—done this before.

"You don't have to do this. You could drop me off at a motel," she said.

"Let's do this my way. Until we can come up with a better arrangement, I think this is our safest option."

They sneaked past the night watchman at the marina. As soon as they were onboard Gillespie's boat, the *Irish Mist*, they separated to their respective staterooms. As they said goodnight, Dan got the final word in. "Lynn, I know there's a lot going on. I'm not the village idiot. For instance, I know you had a prenup with Turner, which means this isn't about money. Anyway, you think about what I said. I've gotta leave early tomorrow morning. For the time being, I think I should go to work like nothing's happened. We can talk when I get home. Goodnight, Lynn."

"Danny, I was wrong about you. I...."

"Go on."

"It's nothing. Goodnight." She closed the cabin door.

\*　　\*　　\*

Gillespie slipped off his boat in the morning. He laughed at himself for feeling queasy about leaving Lynn. Jesse Spooner pulled up at the front gate to the marina right on time. "Good morning, Danny. You look bright-eyed and bushy-tailed for a Monday morning. It's an hour to Pahokee. I'd like to reread the material Turner gave us on the Rolle woman. Why don't you drive? We need to go over a few things before we get there."

"Sure thing. How was your weekend?" Gillespie asked.

"Boring. And yours?" Before he could answer, Jesse changed the subject. "I grew up in the Glades. When a white man showed up in our neighborhood, it was for one of three reasons. Either he was a cop, a bill collector or he was looking to score drugs. The black folks are gonna be mighty suspicious when they see us together. After I explain, we won't have a problem."

"And I was led to believe that only white people were bigots."

\*　　\*　　\*

Clusters of shabby labor camps mark the city limits of Pahokee. The camps were the living quarters for the sugar-cane laborers on contract from the Caribbean. The farm dirt lying fallow was darker than the people who worked it.

Spooner made Dan scrunch down in the backseat. "Danny, stay put." Jesse got out of his car and walked up to a picket-fence in need of paint. When he opened the gate, it screeched. "Hello there. I'm looking for a Mrs. Rolle."

"I'm Sally Mae Rolle. Why you hidin' that white man in your backseat?"

"Oh, you mean that white man?" he said, pointing at Danny who peeked over the backseat.

"Boy, how many white men are you totin'?"

"Just one. He works for me. I'm an attorney. Mrs. Rolle, would it be all right if we come up on your porch? I need to ask you a few questions."

"You say he works for you?"

"Yes, ma'am."

"Ain't nobody stopping you. Boy, don't I know you? What's your name?"

"I'm Jesse Spooner. That's Dan Gillespie."

"Are you the Spooner boy from Belle Glade? The football player?"

"Yes, ma'am."

"Well, ain't that something. Lord have mercy, I went to elementary school with your momma. Don't know what you wanna be talkin' to me about. I done told them other lawyers all I know. Let's go inside. I expect I need to fix you boys some sweet iced tea. This is a hot one, all right." When Jesse gave a nod to Dan, he hurried from the car and joined him on the porch.

Sally Rolle was a heavy woman. She wore tan support hose to press the fluid from her feet, but fleshy bulges squeezed out over the tops of her shoes. She struggled to get up from her rocking chair. Dan offered her his elbow and Jesse held the screen door open. Her living room smelled of pine soap. There were pictures of Martin Luther King and John F. Kennedy on one wall, and a massive bookcase on the other.

"Mrs. Rolle, you must be an avid reader," said Dan. "This is some book collection." He pulled a book out from the bottom shelf, blew off the dust and opened it. It was a copy of *War and Peace.*

"These were my brother's books. He was the reader in the family. I can't hardly see to read. No sir, my doctor told me my sight's failin' cause of my sugar. I just like to look at them. They help me remember Willie. Since my husband passed, all I've got are my memories."

Before Jesse could speak, Dan asked her another question. "I guess your brother was pretty sick just before he died."

"It's true, Willie's lungs were failing. That ain't what killed him. No sir, he drowned in Lake Okeechobee. The police said he fell off the canal bank while he was speck fishin'. Say, I already told you folks about this. Why you askin' me these same foolish questions? Did you say you work for the law firm in Tampa?"

"No, Ma'am. We work for Turner and Turner in West Palm. We've been authorized to make you a very substantial offer."

"Jesse, you should be ashamed of yourself. You go tell that devil Turner, I don't want his money. No sir, I want justice for Willie. May God bless his memory. That's all I want."

"What kind of justice?" Jesse asked.

The woman struggled to her feet and made a shooing motion towards the front door. She looked over the top of her lopsided glasses and shook her head. "Son, if you don't know, I can't help you. I expect ya'll better get. Lord have mercy, I'll bet you're a big disappointment to your momma. Goodbye, Jesse Spooner."

They rode back to West Palm in silence. Finally, Gillespie couldn't stand it. "So, what are you gonna tell him?"

"Tell who?"

"Who? Who do you think? Turner, for God's sake. C'mon Jesse, get with it."

"I was thinking about that old woman."

"Sure is curious how her retarded brother was such a devoted reader."

Dan stared at the sugarcane fields lengthening forever. A yellow crop-duster popped over some high tension wires and then swooped down to start another scud run. A rolling white mist of atomized chemicals spewed from the airplane. Jesse switched lanes to pass a converted school bus. The migrant workers riding in the bus looked down at them as they passed. When Gillespie looked at the workers, he felt guilty.

"Spooner, I'm gonna go out on a limb. I don't know why, but here goes. You need to find yourself another line of work before you get disbarred or end up behind bars as some big white cracker's bitch. I'm giving you the best advice you've ever gotten. Maxwell Turner is a fucking crook. If you hang around, you're gonna get your ass in some deep shit. You know Turner had me bug your apartment."

"I know. I found them."

"You found them? Bullshit. Where did you find them?"

"I found three. One was under my nightstand. Of course, one was in my telephone. The third one was on the light above my kitchen table."

"If I ask you a simple question, can I get a straight answer?"

"It depends on the question."

"Did you ever even go to law school? Wait, let me rephrase that. What the fuck are you up to?"

"I graduated from law school, but I'm not a lawyer, at least not officially."

"Goddamn. I knew it. You're working undercover, aren't you? Is it the FBI or the State Attorney's Office? I bet you lied about failing the bar exam."

"Danny boy, if I answered your questions, I might have to shoot you. Don't look so serious, I'm only kidding. The part about me failing the bar exam was true."

"One more question. Why didn't you say something when you saw me steal Turner's keys?"

"That one's easy. I wanted to stop you from doing whatever you were up to, and I needed those keys myself."

"Spooner, you're full of shit. Like I said before, I was surprised you gave up a career in professional football to become a lowlife ambulance chaser. Now I find out you gave up the NFL to become a cop. Guess that's why we're friends. We're both morons."

"Danny, I'm leveling with you because you're a good guy. I could use some help with Turner. Before you say yes, you should know this Turner thing could get messy, and I mean legally. You've got your career to worry about."

"I don't give a rat's ass about my career, or what's left of 'it,'" he said, imitating quotation marks with his fingers. "How can this get legally messy? Why am I asking you? You're not a lawyer, at least not officially." Dan shook his head in disgust and stared out of the window. I wonder if he's telling me everything. "Spooner, would you mind driving a little faster, I'd like to get home sometime this century. I've got someone staying on my boat you're gonna find very interesting."

* * *

Lynn Allison and Dan Gillespie became inseparable over the next two months. Lynn's living on the *Irish Mist* became a permanent arrangement. When the news reached Max Turner, he was delighted. What better way to keep tabs on his ex-wife?

They ran the *Irish Mist* to Key Largo for a long weekend. On another weekend, they made the fifty-mile crossing to the Bahamas. Jesse had dinner onboard three or four nights a week. He seldom missed cocktail hour.

Both men continued to work at Turner and Turner, and both saw a gradual change in Max's behavior. Max would interrupt a conversation with a partner or place his hand over the telephone mouthpiece if they came within earshot. They were exiled from the Monday morning strategy meetings. Their duties at the firm were reduced to busywork. Every Friday, they would have lunch together and discuss the possibility of Max giving them their notice. Everything changed when Savanna Williams got fired.

On Sunday afternoon, they drove to Belle Glade to visit Jesse's mother. Gillespie waited until he was alone with Jesse before questioning him about Savanna. Lynn Allison had driven Jesse's mother to the First Baptist Church. Lillian Spooner didn't tolerate drinking in her house. Gillespie needed a little help to get straight after a hard Saturday night. The two men sat alone on Mrs. Spooner's back porch, sipping Cokes spiked with Bacardi.

"Lynn asked you to invite Savanna Williams for dinner a dozen times. You said you weren't interested. Either you're gay, or you were setting Williams up. You got Savanna fired, didn't you?"

Jesse knew Dan was eventually going to put two and two together, and had his response rehearsed. "You're the one who told me Turner suspected someone was working undercover. You saw how Max treated us. Turner was looking for an office snitch and I gave him Savanna. What choice did I have? At least she won't be around when the shit hits the fan. In a way, I may have saved her career. Don't worry, Savanna's a smart girl. I'm sure she'll land on her feet."

"You should have told her the truth. What you did was rotten." Jesse couldn't help but smirk. "I did her a favor. Look, it's my job. Speaking of favors, I need one. Don't look so happy. It means breaking into Max's office again. If we get caught, I can't protect you. Do you still have the keys?"

"I'm surprised it took you this long to ask. Of course, I still have the keys. We should use Jimmy the locksmith as our lookout. One thing's for sure—he won't drive off and leave us."

"I was thinking about tomorrow night," Jesse said.

Gillespie didn't answer immediately; instead, he thought about how he could pump more information out of Jesse. "Tomorrow night? You're on. You're not after Turner, are you? It's this Chinese arms dealer, Chang, isn't it?"

"Nelson Chang's the primary target, but Turner knows where all of the dead cats are buried. We believe Chang gave Turner part of the action in an arms deal. What better way to make sure he kept his mouth shut? Turner's so greedy he couldn't say no. Turner came right out of law school doing Chang's contract work. One thing led to another. I'd love to put both of them behind bars."

Dan carefully funneled the rum into his Coke bottle. "So it's the gook. I thought you said you worked for the Bureau. You're an agent with ATF."

"I never said I worked for the FBI, you just assumed it. Let's get the jokes about Waco behind us."

"I'll leave that one alone. If you had passed the bar exam the first time, you could have gone to work for the postal service."

"Very funny. Give me Turner's keys. I've got no right to ask you to get involved."

"C'mon Jesse, you know I can't do that. A man needs a little excitement in his life. Hell, I can't lose my drinking buddy." He decided to tell Jesse about his invitation. "Funny, all of a sudden I've become Turner's newest best friend. He invited me to a pigeon shoot he's hosting at his Okeechobee ranch. Probably see some of my old divorce clients. Turner can't make it, something about a meeting in Washington." When he didn't get a response he carried on. "Let's drink up before your mother gets home," Dan said, draining his bottle. He closed one eye and squinted into the bottle. It was as if he was afraid he might miss a drop.

Jesse took the last swig and said, "Gillespie, you're turning me into an alcoholic."

"You can thank me later. Pass me the rum. I'm getting depressed thinking about Lynn leaving for Africa. I'm gonna miss her. Never thought I'd say that about a woman. I'm becoming a sentimental old fool. Here's to Lynn Allison and that felony favorite, breaking and entering," he said, holding up his bottle. "Spooner, you do know what a felony is? I know you failed the bar exam and all."

"Let's just hope I know enough not to get us arrested."

"I'll certainly drink to that."

*      *      *

The following night, Spooner and Gillespie picked up Jimmy and drove to the Turner building. This time they used the east parking lot.

The break-in ran as smooth as silk. The file on Nelson Chang was still in Turner's desk. Jesse fanned out the sheets of paper and photographed each one of them. Gillespie used the office copier to photocopy all of Turner's son's letters. The work was completed in less than an hour. As they were leaving, Gillespie grabbed two handfuls of cigars from the humidor on Max's desk. They exited the building and jumped into Gillespie's Caddy.

"I got you some more Havanas, courtesy of Turner." He handed the cigars to Jimmy.

"Thanks, but you guys are still buying me dinner," Jimmy said.

"I know what you're gonna say. The restaurant has to use white table clothes. Jesus, the labor laws for the criminals' union are getting tough."

\* \* \*

The next day, Turner stood behind his antique desk. He was too nervous to sit down. He forfeited his usual cigar for a cigarette, and cursed himself for doing so. Something in his office had been altered, but he couldn't identify the change. He summoned his bodyguard to review the building's surveillance tapes.

"I got them, Mr. Turner. They used the east parking lot on Monday night," Bob said, handing him a photograph that had missed Jesse Spooner.

"Gillespie was the Judas all along. Who's the other guy?"

"He's a local locksmith. Crippled prick with a long criminal record. I'm sorry about this. I guess I screwed up."

"I've invited Gillespie to the pigeon shoot on Saturday. Need I say more? Do what you want with the locksmith." Turner walked over to the bay window and looked out at the Atlantic Ocean. He placed his hands behind his back and sighed. "The Lord is a jealous God filled with vengeance and wrath. He takes revenge on all who oppose him and furiously destroys his enemies. It was the cigars."

"The cigars?" Bob asked.

"I filled that humidor myself. They stole my Cohibas."

# 8

# OKEECHOBEE

The weather cleared enough on Saturday for Dan Gillespie to put the top down on his Coup de Ville. It took him an hour to drive from West Palm to Okeechobee. He glanced at the directions he'd scribbled on a cocktail napkin. *There's the pickup truck where I'm supposed to turn off,* he thought. The road was marked with milky potholes from the previous night's rain. He veered to avoid a deep rut and made his own road around a clump of palmetto bushes. The twisted cypress trees lining the dirt road were suffocated in Spanish moss. He gave up looking through the muddy whitewash on the windshield and stuck his head out the window. Up ahead, he saw three men standing in front of a metal cattle-gate. When he stopped the car, one of them walked up to him.

"You are... ?" a man asked, looking over the top of his reflective sunglasses.

"Dan Gillespie."

"Very good, sir." He motioned to another man to open the gate.

Gillespie had heard rumors about pigeon shooting. It was a blood sport for the rich and famous. When Max asked him to stand in for him, he was intrigued. *Old Maxy-boy's doing his best to bring me into the fold. He even put up the two-thousand-dollar entry fee.*

The clearing was surrounded by willowy Australian pines. There was a large tent erected in the middle. After parking his car, he stepped into the tent. Bartenders worked the open bar. Waiters hustled between the tables. Dan eyed the bar, but hesitated. He leaned his Browning 12-gauge in a rack between a Purdey and a Parker Brothers. *These guns cost more than my boat.*

The only seat available was one next to an older woman and her

younger escort. Dan recognized them. She was rich, and her escort
wasn't. Her face had been overstretched by plastic surgery. His hair was
dyed the color of a fox. Much scarier in person, he said to himself. Dan
tried to strike up a conversation, but they brushed him off.

A man walked to the front of the tent and started tapping a glass
with a spoon. "Listen up. Today's shoot is worth one hundred thousand
dollars. I failed math, but we have fifty shooters at two thousand per
head." Laughter rippled through the crowd. "We have some guests with
us today, so I'm going to go over the rules. I'd like to thank Mr. Turner,
who couldn't be here, for letting us use his ranch. Let's hear it for Max."
The man's remarks were followed by enthusiastic applause. "Back to the
rules. As you can see, we have a fifty-foot ring surrounded by a three-foot
fence. You will note three trapdoors inside of the ring. When the shooter
is called, he or she will step forward. Your guns must be opened and
unloaded. Failure to comply with this rule means automatic disqualifi-
cation. On the command 'Load,' the shooter will load. I'll ask if you're
ready. You'll indicate yes with a nod. At your command 'Pull,' a live
pigeon will be jettisoned out of one of the trapdoors. The shooter must
fire both barrels at each bird. If the bird's hit, but manages to fly out of
the ring, it's a miss. All birds must fall and stay in the ring to be counted.
There will be no appeals.

"More about safety. You will note the bird boys. Please don't shoot
them. Shooting a bird boy also means you're disqualified." This remark
was met with hilarity. "I'm sure you saw the men standing around the
perimeter. These men are here to shoot any pigeons you fail to kill. We
don't want an injured bird landing on some Audubon Society member's
windowsill." The crowd's laughter was less energetic. "I know some of
you have disconnected your safeties. I cannot stress this enough, please
be careful. Are there any questions?" he asked, scanning the crowd. "I
guess not. The first two shooters, to your marks, please." The woman
sitting next to Gillespie and a suntanned man stepped forward.

The man was dressed in designer khakis complete with a hat banded
in leopard skin. He twisted his hips trying to get an easy kill on a bird
coming from his left, but the first pigeon came out the right trapdoor;
he missed it with both shots. He was sure the next one would come from
his left, but the bird flew out of the middle trapdoor. He missed again.
Gillespie heard the blast as a perimeter shooter killed it. The contestant

was so unnerved; he had no chance of hitting the third pigeon that did fly out of the left trapdoor. He was zero for three.

It was the old woman's turn. She held her 28-gauge like a mother cradling an infant. She squared her stance and placed the Purdey against her chin. "Pull!" she screamed in a croaky rattle. She stroked the barrel across the sky as smoothly as a great painter would swirl his brush. The shots were fired so close the sound fused into a single noise. That bird and the next two were pulverized into organic dust. She was three for three. Her opponent examined his gun as if it was defective.

As the afternoon bore on, Gillespie noticed a man staring at him. He wore his hair in a ponytail and he had tattoos on his arms. When he stared back, the man looked away. This guy's gotta be one of my old divorce clients, he guessed.

Gillespie was called as the next shooter. He was surprised to find the man with the tattoos walking next to him. "I'm Dan Gillespie. Good luck." He extended his hand, but the man refused to shake it. So that's the way you want it, he thought.

"Mr. Gillespie will shoot first. To your mark!"

He tried to visualize the old woman's shooting. He squared up and fought off the tendency to guess. The first pigeon came out of the left trapdoor. He hit the bird before it could gather any speed and hit it again on the ground for insurance. The next one came from the middle. He killed it easily. The last bird got lodged in the tube. A timeout was called. The bird boys ran into the ring. One of them rung the pigeon's neck and another boy reloaded the tubes with fresh birds. The interruption broke his concentration. He missed his last pigeon with both shots. He was two out of three for the first round.

Gillespie stepped aside to allow his opponent to pass. A shot was fired. The blast knocked Gillespie down. The flash in time was reduced to slow motion. He couldn't move or breathe. He tried to scream, but couldn't. The sulfuric smell of gunpowder filled his nostrils. There was only the ringing. Please God, let this be a dream, he thought. When he opened his eyes, he was looking up at people. They were speaking, but he couldn't hear their voices. There were distorted faces with uncaring eyes looking down at him. His mind raced through a kaleidoscope of his life. It stopped with a vision of Lynn. He felt his bowels ooze. A terrible sadness filled him. The sadness wasn't because he knew he was dying, it was because he wanted to tell Lynn something. His breathing stopped, but he had thoughts. He saw a man's ear. His felt the man's fingers close his eyes. There was nothing he could do.

One hour after Dan Gillespie died, a man pushed Jimmy over the top of the stairs above his locksmith shop. His legless body was vaulted from his wheelchair. The bald man who pushed him reached down and picked up Jimmy's cigar. "Shame on you. Smoking is a nasty habit," the man said, extinguishing the butt between Jimmy's eyes.

\*      \*      \*

Jesse was relieved to find a police car parked at the marina. When he received the telephone call about the accident, he agonized over how he would tell Lynn. Walking down the dock, he passed two policemen headed in the opposite direction. Their expressions meant they had informed Lynn about the accident. He found her curled up in a fetal position in her cabin. There was nothing they needed to say to each other. He sat down on the edge of her bunk and placed his hand on her shoulder. She covered his hand with hers. Jesse stayed with her well into the night. Finally he said, "Lynn, let's get out of here. My mother's expecting us."

The drive to Belle Glade was a silent one. Lynn had planned to tell Dan everything about her involvement with Turner, but she could never find the right time. Jesse had also kept things from Dan. Now it was too late for both of them.

It was after midnight by the time Jesse parked his Chevy in front of his mother's house. The minute Lynn stepped on the porch, the immense woman engulfed her in a bear hug. "Honey, I expect Danny's with the Lord now. I'm gonna fix ya'll some eggs and pork sausage. Son, put her suitcase in my bedroom."

The women stared at each other over the kitchen table. They were too grief-stricken to speak. Lynn looked away and began to sob quietly. Lynn felt she had become a pariah. The men in her life were either terribly flawed or terribly unlucky.

Jesse tried to sleep, but he tossed and turned and never closed his eyes. There was something about Dan's death that didn't make sense.

He was up by six and gone by seven. He bought a newspaper and a cup of coffee at a convenience store. He dropped the paper, and ran to his car. The headline read, "Local Locksmith Found Dead."

Jesse took his time driving back to his mother's house. He wondered if Lynn and Danny had been totally candid about Max Turner. There's something I don't understand about the relationship between Lynn and her ex-husband. I need some straight answers.

For the next two weeks Jesse commuted between his mother's house and West Palm.

Mrs. Spooner was a keen observer, especially when it concerned her son. She was happy to have Lynn as a guest, and she told her so. Lillian watched Lynn's affection for her son change from friendship into something more. She worried about the way they touched each other. When she confronted him in private about his attraction to Lynn, he shrugged it off. Mrs. Spooner never told her son, but she was relieved when Lynn left for Africa.

*     *     *

Max Turner felt rejuvenated by the turn of events. On his first day back from Washington, he was interviewed by a deputy from the sheriff's department. He forced back tears as he lamented about allowing such a repugnant event to take place on his ranch. At the end of the interview, the deputy apologized to Max for the inconvenience. He swiveled his chair around and looked out at the ocean. He lit his first cigar of the day and smiled. Everything was falling into place. The private line on his telephone flashed. It was the secured line reserved for Nelson Chang.

"Are you still in the Seychelles?" Max listened for awhile and then finished the conversation with, "I see. I'd like to explore one more alternative, before I give you my blessing. Goodbye, Nelson."

# 9
# SEYCHELLES ISLANDS

Nelson Chang replaced the satellite telephone on the table next to his deck chair. He had trouble sleeping and was awake before sunrise. The first glimmer of light shone above the Indian Ocean. The reassuring sound of waves lapping against the hull was interrupted by a tape recording: It was the call for morning prayers.

It took thirty-two days for Saudi Prince Waleed's yacht, the *Kingdom*, to sail into the Seychelles Islands from her homeport at Benghazi in the Gulf of Sidra. Two Sikorsky helicopters stayed busy ferrying the prince's guests to and from the airport at Beau Vallon Bay. As one helicopter landed on the *Kingdom*'s fantail; her sister ship hovered over the shoreline. Gray gunboats of the Seychelles Defense Force formed a picket-line offshore.

Sunni fundamentalism had not cast its shadow over the prince's yacht. The strict dictates of the Quran were temporarily suspended. Prostitutes from London, alcoholic beverages and illicit drugs were provided for his guests. The pent-up demand for vices had turned the cruise into an orgy.

Chang Man Ying was renamed Nelson Chang, as a tribute to Admiral Nelson by the British couple who adopted him. Chang was an international arms dealer. Governments in the Middle East juggling their allegiances between the Western democracies and Islamic extremists used Chang. He helped the Arabs funnel weapons into their jihads.

The emergence of China as the next economic juggernaut had elevated Nelson Chang to a behind-the-scenes liaison between the Arabs and the People's Republic.

At sixty-five, Nelson Chang was one of the richest men in the world.

He cultivated the persona of a man without a country; a man unburdened by the fidelities born of patriotism.

Chang reluctantly accepted the prince's invitation to spend a few days cruising in the Seychelles Islands. When he attempted to cut his visit short, the prince protested.

The atmosphere onboard the *Kingdom* was transformed from excessive consumption to sobriety on Chang's last day. The prostitutes were hustled off the yacht before sunrise. The stewards exchanged their western khaki uniforms for traditional Arabic robes. The furniture in the main salon was replaced with pillows and prayer rugs. A green Islamic flag fluttered from the ship's masthead.

Chang stood on the bow watching the emerging sun's fiery display. The smell of Turkish tobacco made him turn around. Prince Waleed was also admiring the sunrise. He wore a long sleeved *thoub*. The red-and-white checkered *shumag* on his head was held in place by a band. When he exhaled, the smoke separated into two strands and disappeared into his tear-shaped nostrils.

"The sunrise is even more beautiful in the desert. *As-Salamu Alaykum*, peace be with you, Nelson Chang," he said quietly. "In the name of Allah, I hope you slept well?"

"A man sleeps better in his own bed."

"I hope you can forgive me for prolonging your stay. I think you will find the meeting I have arranged, how shall I say it, enlightening."

The prince took a few steps towards Chang and spoke again. "We are old friends. Like you, I am also cursed by a western education. Sometimes I wish my father had left me in the desert. Please don't judge us by what you have witnessed. I think it was the philosopher Spinoza who said, 'Desire is the very essence of Man.' I'm afraid our steadfastness is challenged by the forbidden fruits of the West."

As soon as the prince sensed Chang had accepted his explanation, he switched to another topic. "Nelson, are your friends in Beijing pleased by the developments in the Sudan?"

Chang took his time in answering. "I would have to say, yes. We know any military adventures in Africa would be thwarted by the Americans. Better to let our Arab friends take control of Africa from within."

"The Islamic movement is spreading over Africa like a great tidal wave. I'm curious, how many Chinese are working in Africa?"

"Thousands. Seven hundred Chinese companies are operating in forty-nine countries on the African continent. We just completed the presidential residence in Zimbabwe, a gift for Robert Mugabe.

"The Middle East has less than forty years of oil left. China must have strategic minerals if she is to challenge the United States. The destinies of our two great civilizations have been written here. Allah will convert these savages. Together, we will reap Africa for a hundred years," the prince reiterated, to make his point.

The conversation made Chang uncomfortable. He walked over to the railing and looked towards the Horn of Africa. His thoughts drifted back to his last briefing in Beijing. The Chinese thought of Arabs as only slightly more advanced than Africans in human evolution. Their union was one of convenience, certainly not preference. "Your Highness, I understand the Canadians have abandoned their oil interests in the Sudan." He turned around expecting the prince, but he was gone.

Prince Waleed climbed to the bridge where he could look down at Chang undetected. Chang was an enigma to the prince. He was devoid of religion and family. He sensed that to trust Chang would be a grave mistake. Our association is one of mutual mistrust, he thought. Chang walked up to the bowsprit. The man's slanted eyes were encased by folds of leathery skin. As he observed Chang, a bilious taste filled his mouth. Someday China *will* inherit the earth. What a ghastly place, he reflected.

Later that morning, Chang was ushered into the main salon. The prince greeted him in the traditional Arabic manner with his palms turned up. There were two men standing next to the prince. Their skin shined like anthracite. Chang guessed the larger man was a general by his uniform. A glossy scar starting at the corner of his left eye disappeared into his beard. The scar had damaged his facial muscles, turning his expression into a permanent snarl. His face was so twisted; it looked like two opposite thespian masks grafted together.

The general's interpreter was a small man. He had snakelike eyes framed by thicketed eyebrows. One eye was lazy and gazed off in a different direction from the other. Chang took a step back, hoping to avoid the traditional cheek-kissing. His hopes were dashed as each man was introduced to him. Chang wiped his face and sat down.

"Mr. Chang, this is General Muhammad Nur of the Sudanese Army," the prince said, introducing the larger man who scowled at

Chang. The general has information about your friend's son, Arthur Turner."

"General, Mr. Chang represents the Chinese National Petroleum Corporation. This company has completed construction of the first oil refinery in the Sudan. Sixty percent of Sudanese oil is exported to China. I'm sure your superiors in Khartoum would want you to help him. To make sure we have your undivided attention, I have provided you with a small token of my appreciation." The prince handed the general a briefcase.

Chang listened to the general lecture him about his military exploits on the Sudanese frontier with Chad. He knew the Janjaweed militias had killed four hundred thousand Africans in the Darfur and had driven two million more from their ancestral homes. The Islamic armies had castrated men and raped women in their so-called Holy Jihad. The world condemned the scorched-earth policy as a religious genocide, but Chang knew there was another motive. The Darfur region contained vast oil reserves. Once the land was cleared of human interference, the Chinese could start exploring for oil. "Yes, yes," said Chang, interrupting him. "I'm sure you will prevail in your military endeavors. Tell me what you know about the American, Turner." Chang waited impatiently for the translation.

The general opened the briefcase and patted the money listening to Chang's translated inquiry. His damaged mouth could not contain the saliva as he answered. When he stopped speaking, he ran his finger along the scar on his face. He discreetly wiped the spittle on his robe.

"The general says Turner lives in a refugee camp known as Mangalatore. This place is north of the Ugandan border. He's curious to know what you want with this man. He says if you wish him to rescue the man, he feels he should return your gift. It would be a most difficult undertaking. The savages are fierce fighters. A *Dinka* warrior has already scarred him." The interpreter outlined the general's scar on his own face to make his point.

"Ask the general if it would be easier to kill the man," said Chang.

The interpreter asked the general. He answered a few seconds later, saying, "It could be done. The general wants to know what evil thing this man has done to his father that would make him want to kill his own son."

"Tell him, that's not his concern. I will let him know of my friend's wishes. Tell him my friend is a generous man." The interpreter relayed Chang's remarks. He decided not to translate the general's opinion about the brutality of a father ordering the execution of his son. A few minutes later the general and his interpreter got up to leave.

Chang watched the general's helicopter disappear into the washed-out haze. The renewed sunlight turned the coconut trees along the coastline from black to green. The first gasp of day produced a chilly breeze. He shivered and closed the collar of his linen jacket to ward off the coolness.

Prince Waleed studied Chang, but his poker face gave no insight to his thinking. "Nelson, you look perplexed. What's your opinion of the general?"

"Someone once said, 'Men never do evil so completely and cheerfully as when they do it from religious conviction.'"

"The man you quoted was Pascal," said the prince, wiping the last vestiges of sleep from his eyes. "These Africans are like barbarous children. That's precisely why we must control them. I've heard it said that the United States and China will fight a great war. Maybe that war will be fought here in Africa. Come Nelson, let us eat. It's too early for such depressing thoughts. It's given me a headache."

"I'll join you after I make an overseas call. My friend's anxious to hear the news about his son."

# 10
# ZIMBABWE

As soon as Lynn recovered from her jetlag, Helen and Rigby organized a small dinner party in her honor. It was late when the guests left. Lynn retired to her bedroom. The Croxfords sat alone on their veranda listening to the cricket concert. A pearl-spotted owl's whistle quieted the crickets.

"Rigby dear, I have something I need to talk to you about."

"Anytime you call me 'dear,' I know it's serious."

"It's nothing bad. It's just something we need to discuss."

"Let's hear it. I'm breathless with anticipation." He pulled her in and kissed her on the cheek.

"Lynn has an American friend coming to Zimbabwe to visit her. Her friend's a man. I've invited him to stay with us."

"So, what's the big deal? Lynn's a grown woman. What's the man's name?"

"Jesse Spooner. He's a black man."

"When you say 'friend,' what exactly do you mean?"

"I think Lynn's in love with him."

"Helen, have you lost your mind? You know we don't mix the races in this country. Our friends will think we've lost the plot. That man is not staying on my farm. Helen, you're gonna have to make a new plan. What in God's name were you thinking? No sir, not on my farm. Maybe it'll happen one day. Thank God I won't be alive to see it."

"Are you through? I don't care what our friends think. You claim to be this great champion of the blacks in this country, but when it means complete integration you go ballistic. I hate to enlighten you, but the world will change with or without Rigby Croxford. And another thing, this is not *your* farm, it's *our* farm. I'm very disappointed. I'm not surprised, just disappointed."

"You're disappointed! You should have asked me about this beforehand. I'm going to bed." He got up, walked over to the wooden railing and flicked his cigarette butt into the blackness. "Helen, I love you, but you still don't understand Africa or Africans."

The night was unpolluted by a moon. The stars seemed to reach endlessly into the blackness. Helen heard a distinctive series of whistles rising in sequence and ending in a "wheeoo-wheeoo" sound. It was the male owl warning his rivals. Maybe I don't know Africa, but I do know you. It might take a little of the silent treatment, but you'll come around. You just needed to show off your maleness. Just like the owl, only bigger, she continued thinking.

It didn't take the silent treatment to bring Rigby around. He apologized to his wife the next day. Of course it would be all right if the man stayed with them, just not in the same room with Lynn. Helen accepted her husband's change of heart with pride. It wasn't a total victory, but it was a step in the right direction.

What Helen didn't know was that her husband had plans for Jesse Spooner. Jesse was to land at the Victoria Falls Airport in five days. The town was over two hundred kilometers from the Croxford farm. Jesse's visit overlapped a previously scheduled Cape buffalo hunt. Rigby could have turned the hunt over to his partner, but that wasn't about to happen. He would pick Jesse up at the airport and take him out into the bush to finish the hunt. If his plan worked, Jesse would be headed home in a week.

*      *      *

Jesse slept for most of the fourteen-hour flight to Johannesburg. He waited in line with the other bedraggled passengers to clear customs at the airport. Finally, Jesse presented his passport to the uniformed agent who smiled and welcomed him to South Africa. When he slid his ATF weapons permit across the desk, her smile curled down into a frown.

"Sir, I need to check with my superior," she said, folding the permit inside of his passport and then walking away.

In a few minutes, the customs agent returned with a man following her. "Mr. Spooner?" the man inquired without smiling. He stared at his passport picture and then looked up at him reflectively. "Mr. Spooner, what's your purpose in South Africa?"

"I'm transiting through to Zimbabwe. My flight to Victoria Falls leaves in four hours. Is there a problem?"

"No problem. Your papers seem to be in order. The security rules changed after 9/11. I'm sure you understand."

"Of course. Is there anything else?"

"If you change your travel plans and decide to stay in South Africa, you must contact my office. Goodbye, Mr. Spooner." He handed him his passport.

Jesse checked his luggage at the Air Zimbabwe desk for the flight to Victoria Falls. He bought a copy of the foreign edition of the *London Times* and found a seat in the terminal.

A heavily accented woman announced the arrival and departure of flights to and from exotic sounding places like Katmandu and Lusaka. Bearded Arabs kneeling on their prayer rugs chanted quietly in the corners of the building. West Africans dressed in brightly colored robes and matching madras turbans studied the monitors for undated flight information.

A tall African sat down next to him. He was wearing a rumpled business suit and splayed tie-up shoes. Jesse smiled and said good morning to the man, but got no reaction. He glanced at a flight monitor. He noticed the flight to Victoria Falls was flashing on the screen. The ticket agent was polite but nonchalant as she explained the flight had been delayed three hours. She told Jesse that he should check with her later to make sure the flight hadn't been canceled.

Bored and stiff from sitting, he walked out of the building and into the brisk morning air. A car stopped next to him. The driver stuck his head out of the window and shouted. Jesse moved closer to hear the man. "Mister, do you need a taxi?"

"Why not?" he said, getting into the backseat. "Why don't you give me a tour of the city? Were you born here in Johannesburg?"

"I'm from Mozambique," the driver answered. He adjusted the rearview mirror to look at Jesse. He was missing his left hand and had trouble moving the mirror into position. "Are you from England?" the man asked.

"I'm an American."

"America is number-one. In America, everybody's rich." He made a finger-rubbing gesture of making money. "Would you mind if I collect a friend?"

"No, I don't mind."

The road sliced through the industrial section of Johannesburg. There were factories topped in belching smokestacks on one side and squatter-camps on the other. The camps were composed of squared shacks roofed in corrugated metal. The shanties were packed so tight they suffocated the land. A dusty haze blanketed the districts. Barefoot children with popping bellybuttons played soccer on the outskirts. Women hung clothes on the perimeter walls built to hide the eyesore. They turned down a dirt road. Jesse moved uneasily in the backseat.

The driver stopped in front of a dilapidated building. A man left a group of four men and approached the car. The man's dreadlocks looked dirty. His eyes were hidden behind sunglasses. The driver rolled down the window. They talked in pigeon Zulu. The man with the dreads smiled over the top of his shades and then slid into the front seat. Jesse touched his 9mm. Jesse watched the other men run to a pickup truck. The car pulled away with the pickup following close behind. The driver's cell phone rang; Jesse guessed it was someone in the truck.

"You aren't going to give a tour, are you?" The man riding in front reached for something in the glove-box. Jesse grabbed a fistful of dreads and pressed the barrel of his revolver against the man's temple. When he looked back, the truck was gone. "What were you going for?" he asked, pointing at the glove compartment. "Take it out slowly." He yanked the man's head back. The man retrieved a book entitled: The Tourist Guide to Johannesburg. Jesse released his hair and slumped back inside the seat. The man whispered to the driver.

"What did he say?" Jesse asked.

"He asked me if everyone in America is crazy. Mister, do you still want the tour?"

Jesse stared at a group of children waving at him. "Forget the tour. Take me back to the airport. Sorry, I got carried away."

*       *       *

The archaic DC-9 landed with a thump at the Victoria Falls Airport. The terminal was in need of paint. The airport's baggage handlers were barefooted and could have passed for beggars. They fought over the more expensive-looking luggage. One of them tried to strike up a conversation with Jesse, but he ignored him.

As Jesse stood in line with the other disembarking passengers he saw the man who had been described to him. Rigby Croxford stared back at him. They acknowledged each other with smiles. Croxford was bigger than he had expected. Deep laugh wrinkles spread from the corners of his eyes. His hair was clipped in a buzz-cut. He wore khaki shorts and sandals. Jesse wiped his sweaty hands on his pants.

Rigby felt out of sorts and he didn't know why. Jesse Spooner was lighter-skinned than the Africans standing around him. Rigby shrugged off his reluctance and stepped forward. "You must be Spooner. I'm Rigby Croxford." They shook hands, but their eye contact was brief.

"I can't believe your flight made it," said Rigby. "It's bloody amazing. There's not a spare part in Zimbabwe. Our planes are held together by bailing wire and electrical tape like everything else on this buggered continent." Rigby omitted the local joke about the perils of flying with black pilots. He handed Jesse a warm bottle of beer. "This'll help settle your nerves. We better collect your luggage before someone pinches it. Let's hope they put your bags on in Joburg." He omitted another local joke, about the idiocy of Africans running the airlines.

"They can't lose my luggage with only five passengers."

"This is Africa. Anytime something can go wrong, it usually does." The men walked over to the suitcases. "I see my bag."

"Grab it. I'll bring up the vehicle," Rigby yelled over his shoulder.

The road to Victoria Falls had no traffic except for one donkey-drawn cart hauling firewood. Heat waves curled up from the tarmac like gas fumes. The dry wind made Jesse's eyes feel sandpapery. Both men had practiced what they would say to each other, but had trouble cracking the silence. "How's Lynn doing?" Jesse asked.

"She's fine. How was your stopover in Johannesburg?"

"It was interesting. Look Rigby, there's something I need to get off my chest. I hope you're all right with me coming over here. I mean, with the black-and-white thing."

"It's not a problem. C'mon, man, you're in Africa now." Rigby stuttered slightly as the words lodged in his throat.

"I'm glad that's over. I can't tell you how much I worried about meeting you. To tell you the truth, I never thought a woman like Lynn would ever give me a second look. She's very special."

"She is indeed. Do you mind if I smoke?" He lit a homemade cigarette before Jesse could respond.

"Those things will kill you."

"Spooner, you'll discover that everything on this bloody continent is keen on killing you. Smoking is about the safest thing we do in Africa."

Jesse's confession released the tension. He propped his head against the window and closed his eyes. Rigby glanced over at him. He remembered his wife's words, "Please, just give him a chance." Helen hasn't got a clue, he thought.


They drove over the Masuie River Bridge just as a troop of baboons were crossing. The dominant male lagged behind giving his troop time to cross. His red-bottomed females slung their babies under their bellies and loped down the embankment. The troop leader swaggered behind them. Without warning, he sounded a thunderous bark, which evoked panic in the troop. When they reached the river bottom the flare-up ended.

Two skinny women waved from the far end of the bridge. They had babies strapped to their backs. Rigby pulled over, and said something to the women. They jumped up into the back of the truck.

"They're members of the Shona tribe.

"Interesting," said Jesse, glancing back at the women.

Vic Falls had atrophied in recent years. The road ran downhill and disappeared into some mopani trees. Beyond the trees there was mist rising from the waterfalls. "The Shona named this place *Musi oa Tunya*—it means the smoke that thunders," Rigby explained. When he slowed down at a railroad crossing, the hitchhikers swung down off the back of his truck and merged into the throng of natives.

Croxford drove at a snail's pace, giving Spooner time to absorb the primal scenery. Raggedly dressed women carried bundles of firewood and sacks of cornmeal on their heads; their bowed legs seemed too frail to support their loads. Their husbands, unburdened by portage, led the way. Feral children harassed white tourists with offers to exchange currencies. I wonder what he's thinking, Rigby thought glancing over at Jesse.

Jesse stuck his head out of the window. Strange odors fought for supremacy of the air, but to Jesse the town smelled like a musty barn. "My God, it's wonderful, isn't it?" Spooner remarked.

"Wonderful? Say, let's stop by the Vic Falls Hotel for a drink. You do drink?"

"Of course I drink. What did Lynn tell you about me?"

"She said you were a serious football player. I've never liked soccer. Rugby's my game."

"American football is like rugby. I've never played soccer in my life." Jesse sensed a combative tone in Rigby's remark. He looked at Rigby and thought, so this is how it's gonna go down.

\*     \*     \*

The Victoria Falls Hotel had dark mauve window frames and doors contrasted against cream-colored walls. Mango trees heavy with green fruit shaded the front lawn and gardens. African women, some carrying babies on their backs picked weeds from the flowerbeds by the entrance.

"How about ordering me a whiskey? I need to use the loo," Croxford said.

The rain tree behind the hotel had sprinkled its purple-colored flowers on the lawn. Hand-watering had sweetened the grass, making it green and lush. A family of warthogs grazed on the lawn. The rumbling sound of the Zambezi River ascended from the gorge below the hotel. When Jesse walked on the lawn, the warthogs stopped eating and took notice.

The patio bar was decorated with mounted animal heads and framed black-and-white photographs. The only customers were two white men and their black lady-friends. One man's shirt was unbuttoned to his navel. The women wore wigs and heavy makeup. Both had long, hooked, purple fingernails. No longer willing to endure their pointy high-heeled shoes, they had placed them on a table. One woman giggled with her bare feet in the larger man's lap. The other couple stood next to a piano, where an elderly African wearing a tuxedo struggled with his rendition of the *Horst Wessel Song*.

The hotel manager met Rigby as he emerged from the loo. He shrugged and nodded over his shoulder at the men. "What's going on?" Rigby asked. "Those two Germans and their hooker friends are giving my bartender a hard time."

"Barkeep, another round, *ndapota*," Rigby yelled. He held up two fingers to confirm the drink order.

"Say, friend, are you a local?" the larger man slurred in a German accent.

"I am indeed. I was born here, actually. Rigby Croxford, at your service."

"How about telling this *kaffir* we want some good German lager." His remark evoked hysteria from his friend. The hookers giggled nervously.

"I'll take care of this," Jesse whispered.

"Spooner, if something happens to you, my wife will kill me. If either kraut talks to you, I want you to say the word, '*Arschgeige.*' Think you can handle that?" Jesse nodded as Rigby stood up.

"I take it you're both from Germany," Rigby said, getting up and walking over to the men. The Germans' faces were locked in inebriated grins, but both managed affirmative nods. The piano player stopped playing. The bartender suspended polishing a wineglass.

"We're from Hamburg."

"I see. I'll bet you both have families back in the Fatherland. Did you know forty percent of the people in this part of Africa test positive for HIV?"

"What's this got to do with you?" the big man snarled.

"Of course that wouldn't matter to a couple of pigs like you two," Rigby said, sitting down at the Germans' table. The two hookers grabbed their shoes and ran for the door.

"Is your pet *rhesusaffe* along for protection?" the big German asked, glancing at Spooner, who yelled "*Arschgeige.*" The German seemed unnerved at being called an asshole by someone he had just called a pet monkey.

"Him? Oh, I won't need him. You see, I'm a man of few talents, but one of them is flogging men. During our war, I killed men a hell of a lot tougher than you two baboon turds. Funny thing about killing men, once you get over the horror, it's extremely exhilarating. Steven will back me up," Rigby said, looking at the bartender. "Steven, am I telling them the truth?"

"It is true, sah," the bartender said. The piano player nodded in agreement as did the manager.

"My only regret was that I was too young for the Second World War. I could have had the distinct pleasure of killing Germans. Let me ask you both a question. Have either of you been swimming in the Zambezi?"

"*Nein*, the river is full of man-eating crocodiles."

"I wouldn't worry about the crocs. This hotel sits above a three hundred-foot gorge. When I throw you both over the cliff, your bodies will be crushed on the rocks."

The color drained from the Germans' faces. They pushed and shoved for access to the narrow doorway. One of the hookers reappeared to retrieve a shoe. The piano player started banging out *Lili Marlene*. Rigby walked back to the table where Jesse was waiting. "Let's get out of here before I end up in jail. Cheers, Steven."

"*Lisale kuhle, Baba,*" the bartender said.

"I didn't know whites and blacks fought on the same side in the Rhodesian War," said Jesse, climbing in the truck. "What did that Nazi prick call me?"

"Of course we fought on the same side. The bartender fought on the other side. He was an insurgent, and a damn effective one, I might add. We captured him in Mozambique. As far as what the German called you, I haven't the slightest," he lied. "If it's any consolation, you called him an asshole."

It wasn't enough, Jesse thought.

\*    \*    \*

Jesse slept for the first part of the drive to the Matetsi hunting camp. A bone-crushing bump in the washboard road jarred him out of his cat-nap. A Land Rover drove up behind them. The driver flashed the head-lamps and waved them over. Croxford looked in the rearview mirror and cursed. "Shit. I wonder what *he* wants. Spooner, you're about to meet Zimbabwe's worst nightmare."

Ian Rhodes had been a South African military advisor during the Rhodesian War. After he received a confiscated farm, it was widely suspected that he had been a mole working for the Russians. He was especially despised by the natives, who nicknamed him 'Fisi,' which means hyena.

The English, having never been a particularly attractive people, sent some of their more unsightly daughters to India and South Africa in search of husbands. Rhodes was the by-product of such a union. He had inherited the ugliest features from both of his homely parents. He had more hair growing out of his nose and ears than on top of his head. Thick eyeglasses magnified his watery eyes. His face was dotted with blackheads and ruptured blood vessels. A network of acne scars stretched like a spider web across his forehead and cheeks.

Both trucks screeched to a halt. Armed soldiers ran forward and surrounded Croxford's truck. Croxford got out and told Spooner to stay put, but a soldier pulled Jesse out and pushed him to the ground at gunpoint. After the dust settled, Rhodes walked forward.

"Sir Fisi, what brings you out to the bush? Did your bla— mistress run away again?" Rigby almost said 'black mistress,' but stopped in deference to Jesse.

Rhodes's attempt to camouflage his crooked teeth would have been more effective had he not used such a toothy English accent. "I'm afraid you're both under arrest."

"What's this rubbish you've cocked up?" demanded Rigby.

"I received an urgent communiqué from the police in South Africa. Seems your friend's carrying a concealed handgun. You're both guilty of weapons trafficking. Search their vehicle," Rhodes ordered his men.

"Spooner, what's he talking about?"

"I have an international permit to carry a pistol. It's in my wallet."

"Sergeant, bring me his wallet." Rhodes spread the contents of Spooner's wallet on the Rover's bonnet. "We have a law against handguns in Zimbabwe. As I suspected, this permit is worthless. Your friend might survive an African prison sentence, but you won't, not at your age," he said, smiling at Croxford. "Bind their hands and put them in the lorry."

"Wait just a minute, Rhodes. I wonder what your friends at Central Intelligence will say when I tell them about your illegal ivory-exporting business."

"What are you talking about?" Rhodes's brow knitted from irritation. He looks too nervous not to be guilty, Rigby reasoned. "Fine. Let's let the authorities sort this out."

"Croxford, I'd be careful about making inflammatory accusations. Concerning your friend, I might be willing to look the other way."

"Good. Don't look so worried, I'm no squealer." Rhodes had one of his men cut the plastic tie-wraps on Spooner's wrists. He tossed Jesse's wallet on the ground and walked away. His truck made a U-turn and disappeared over an incline.

"Bugger, I was saving that ivory scam. Spooner, you can get up now, he's gone." Rigby started the truck and began to pull away. "My friend, you've got some explaining to do. Let's start with Max Turner."

"It's a two-way street. You haven't been straight with me, Croxford."

"What the hell are you talking about?"

"You really aren't wild about me coming over here, are you? Just be honest with me."

"Why Jesse, you've got that American civil-rights chip on your shoulder. This is Africa my friend, not the United States."

"So you're saying—there's no racism over here?"

"Not like there is in the States."

"I see. I understand your daughter's a doctor and she lives in South Africa. What if you found out she was seeing a black man?"

"That wouldn't happen in a million years," Rigby blurted out.

"I rest my case," Jesse responded. He sighed and shook his head.

The silence was uncomfortable.

Jesse was the first one to speak. "My mother said I was crazy coming over here. Are your parents alive?" he asked, trying to bridge the discomfort.

"They're both dead. My mother died of a broken heart after my father was beaten to death by terrorists during the war."

Well, that's just great, Jesse thought.

"Look Jesse, the war was a long time ago. Tell me what you know about Max Turner? Lynn said something about you investigating Turner's Chinese business partner," Rigby said, changing the subject.

Jesse told him about his recruitment by the Alcohol Tobacco and Firearms Agency. As a special agent, his assignment was to gather intelligence on Nelson Chang. Chang was an international arms trafficker. Turner had been Chang's silent partner for twenty years. Because of his law degree, Jesse was selected to work undercover at Turner's firm. When Jesse mentioned losing his job because of his affair with Turner's ex-wife, Lynn, he sensed Rigby didn't believe him.

The silence returned as Rigby digested the concept of Lynn and

Jesse's involvement. Finally, he spoke, "Maybe I should have lied when you asked me about my daughter. You think I'm a bigot. I'm afraid it's not that simple in Africa. Let's get to know each other before we make judgments."

"Fair enough," Jesse answered. He was sure Croxford was a bigot, but for some reason, he trusted the man. "Tell me about this buffalo hunting business. It can't be that dangerous. They look like dairy cows."

"A year ago, my partner, Hansel Martin, was gored by a buffalo. His hunting client was a French Baron. After what happened we changed his title to 'the Baroness.' The buffalo hooked Martin in the groin and tore a massive gash. Stuffed his testicles all the way up to here," Rigby said, pointing to a spot below his chest plate. "Spooner, does this sound like a dairy cow?"

These people are crazy, Jesse thought. "So, what happened to the Frenchman?" he asked.

"The Baroness climbed a thorn tree. Took the camp boys an hour to coax him down. Martin reaches down and finds his balls are missing. That's when he begged his tracker to shoot him. Martin's a real ladies man and he figured his life without testicles would be somewhat limited. The tracker tried, but couldn't pull the trigger. Eventually we get Martin medivacced to a hospital. Indian doctor specializing in animal trauma wounds puts him all back together again. While he's recuperating, we organized a party to celebrate his recovery. After some hard boozing, we decide to move the party to Martin's hospital room. When we get there, he's knocked out from the drugs. His girlfriend pulls the sheet down to take a look at his wound. Christ, his scrotum was the size of a rugby ball. After he comes out of the anesthesia, we tell him his doctor has performed the first testicle transplant in history. He now had the balls of the buffalo that nearly killed him. It was one hell of a party."

I was right; these people are crazy, thought Jesse.

"Don't look so concerned. Most of these buffalo hunts are routine," said Rigby.

"I was thinking about a friend. He got himself killed shooting pigeons."

*     *     *

Few landscape painters are gifted enough to capture an African sunset. The rust-colored iron dust from the African deserts transforms the setting sun into a vivid orange ball. The sky comes to life in blushes of lavender brushed over shaded streaks of pinks and reds. Rigby parked on a cliff overlooking the Zambezi Valley. In the stillness of dusk, they heard voices. The chatter came from the hunting camp that lay nestled in a grove of umbrella acacias. Jesse was spellbound, which was disconcerting for Rigby.

Rigby's partner met them as they climbed out of the truck. The cook handed out glasses of whiskey. Spooner wolfed his down in two swallows.

"You must be Spooner," the man said, leaning on a cane with one hand and reaching out to shake hands with his other. "I'm what's left of Hansel Martin. I guess Rigby told you about my episode with the buffalo."

"Every gory detail. You're lucky to be alive."

Before Martin could respond, Rigby interrupted. "How are the clients?"

"They're resting before dinner. He's near seventy. His wife's half his age. Shot a respectable kudu two days ago. He's a typical American— lots of name-dropping and bragging about money. Sorry Spooner, I forgot you're a Yank."

"Don't sweat it," Jesse said. "I think I'll take a nap before dinner."

Martin waited until Spooner disappeared into his tent. "He seems nice enough. Good-looking chap. What's your take on him?"

"He's only been here a few hours. I plan on doing some heavy walking. Our Mr. Spooner's coming with me. Ask me the same question tomorrow."

"Rigby, I'd be careful, he looks very fit."

"Nonsense. He's bulked up from weightlifting. I'll walk this guy until he drops. The big ones never last."

*     *     *

Jesse slept soundly, but he woke up before sunrise. When he thought about Lynn Allison, a dull ache filled his belly. I wonder what we'll say to each other. Better keep the meeting prim and proper in front of old Croxford, he thought, looking at Rigby's tent.

The nights in Africa belong to the predators, but the mornings are reserved for song birds. The animals make a temporary truce to suckle their young. The animal screeches and screams of the darkness are replaced by the mournful cooing of wood doves. The loud bark of a baboon startled Jesse. He rolled over on his side and looked through the tent mesh. A spider had spun its web between the tent poles. The diamond-shaped web glistened with early-morning dew. He reached under the tent flap and plucked one of the web's silk threads. The architect scrambled to reclaim a cocooned tsetse fly.

Rigby emerged from his tent. He realigned his genitals with one hand, closed off a nostril with two fingers of the other and snorted a glob of phlegm into the dirt.

"You need to stop smoking. Come take a look at this spider and tell me if it's poisonous," said Jesse.

"I don't have to look at it. It's like I told you before—everything on this continent's poisonous, including the advice. How'd you sleep?"

"Like a baby," he lied.

"My friend, you're in for a fair amount of walking. Dress lightly. It's cold now, but it'll get hot in a couple of hours. I can't have you dying from heatstroke."

"Yes, *Baba*," Jesse answered.

"Say, does that spider have black and yellow stripes?"

"Wait just a minute. Yes it does."

"It's a leaping button spider, probably a female. The females have the rather nasty habit of eating the males after they mate."

"But are they poisonous?"

"The African button spider's responsible for more deaths in Africa than venomous snakes," he responded.

Jesse's scream made Rigby laugh. He wished the spider story was true. Let the games begin, he thought.

*     *     *

Croxford had had similar problems with other hunting clients, but this one was especially troubling. The client, clearly in the waning years of life, went to bed early. His wife, who was having a life-and-death struggle with the aging process, continued drinking well into the night. Her hair was blonde, but after two weeks on safari, her roots told a different story. She troweled her makeup on like a bricklayer filling in cracks. Her enhanced breasts struggled against the confines of an open blouse. She was a woman who believed all men were hopelessly attracted to her. Her flirtations with Jesse started out innocently enough, but quickly became touchy-feely. Jesse was clearly uncomfortable, and when Rigby told him he needed to get a good night's sleep, he jumped at the chance to excuse himself. When Martin and Rigby excluded the woman by conversing in Afrikaans, she got the message and went to bed.

*     *     *

Late rains in Africa are a blessing for farmers, but a curse for hunters. The animals don't congregate at waterholes making them hard to find. Rigby's plan was to drive twenty miles and then walk back, hoping to stumble on fresh buffalo spoor. The group drove out as the sun peeked over the hills of Matetsi. Blue helmeted guinea fowl trotted along in single file just out of reach of their churning tires. The birds would flush and then land on the road as if they were engaged in a game of chicken. Croxford and Spooner rode in the back with the two Matabele trackers and the black game scout. Rigby glanced at Jesse. His bubbling enthusiasm for Africa was scratching at Rigby's nerves. Spooner, let's see if you're still so cheerful tonight.

The game scout was a Shona. His job was to enforce the game laws. The man rapped his knuckles on the truck's cab and jumped out before they could stop. His scowl scrunched up as he disappeared into the bushes with a roll of blue toilet paper stuck over the barrel of his Kalashnikov. This ritual was repeated four times before Rigby exploded. "Enough is enough! Martin, I need the first aid kit."

When the man reemerged from the bushes, he looked clammy. Rigby emptied some pills in the man's hand and handed him a canteen. He bowed and seemed appreciative. With his rebellious bowels calmed, they made better progress. One of the trackers yelled to stop. Everyone got out of the truck and encircled the man, examining some animal tracks.

"How much time has passed since the buffalo made this spoor?" Rigby asked.

"The *nayati* passed water here six hours ago," the tracker said. He smelled a handful of the sand infused with urine. "The old bull will seek out the shade of an acacia to chew his cud."

Croxford, Spooner, the game scout, and the trackers started walking. Martin drove the client along a dirt path paralleling their route. If the trackers found fresh buffalo spoor, they could bring in the client.

"Spooner, stay close to the trackers." He engaged a cartridge into the chamber and slung the rifle onto his shoulder. "Watch where you step. This area is loaded with black mambas." Rigby's eyes twinkled. His mouth curled around a cigarette in a smile.

They walked for three hours. Spooner shaded his eyes and squinted up at the white sun. Sweat burned his eyes like whiskey. Fatigue made him clumsy. He stumbled on hidden rocks and got entangled in the hookthorn bushes.

At first, Rigby called out the names of animals and birds. "There's a lilac-breasted roller on that limb," or "Look, that's a nice waterbuck." Fatigue sapped his enthusiasm.

It was an undeclared war between them. Rigby had walked the hills of Metetsi for thirty years, but Jesse was younger. Africa was hot, but so was football practice in August. After five hours of hard walking, Croxford conceded. His voice sounded raspy. "Spooner, let's stop and give the trackers a chance to rest."

"This is unbelievable. The game scout seems to be feeling better. What kind of pills did you give him? How many did he take?" Jesse asked.

"It was Imodium. He took the whole lot, actually."

"The whole bottle?" You can't be serious."

"I wouldn't worry about him. Africans are tough."

"Would it be all right with you if I run up that hill? It looks like a great place to take a photograph."

Rigby shook his head. "Spooner, if you're crazy enough to climb that hill—have at it. We'll wait for you."

Jesse climbed the hill. When he was sure Rigby couldn't see him, he collapsed behind some rocks. He held his canteen up and poured water over his head. I'd rather die than let you win, he thought, peeking down at Croxford. He saw movement out of the corner of his eye; it was a large brown snake. The snake's tongue flickered. The inside of its mouth was velvety black. The mamba's eyes fastened on Jesse as he backed away. Jesse hurdled a boulder, lost his footing and then slid down the hill on his backside. At the bottom, he jumped to his feet like nothing happened. Rigby laughed. "See any snakes? Before Jesse could answer, one of the trackers reappeared. Rigby sent the other man to bring back the client.

He exhaled some smoke and then turned to Jesse. "The tracker found buffalo spoor. Are you carrying your peashooter?" Rather than answer, Jesse took the 9mm. out of his pocket and offered it to Croxford.

"Nice weapon. I reckon you need two bullets. If things go badly, you could shoot me and then shoot yourself. A slingshot would do more damage. It takes a big piece of lead to stop a buffalo. A wounded Cape buffalo is like a runaway freight train. These old solitary bulls can be irritable without those extra eyes and ears of a herd to warn them." Jesse was too rattled to hear everything. You're wrong when you said I need two bullets, thought Jesse. I only need one.

"Martin says the client's an excellent shot, but he's over seventy." Spooner, this is no time to be a hero. Run like hell, if I tell you to. Try to keep me between you and the buffalo. Got it?"

"And how fast can they run?"

"A buffalo can outrun the fastest football player in the world."

"So I should only be concerned about outrunning you and the client."

"I guess you could look at it that way. Spooner, a couple of hundred years ago, your ancestors hunted Cape buffalo with spears. God only knows, how many of them got killed. This is two thousand pounds of rage, not a Holstein."

Before Jesse could say something clever, the client and a tracker walked out of the underbrush. The client was laboring heavily. His safari khakis were soaked in sweat. He handed Rigby his rifle. Rigby checked the safety and gave it back to him.

Their walking was purposeful. One tracker checked the wind direction by sprinkling bits of grass. One hour labored into two and the guns grew heavier on their shoulders. Jesse sensed that nothing would make Croxford happier than to see him chicken-out. It'll never happen, he thought, laughing at himself. Rigby, I'm a bigger fool than you are. He stepped on a twig and cringed. His apologetic expression was not received well by Rigby. The head tracker's behavior changed. He placed his finger to his lips, pleading for them to move quietly.

The Cape buffalo stood motionless in the elephant grass watching his pursuers. The bull was two years past his last breeding. The younger bulls would not tolerate his presence and the cows, sensing his frailty, shunned him. His flanks shuddered from pesky insects. Red-billed ox-peckers feasted on the ticks attached to his back and neck. The bird's chirping warned him. For the moment, the buffalo's aggressive nature was conquered by its fear of humans. Shiny strings of drool hung from his wet muzzle. The bull's drooping horns were caked with dried mud. His shoveled ears were shredded from failed lion attacks. The bull grunted, and bolted. The report from the client's rifle boomed like thunder. "What the fuck? I didn't tell you to shoot," Rigby screamed.

"I hit him," the hunter yelled.

"Oh, you hit him all right. Bloody Portuguese heart shot. Right up the bung. Isn't this a lovely cock-up? You there, check the spoor for blood," Rigby yelled to one of his trackers.

The tracker showed Rigby a handful of bloodied semi-digested grass. The buffalo was gut-shot. "Take the client back to the truck," he told the tracker. "Give me his weapon." He cocked his hat to shade his face from the sun's glare and grinned at Jesse. "It's my job to put him out of his misery. There's no need for you to get involved in this. Why don't you follow them back to the truck?" Rigby said, nodding at the client.

"Oh, no you don't. I wouldn't miss this for the world."

"Suit yourself. Just stay out of my way."

It would take the client and the game warden an hour to reach the truck and another hour for Martin to walk back. Rigby looked at the setting sun. There wasn't time to wait for Martin. He handed Jesse the client's rifle. "Spooner, ever use one of these?"

"Not under these circumstances."

"When I told you these buffalo hunts were routine, I guess I mis-spoke. Don't look so worried, he may already be down."

They followed the buffalo's blood spoor. The grass was so thick they had trouble seeing each other. When the tracker held up his hand, they froze. He was listening for tickbirds.

The old bull needed water to quench the fire in his gut. The scent of water led the buffalo into a box canyon. The blackened sides of the gorge were streaked with white crystallized urine stains from hyraxes. The animals scampered into the fault crevices. Red aloe plants and strangler figs clung to the rocks. Howling baboons raced along the upper rim. "The old *nayati* waits for us by the waterhole," the tracker whispered to Rigby. "The hunter has made a very bad shot." He pointed at a scrape mark in the sand indicating that the buffalo was dragging his intestines.

"This is as far as you go, Spooner," Rigby said. I'll send one of them back for you when it's over."

The wounded buffalo watched his tormentors from the shade of a fever tree. Vultures waited impatiently on its limbs. Marabou storks circled above the tree. The water had not eased the buffalo's pain. The bull slung his muzzle to shoo away the flies.

Rigby's first shot was accurate and so was his second. Both bullets buried into the buffalo's chest. A rush of adrenaline fueled the animal's rage. The bull crashed into the shallow water and charged straight for Rigby. Rigby broke open his double and slammed two solids home, but when he looked up, he realized there wasn't time to fire. He was sure he would be gored. He feinted left and dove to the right.

The crack of Spooner's rifle rang out. His shot missed the animal's vitals, but the .458 slug smashed into its foreleg. The femur snapped causing the bull to cart-wheel. The buffalo came to rest in a heap at Rigby's feet. Jesse ran up and fired another shot into its brain. The animal's death bellow reverberated in the gorge.

After the dust cleared, Rigby touched the buffalo's eye with his gun barrel. "He's finished," he said, going down on one knee. "God damn you, Spooner. I thought I told you to stay put. I'd already made up my mind about you, and now look what you've done." After examining the wound that killed the animal, he turned to Jesse. "Thanks for saving my life," he said, still breathing hard.

"It was my pleasure," Jesse answered, mimicking a British accent.

The trackers started to sing. One of them cut the animal's stomach open. The buffalo's innards spilled out on the ground saturating the air with the smell of rotting marigolds.

"What's the song about?" Jesse asked.

"It's an old Matabele hunting song. They're singing about you, Jesse. It's really quite an honor. Oh, there's one more thing. They're saving its testicles for your dinner. A bit chewy, but a real delicacy. Spooner, you look green. I hope you're not going to be sick. Can't let them see their hero pitch his cookies." He handed his canteen to Jesse.

*    *    *

The next morning they left *Metetsi* for the two-hundred-kilometer drive to Rigby's farm. An air of civility replaced their misgivings about each other. After three hours, Jesse took over the driving. Their conversation was lighthearted. Jesse was careful not to mention Lynn Allison. He didn't want to press his luck. Rigby asked a question. "Say Jesse, just out of curiosity, where were you trying to hit that buffalo?"

"If I told you the back leg, would you believe me?"

"No way."

"I didn't think so. Tell me about the lion hunt with Max Turner. I saw the lion's head in Max's den."

"What did he tell you?" Rigby asked.

"Just that he shot it. He said something about a man getting killed."

"Did he, now? The man was a friend of mine." When Rigby wouldn't elaborate, Jesse decided not to press the issue.

Thinking of Sam triggered one of Rigby's flashbacks. *"Gentlemen, I'll not bore you with politics. Politics is the business of pimps. We're military men. We fix what politicians bugger. What do you know about the Johnston attack?" the colonel asked.*

*"Sir, I grew up on a farm next to the Johnston place. I attended Plum Tree with Seth Johnston. When I heard about the raid, I was horrified," I said.*

*"The terrorists came over from Mozambique. They made Mr. Johnston watch, while they raped his two daughters. One girl was only eleven. The older one had just turned twelve. When they finished, they killed them. Mercifully, they also killed Johnston. The barbarity is beyond belief."*

*"Sir, I had no idea," I said.*

*"Any news on Mrs. Johnston?" asked Willie.*

*"I thought you knew. Mrs. Johnston hanged herself yesterday."*

*I was speechless as was Willie. "Take your time, gentlemen. These are bloody hard times," said the colonel. I remember seeing the lust for revenge in Sam's eyes.*

*The colonel droned on about the need to stop the attacks on the farmers. He concluded by saying, "Your job is to locate that camp and call in an air strike. I want that camp incinerated. We must send a message, if you harm our women and children, the consequences will be horrific."*

Jesse reached over and touched Rigby's arm to wake him. Rigby yawned and rolled his head to work out the stiffness in his neck. "How far is it to your farm?" Jesse asked.

"Not far. We need to stop at the next farm for petrol. I should warn you about these people. They're our version of what you call rednecks. The farmer's name is John William. He has five daughters. They ripped the pants off of the last stranger I brought here."

"This sounds like more of your bullshit."

Undeterred by Jesse's skepticism, Rigby continued. "These people have lived here so long—nobody knows where they came from. Some say John William's the missing link. He has five daughters. One's an albino with Tourette syndrome and a stuttering problem. We named her 'Velma the Vulgarian.' All of his daughters weigh over fifteen stones. That's two-hundred pounds to you. Seems like they're always pregnant.

"They keep a three-legged, one-eared hyena as a pet. They named him Oscar. They raised him from a pup. Couple of years back, Oscar tried to hook up with a pack of wild hyenas. Naturally, they mauled him. That's when he lost the leg and his ear. If Oscar tries to sniff your private parts, I'd let him. He gets testy if he's rejected." Rigby couldn't control his laughter.

"I'm not getting out of the truck."

"It might be better."

"You said his daughters are always pregnant. What happened to their husbands?"

"You've just touched on one of the great unsolved mysteries in this country. My wife says it's like 'Where did the Mafia bury Jimmy Hoffa?' The way I see it, there are two possibilities. Either John William's the father or it's Oscar. The kids are so ugly, it could be either one."

They left the tarmac and turned onto a corrugated road running uphill. The William's place was a makeshift series of wooden shacks. There was a tireless tractor and the remains of four trucks jacked-up in the front yard. The three-legged, one-eared hyena played with two children in the dirt. Oscar licked one child's head. The other kid tried to stick a bone in Oscar's unprotected ear hole.

John William rocked back and forth in his rocking chair. There was a rusty shotgun in his lap. He wore nothing but a dirty blanket draped over his hairy shoulders. On the forward rocks, Jesse could see his genitalia. Jesse smiled and waved nervously. The man's eyes gave no indication of mental acuity. John William's beard was soiled with the evidence of his last feeding. His lips formed a circle as he ejaculated a snotty mixture into the dirt.

"Why Jesse, I do believe John William likes you," said Rigby getting out of the truck.

"How do you know he likes me?" Jesse asked.

"Because he hasn't shot you," Croxford whispered. "Sir John, how's the family?" Croxford inquired, getting no response.

"I'm locking the doors," Jesse yelled.

Five heavyset women encircled their truck. One woman pressed her milk laden breasts against a side window. Two others started to lick the windshield. Some children climbed up on the hood. The more adventurous ones used the truck's roof as a trampoline. Oscar balanced on his rear leg and peered into the back window.

A woman knocked on Jesse's door, but he ignored her. He guessed she was the albino, but she was so dirty he wasn't sure. The same woman continued to knock until Jesse cracked the window open. Her words were so muffled he rolled the window completely down. "I beg your pardon," Jesse said.

"I said, you can kiss my ass, you cock…cock…sucker." She tried to re-swallow her profanity, but couldn't. She seemed pleased when her sisters found her comment hilarious.

Jesse knew she was Velma, the stuttering albino. "Get me out of here," he screamed.

After Rigby filled his truck with petrol, the men drove away from the farm leaving rolling dust filled with children running in their wake. "Spooner, if you're interested in any of his daughters, just say the word and I'll turn around. I think old John kind of fancied you for himself."

"Please tell me you've run out of surprises."

"You've taken my best shots and you've passed with flying colors. Here, take a drink of water. You look shaky," he said, handing Jesse his canteen. "My farm's just over the next ridge."

The winding road to the Croxford farm was lined with blooming bougainvillea and blue flowered jacaranda trees. The fields on the right looked weedy and unattended. To the left there was a herd of zebra. The stallion watched them, but his females continued to graze. Jesse saw a giraffe gliding between some woodland acacias. The shadows from cotton ball clouds moved lazily over the rolling hills.

"It's beautiful. I didn't know you had wild animals on your farm," said Jesse.

"It was my wife's idea. I fought it, but she won the argument."

"What crops do you grow?"

"We did grow wheat and tobacco. We stopped planting four years ago. If we plant, we're afraid the government will confiscate our farm. This land has been in my family for over a hundred years. Someday, I expect to die defending it."

They slowed down as they approached some thatch-roofed huts. The men standing around the huts glared back at them. Rigby didn't acknowledge them. "Squatters or war-vets as they call themselves, sent here by Mugabe to run me off my land."

"I can't blame you for trying to hold on. It's not like I thought."

"Spooner, forget everything you think you know about Africa. For starters, the unemployment rate in Zimbabwe is eighty percent and our inflation rate is a zillion percent. Mugabe's a rabid baboon. Ten years ago, we had fifty black families living on this farm. My wife insisted that we send the brighter kids to college. It damn near bankrupted us."

"What happened to the college-educated kids?"

"They're afraid to come back to Zimbabwe. They're seen as a threat by the men in power. It's the same story all over Africa."

"You were right. Africa really is a mess."

\*     \*     \*

Helen and Lynn walked out of the house to meet them. Black servants unloaded their luggage. They knocked the dust off and followed Helen and Lynn up on the veranda. The introductions were slightly awkward. There was the usual small talk, but the atmosphere was contrived.

"Is Africa anything like you expected?" Helen asked Jesse.

"Dr. Croxford, your husband has shown me things I could never imagine."

"I hope you didn't subject him to those dreadful people," she said, turning to her husband.

"That family is one of the great tourist attractions in Zimbabwe."

"My husband has a weird sense of humor. Rigby dear, let's go inside. There's something we need to discuss."

Jesse didn't stand up. He thought the couple wanted privacy. "Jesse, this includes you," said Helen.

Rigby's mind raced through the possible scenarios. The two couples sat around a table. Helen spoke first. "Maxwell Turner's here," his wife blurted out.

"I'm not following you," said Rigby.

"Turner's here in Zimbabwe. He wants to hire you to help him get his son out of the Congo. Before you go ballistic, hear us out. Lynn, give him the background on your stepson."

"I don't want to hear another word about Max Turner or his son. Spooner, what've you got to say? Let's start with the truth. By the way, I know you still work for your government. Carrying that pistol was proof positive." Rigby turned to Lynn. "Why do I get the feeling you planned this?" He waited for a response. When he didn't get one, he threw up his hands in frustration. "Please, somebody say something."

Jesse got up, put his hands in his pockets and walked over to the railing. He turned to face Rigby. "Everything you said is true. Coming over here was my idea, not Lynn's. Our motives are not the same. Lynn wants to save her stepson. I'm part of an investigation involving Max Turner and Nelson Chang selling classified information to the Chinese Government. On a personal level, I believe Turner was responsible for the death of a good friend." Jesse turned to face Lynn. She looked tearful. "I wouldn't be averse to killing Max," Jesse said.

"Shame on you Jesse," Rigby said. "All this talk about killing Max is meant to butter me up. Listen to me for a second. I know the Congo. I fought there as a mercenary. The Congolese are proper Africans, not like the Africans you see around here. The ones around here talk on cell phones. We're talking about cannibals who file their teeth and run around naked looking for someone to eat. The Congo's dangerous."

"Arthur isn't in the Congo," declared Lynn. "He's in the Sudan, the Darfur region to be exact. Sorry, Helen, I should have told you."

Croxford sprinkled a pinch of tobacco on a piece of paper, licked the edge and rolled it. After he lit the cigarette, he picked a piece of errant tobacco from between his teeth and smiled. "Well now, that's lovely news. The Sudan's even more dangerous than the Congo. I hunted elephant in the Sudan thirty years ago. We used camels as pack animals until we heard that if the Arabs captured us, they'd eat us and rape the camels. Or maybe it was the other way around. This ought to be interesting."

"Does that mean you've decided to lead the rescue?" Helen asked.

"Lynn, arrange a meeting with Turner. Jesse, does he know you're in Zimbabwe?"

"I don't think so, but I wouldn't bet my life on it."

"Bad choice of words. I need a promise that you won't interfere?"

"I'm hoping Arthur Turner will be a friendly witness against Nelson Chang. I promise I won't get in the way."

Rigby held up his hand to stop them from speaking and turned his back. He stared out at his land. There was a snake eagle soaring high above the green hills. It's so peaceful here, so tranquil, he thought. They have no way of knowing how bad this could get. He shook his head and turned back to face them. "If we're gonna do this thing, I've got lots to do. I said 'we,' because I need all of you to go as far as the Central African Republic. Helen, I'll need your medical expertise. I'll play the safari guide, and you two will be my clients," he said, nodding at Lynn and Jesse. "Once we get to the Sudanese border, I'm on my own. This rescue will be damn expensive. Just the bribes will be a fortune."

"Max says he's willing to pay you a half a million dollars," Lynn said.

"You tell Max I'll do it for expenses. This isn't about money, it's personal."

"We'll take the money," Helen demanded.

"In that case, let's get the money in advance," Rigby insisted.

Her husband's words made Helen uneasy. She had hoped time would heal his war wounds, but she realized a long time ago there was no magic cure. Does he want the money upfront, because he plans to settle an old score? She had no way of knowing.

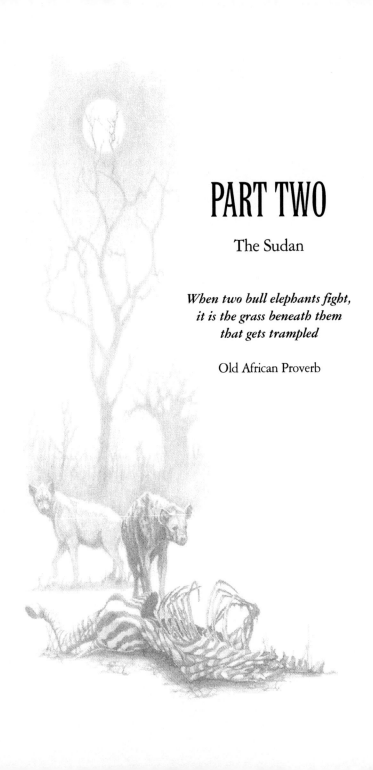

# PART TWO

## The Sudan

*When two bull elephants fight,
it is the grass beneath them
that gets trampled*

Old African Proverb

# 11

# THE DARFUR REGION, SUDAN

Arthur Turner squinted as he proofread his letter. He moved upwind from the smoke. His assistant, Abel Deng, a Dinka boy, handed him a cup of bush tea. Turner sniffed the contents and scowled. The boy's expression changed to a gap-toothed grin.

"This tastes like cow piss. I'm afraid to ask what you boiled to make it."

"*Khawadja*, the tea is brewed from swamp reeds. There were days in the Sahel when I prayed to God for 'cow piss' to quench my thirst. I ate mud for the wetness. Some days, my uncle gave me his urine to drink. I was so thirsty I cried, but my tears wouldn't flow. My people have always bathed in cattle urine, but the Arabs have stolen our cows. I think that's why many of us are sick."

"The Dinka are sick for many reasons. When you finish medical school, you will understand these things. Tell the women if they leave the camp to search for firewood they might be kidnapped." He waited until Abel's back was turned before pouring the tea on the ground. He picked up the letter and resumed his proofreading.

> My dearest Lynn,
> It has been two months since our last attack. The Sudanese rebels continue to steal most of the food and medicine sent to the Darfur. Since my last letter, the English doctor has left the refugee camp.
> If you could send me a copy of Jamison's Diseases and Mortality of Sub-Saharan Africa, it would be greatly appreciated. Mail it to the same address in Kampala.

For the first time in my life I feel like I'm making a difference. I work with an Italian nurse and two French nuns. We work twelve-hour days. The work is the most satisfying thing I've ever done.

My personal problems seem trivial compared to what these people are enduring. The president of the Sudan has declared that he wants this country to be an Islamic state. There is a movement to kill all of the Christian males in the Sudan. Pregnant women are killed, fearing they might be carrying a male baby.

Thousands of boys have left their villages to avoid being massacred. The boys, some as young as five, marched single file across the desert into Ethiopia where they hoped to find a home among the Christian majority. They walked at night to avoid detection by the Arabs. Many of them died during the march. The Dinka girls have fared no better. They have been raped and killed. Malnourishment and exposure killed thousands. The Janjaweed continued to attack the children until they crossed into Ethiopia.

The Ethiopians are plagued with another famine; as such, they couldn't afford to share their food. Faced with starvation, some of the boys went in search of food. They stole some pumpkins from the local farmers. That's when their world got turned upside down. The next few words are exactly as they were told to me by a Dinka survivor. Lynn, the story is so brutal it defies the imagination:

"We had nothing to eat for five days. Some of the boys left the camp to search for food. They brought back pumpkins and tortoises. The People's Protection Brigade came to the camp with soldiers. They demanded we turn over the boys who raided their crops, but we refused. I remember my uncle reciting an old African proverb: 'When two bull elephants fight, it is the grass beneath them that gets trampled.' The next day more soldiers came to the camp. They told us that we must leave and go back to the Sudan. My uncle asked if they would reconsider. A soldier shot him in the face.

The camp is on the Gilo River. The river had risen above

its banks. Few of us could swim. Gunfire forced us into the water. When they ran out of bullets, they used their rifle butts to smash the heads of the smaller boys. A helicopter fired bombs into us as we gathered on the bank. The river turned red from the blood. The first boys were crushed by those who followed. Crocodiles fought over the bodies. I tried to hold on to my brother, but a crocodile pulled him under. Somehow, I reached the other bank. When I looked back, I thought the end of the world had come."

Lynn, we heard rumors that as many as eight thousand boys may have died in the Gilo River. I apologize for this disorganized letter. I'm writing between treating cases of cholera. I missed my calling. I am a far better healer than a lawyer. Please see that Ashlyn gets the enclosed sealed letter.

All my love,
Arthur

Arthur stared at the glowing embers. There was wheezy coughing coming from some of the mud huts. The stench was a mixture of human waste and the sour smell of sweat. Some of the refugees were too weak to make it to the latrines. He strained to hear a mother humming to her baby. The Dinka embraced their shortened lives with such enthusiasm. This is such a living hell, I wonder why I love it, he thought.

He opened a book entitled Introduction to Parasitological Studies in Cameroon, but before he could find his place, Abel Deng reappeared in the dull glow. Two white-haired black men stood behind the boy. Their cadaverous features were obscured in the flickering light. Both men were naked from the waist up and skeletally thin. When they stepped forward, he could see the intricate scarring on their foreheads, indicating they were tribal elders.

"Khawadja," said Abel, "these men have traveled from the Kangen Marshes in the Sudd. They say there are young Dinka girls hiding there. There is little food and many of them are sick." The two men escaped the shadows and stepped into the light. One of them wobbled and grabbed Abel's shoulder for support.

"Have you been injured?" Arthur asked the man. The old man looked down. Encouraged by Abel, he stepped forward. His skin sagged from malnutrition. He unhooked his pants and let them fall to his ankles. His uncircumcised penis drooped above a festering wound where his testicles should have hung. Streaks of septic pus glistened in the light.

"How many days have passed since the Janjaweed did this to you?" Arthur asked.

"Ten days," the old man answered. He showed no indication of pain, only embarrassment.

"And you walked here from the Sudd. Surely, God will smile favorably on you in the next life. I am honored to meet you." He felt the man's forehead. "His temperature is elevated. Abel, bring my medical kit. We need to get an antibiotic in him." Arthur looked away and muttered, "Will the insanity ever end."

"A thousand blessings upon you," said the injured man. "I will never see heaven. A man cannot reach the next life without a son to guide him. All of my sons have been butchered by the Arabs." Sadness filled the moment.

"Don't the Dinka believe an adopted son can show you the way to the next life?" asked Arthur, trying to lift the man's spirits.

"Ouch, I have been bitten by a scorpion," the old man barked as Abel stuck the syringe into his wrinkled buttocks.

"Sorry, the needle is sterile, but dulled by a hundred injections," said Abel. "The *Khawadja* has taught us not to be wasteful."

"My friends, I must say goodnight. I leave for the Sudd in the morning," Arthur said. The Dinka men bowed and left him.

The next morning, the injured man was waiting next to the Land Rover for Arthur. Abel Deng complained about not being allowed to go, but his words fell on deaf ears. If they were stopped by the Sudanese Liberation Army, Abel would be conscripted. If they were raided by the Janjaweed, the odds of him surviving weren't good. Arthur spoke to Abel as he was leaving. "Abel, I'm leaving you in charge."

"Are you sure I'm ready?" Abel asked.

"Someday you'll be in charge of a camp. Don't worry, you'll do just fine. Goodbye," he said, shaking the boy's hand. Abel watched Arthur's truck disappear behind the sand dunes.

The Darfur was held hostage by the dry season. Only the Bahr-el-Jebel or White Nile fed water into the lower regions. The earth was cracked and buckled from a lack of rain, which made the driving difficult. Arthur worried about being seen from the air. He slowed down to reduce the road dust.

On the first day, Arthur's convoy came upon three scorched villages. Only the walls of the huts were left standing. Everything had been burned.

The skeletal remains of the cattle defined the Arab's plan. In Dinka society, cows are the essence of life. Without cattle, there is nothing. What animals the Arabs didn't steal they slaughtered, hoping to force the Dinka from their land. Driving across the parched earth, Arthur realized how successful the ethnic cleansing had been. Only the vultures are thriving here, he thought, squinting up at the specks circling above him.

The last village they came to was still smoldering. A scrawny yellow dog straddled the remains of a calf. When the men got out of the truck, the dog lowered its head and snarled. An old woman crawled out from under a demolished hut. She was naked and tried to cover her private parts with her hands. Her breasts hung like black leathery pouches. A few tuffs of white hair covered her skull. She wore a necklace of white crocodile teeth. When they offered the old woman water, she gulped it down and dropped to her knees. When she recognized Arthur Turner, she squealed and shuffled up to him. She sighed and placed her head against his chest.

"*Khawadja*, I am sickened to have you see me. The Janjaweed have killed and stolen everything in the village, even my clothes. It's not safe for you here. You must leave this place before they return."

"How far is it to the Kangen Marshes?"

"Not so far. Why do you go to the swamps? You will find nothing but blood-sucking mosquitoes. Even the hippos have been killed by the Arabs."

"We've come to rescue the Dinka women," Arthur answered.

"I was fishing in the swamps yesterday. There are no Dinka women in the marshes. I think maybe you play a joke on me," she said, giggling.

"Tell her about the women," he demanded, turning to the old man he treated the night before. The man looked panicky.

"Please tell me we didn't drive all this way on some wild goose chase. Well, just don't stand there. What have you got to say for yourself?"

"It was only a small lie," the old man said, looking away.

"Why would you lie?"

"Our spies warned us about an attack on the camp. The Arab devils were coming to kill you. You have many friends in the Sudan. The
deception was Abel Deng's idea. He was afraid you wouldn't leave. I was
following orders."

"You old fool, what have you done?" Arthur yelled, running to the
Land Rovers.

The minutes ticked by like hours as Arthur raced across the desert.
He was so preoccupied by worry; he hit a petrified tree stump. The truck
became airborne. After skidding to a stop, he jumped out and crawled
under the vehicle to inspect the damage. A broken shock absorber made
the vehicle sag. He ran back, jumped into the other Land Rover and
drove away.

Two hours later, he saw a plume of black smoke mushrooming up
into the cloudless sky. At that moment, he had a premonition that Abel
Deng was dead.

*     *     *

General Mohammad Nur used binoculars to survey the carnage his
men had wreaked on the refugee camp. His view was clouded by the
dust kicked up by the Sudanese Army helicopter touching down three
hundred yards behind him. The gunship's rocket launchers and her 12.7-
millimeter machine guns were empty. Nur had ordered the pilot to fire
everything into the refugee camp. The black billowing smoke looked
like the tentacles of a black octopus. The mounted militiamen paraded
past the general. The plundered loot they carried in their saddlebags was
rubbish, but to the victims, the objects were priceless. A few skinny cows
and some captives were also marched in front of the general. He seemed
more interested in the human contraband. Abel Deng was one of the
boys captured in the raid. The young boys were valuable assets to the
general. He always needed fresh recruits for his children's army.

A large bellied man wearing crossing ammunition bandoliers swung
down out of his saddle. His lathered horse pranced on the rein. He
handed the general something wrapped in a bloodied rag. Nur unraveled
the contents and looked at the Arab. "Do you think I'm stupid? I ordered
you to bring me the *Khawadja's* right hand. This is a woman's left hand.
You cut off her finger to steal her wedding band. The man fell to his
knees and begged for mercy. Without hesitating, General Nur fired a

pistol shot into the man's brain. As he walked away, he rehearsed what he would tell Nelson Chang.

*     *     *

The Janajweed had deserted the camp by the time Arthur got there. The Arabs had killed everything, except the old people who were seen as unworthy of the bullets needed to kill them. The Italian nurse had escaped in the confusion. The two French nuns were not as fortunate. Their handless bodies lay naked in the sun. Arthur buried his face in his hands. The fact that Abel's body wasn't found meant he was probably kidnapped. It was a small consolation.

An animal's bellowing made him look up. The camel staggered to keep weight off of its broken foreleg. Bone protruded through the skin. Arthur retrieved a pickax from the back of his Land Rover. He walked up and buried the ax between the camel's eyes.

The next morning, Arthur lowered himself into the camp's well. The Arabs had dumped bodies down the well hoping to foul the water. The villagers helped him haul up two corpses, which they buried with the others.

That afternoon, he collapsed under a desert acacia. Through the leafless branches, he stared at a long line of white-backed vultures gliding effortlessly towards the camp. The scavengers of the Darfur had learned to equate black smoke with food.

*     *     *

# 12

# ZIMBABWE

Rigby Croxford drove to Victoria Falls alone. It gave him time to formulate a plan for Arthur Turner's rescue. It also gave him time to reflect on Sam Mabota's death. It was Max Turner's blunder that killed Sam, yet Rigby blamed himself.

He decided to use the patio bar behind the hotel for the meeting. The spent .375 brass casing from Turner's rifle lay on the table next to his chair. A smartly dressed waiter walked across the lawn with Max Turner in tow. Rigby had made it clear that the meeting was to be between the two men. Turner's bodyguard and a woman stayed seated at the bar.

"I can't thank you enough for agreeing to meet me," Max said, shaking hands. Immediately, his eyes were drawn to the cartridge on the table.

"I'm afraid it's not quite that simple. We need to clear up a few things," Rigby said, tossing the cartridge at Turner who caught it backhanded.

"God forgive me, I panicked. I lied because I was afraid you wouldn't help me."

"Why didn't you just ask me in the beginning? Why waste time on a hunting safari?"

"If you remember, we got off to a rather shaky start. I never got a chance to ask you. I'd give anything if it never happened. I know that man was a good friend. I'm sorry." Max looked at the ground. "I don't know how much my ex-wife's told you about my son. If you knew Arthur, you'd understand why I'm doing everything I can to find him."

"Got any surprises before we discuss the rescue?"

"I can never pay you enough. Tell me what you want me to do."

"Leading this rescue has nothing to do with you. I'm doing this for Lynn. I wanted you to know, before we get into the particulars."

"I understand. The important thing is for me to get my son back. I just pray Arthur's still alive."

Rigby outlined the plan. He would use the Central African Republic as a base. Posing as big-game hunters, they would establish a base-camp on the Sudanese border. From the camp, Rigby would cross into the Sudan and hopefully rescue Arthur. Of course, there were a thousand obstacles, but there was no reason to discourage Max with the details.

"This rescue attempt won't come cheap. Bribes are a way of life in that part of Africa. I'll need an airplane standing by in Uganda. And I'm gonna need some special weapons."

"I don't care what it costs. I'll have my bank wire the money."

"The aircraft needs to be a bush plane, one that can land in the desert. I need four Remington M-24 sniper rifles, two with night scopes, plus two hundred rounds of ammo. Here's the tough one—I want two Barrett fifty-caliber rifles with fifty rounds of standard ammunition and twenty M-1 incendiary rounds."

"I'll have my contacts get on this. Sounds like you plan on conquering the entire Sudanese Army."

"This is a military operation. If there's one thing I've learned—always expect the unexpected. Oh, there's one more thing, Lynn wanted me to ask you about a friend. I think his name is Jesse."

Max's expression masked his curiosity. He faked a lack of interest and answered the question. "Jesse Spooner worked for my law firm. He just wasn't cutting it, so I had to fire him. That's all I know." He waited for a response. When he didn't get one, he continued. "Back to the rescue, what kind of a timeframe are we talking about?"

"I'm ready to move as soon as you secure the aircraft and the weapons. Dutchy should be here in two days."

"I'll take care of my end. Give me a week. Like I said, I can never thank you enough." Max stood up, shook hands and left. Rigby studied Max's walk. It was a weightlifter's swagger. Well, at least he doesn't know Spooner's involved. Jesse was right; he didn't blink an eye when I asked for the Barrett-50s, which means he's still involved in arms trafficking.

God help me, I do love the hunt, he thought. Using his hand as an imaginary pistol, he aimed his forefinger at a spot in the middle of Turner's shoulder blades. "Bang," he whispered under his breath.

*     *     *

Helen remarked that their farm looked like the staging area for the invasion of Normandy. The weapons were delivered, as promised to the Croxford farm on time. Rigby and Dutchy spread the camping equipment, medical supplies and a hundred other items on the lawn. They concealed the Barrett fifty-calibers in a false bottom under one of the Land Cruisers. The house servants helped them load the vehicles. At the end of the day, the three men gathered on the veranda for sundowners with Lynn and Helen.

"Couldn't we get arrested for smuggling?" Helen asked.

"Jesus, I hope not," Rigby said. "To be on the safe side, I'll drive the lead vehicle with the hidden fifties through the border crossings alone. That way, if I get caught, you can try to bribe the guards. Every border guard in Africa has his hand out. I assure you, it's the least of our worries. And we've got Jesse here as our second line of defense."

"I'm sure I couldn't pull any strings," said Jesse. "Not over here."

"Old Maxy sure delivered those fifty calibers in a hurry. Makes you wonder if we should have ordered something bigger," Rigby directed at Jesse.

"It makes me wonder what the bad guys are using."

"Yikes. I never thought of it along those lines. Wish I hadn't." Rigby rubbed the black stubble on his chin. He drained the last of his whiskey and shuddered when it hit bottom.

"Dutchy, you got any last-minute thoughts? You know, when I look at the superior job I did in sewing your scalp back on, I realize I missed my calling. I would have made a damn fine surgeon."

"*Ja*, my wife says I'm better-looking now." The Dutchman laughed as he examined his head in a window's reflection.

"Cheers! Here's to a successful hunting trip," Rigby said, holding up a beer bottle. His face showed the evidence of a smile, which irritated Helen.

"Why so gloomy?" he asked, looking at his wife.

"Your exuberance always makes me nervous."

Rigby erased his smile. "Okay, let's talk about where we're headed. We'll take the Pan African highway north. I reckon it should take us five days of hard driving to reach Tanzania. It makes sense to camp away from the villages. Africans are curious. No sense in tipping our hand. Anyway, once we get to Mwanza on Lake Victoria, I've got a good mate to look after us."

"Are you talking about Seth Johnston?"

"Yes, love. Seth runs a ferryboat on the lake. The ferry makes a weekly run north from Mwanza to Entebbe. We'll take the ferry north. There's the security issue, and Lake Victoria's over three hundred kilometers long. It'll give us a rest."

"Poor Seth," said Helen. "What happened to his family was so sad. I'm surprised he's still in Africa."

"What's his story?" asked Jesse. It was too late for a retraction. He wished he hadn't blurted out the question.

"During the bush war, Seth's two sisters were raped in front of their father, who was killed with the girls. Poor Mrs. Johnston hanged herself. Seth and I were classmates at Plum Tree. After Mugabe confiscated his farm, Seth moved to Tanzania. Yesterday was the first time I've talked to him in thirty years."

That's the last time I'll ever ask him about one of his friends, Jesse promised himself.

The next morning, they left their farm for the uncertainty of central Africa. Jesse and Rigby led the group in the lead vehicle. Dutchy and the two women followed in the backup truck. Rigby was right: Greasing a few palms made the border crossings a cinch. After five days, they entered the port town of Mwanza on the southern shore of Lake Victoria in Tanzania.

*     *     *

The Kisumu ferry was in need of spit and polish. Her sides were zebra striped in human feces. The heads were holes cut out over her gunnels. The tropical humidity had blistered her paint with rusty boils. With her stern ramp extended, she looked like a beached crocodile with its jaws opened.

Rigby and company drove their trucks up onto the ferry. The vehicles were blocked by two freight trucks, one transporting giant mahogany logs, the other loaded with green bananas.

Seth Johnson met them at the top of the gangway. Most of Seth's face was hidden behind a red beard. The equatorial sun had etched deep tread marks into his forehead. Seth's skin looked yellowish, like he had been visited frequently by tropical malaria. Few men who had looked into his eyes would ever forget the deadness. Johnson barked in Swahili, ordering a man to carry the luggage to their respective cabins. He was perplexed by Jesse and Lynn traveling together, but he handled it.

"I hope you weren't expecting the QE2. The cabins are a bit frightful. Why don't you tell my boys about your sleeping arrangements? Helen, I'd like to borrow your husband if I might. I promise I'll have him back in a jiffy."

Seth grabbed Rigby by the arm and pointed to the wheelhouse door. "Helen, could you have a look at my first mate? We haven't seen a doctor around here in six months," he yelled over his shoulder.

Dutchy stayed with the trucks to keep any natives with sticky fingers from pinching their equipment. Lynn assisted Helen with her medical examination of Johnston's first mate. Jesse followed Seth and Rigby forward to the wheelhouse.

"It's been a long time, mate," Seth said to Rigby.

"I reckon it's been thirty years. What did you find out?"

"When you get to Kampala, you'll need to contact the British Embassy. Two limeys, Graham Connelly and Ian Laycock are your best bet. They're the best-connected Europeans in Uganda. They're expecting your call. You know, when this thing happened, it scared the crap out of every white man in central Africa. The reward for the missing American was so big—I thought every bloody *munt* on the continent was plotting to kill me for the reward money. Sorry, I meant to say 'native,'" he said, looking at Jesse.

"Don't sweat it. Remember I've spent the last three weeks riding around Africa with David Duke here," Spooner said, putting his hand on Croxford's shoulder.

"Quite right. Cheers," Johnson said, bumping fists with Jesse. Seth looked puzzled trying to place David Duke, the white supremacist. "Anyway, the Sudan's a fucking nightmare. You're gonna have your hands full. Arabs killing natives. Natives killing natives. Just the usual fun and games. Damn thrilling show. Almost wish I was going along."

"I was hoping you might say something like that," said Jesse. "Why don't you take my place?"

"I said almost. Say Jesse, what kind of work do you do back in the States?"

"Not much, just the usual fun and games." His smile indicated he was unwilling to elaborate.

"Excuse me for a second," said Seth. "We need to be getting underway." He gave the signal to close the ramp, which crammed the rest of the Africans onto the already overcrowded ferry.

"Mr. Spooner, could you give us a few minutes alone? We've got a little catching up to do."

"That won't be a problem, Captain. I'll check on the ladies." Johnston waited for Jesse to close the wheelhouse door before speaking. "Who'd of thought it would come to this?"

"Sorry. I'm not following you," said Rigby.

"My God, a white woman of quality traveling with a black man—I swear, I don't understand it," acknowledged Seth.

"Spooner's a good man. Did you hear about Sam Mabota? He died down in Mozambique? Jesse reminds me of Sam."

"I heard a lion killed him."

"You heard right." Rigby caught a fly in the air and listened to it buzzing in his hand. "I had a dream about your father." When Rigby saw a flash of sadness spread across Johnston's face, he apologized. "Sorry Seth."

"How are things going in Zim?" Seth asked, averting the topic.

"Fucking awful. Mugabe's a catastrophe. If I knew I was dying, I'd shoot that hyena."

*     *     *

Seth Johnston blew the all-aboard whistle three times, each stream-driven hoot was longer and more mournful than the one before it. A swirling cloud of black diesel smoke enveloped the ferry as she idled out into Lake Victoria. The Kisumu ferry was licensed to carry a hundred passengers. Three hundred Africans swarmed over every available inch of deck space. Most of them were raggedly dressed, but a few wore their Sunday best. Some women carried live chickens. One man balanced a hindquarter of bloodied beef on a rickety bicycle. The lower deck had turned into a seething, living organism.

Seth throttled up to cruising speed. The ferry's Lister diesel engine beat the water into a white foamy wake. A sultry breeze washed over the deck. At times, the air was perfumed by unseen tropical flowers, but intermittently it was overwhelmed by the smell of rotting fish. Villages dotted the otherwise monotonous shoreline. Flocks of scarlet-winged flamingos and white pelicans played a visual hide-and-seek game in the man-made smoky haze.

Their first stop was Rubondo Island. The minute the ferry dropped anchor, dozens of dugout canoes with furled lateen sails rafted up. One Luo fisherman tried to peddle a Nile perch; the fish was longer than a man. A spindly native tried to sell them a dead monkey. When he became too persistent, Johnston yelled at him. Reassured by the distance between them, the old man swung the monkey over his head and cursed him.

Lynn Allison turned to Seth Johnston. "Is this what they mean when they talk about bush meat?"

"Bush meat includes everything from porcupines to chimpanzees—anything that runs or crawls. In the Congo basin it might include an occasional Pigmy, albeit a slow one." Seth's laughter was met with unbelieving stares. His answer was an obvious shot fired across Jesse's bow.

"Tell me he's kidding." Jesse's expression revealed discomfort at being ancestrally linked to cannibals.

"Let's have another drink before dinner," Johnston suggested.

"I think I'll pass on dinner," said Jesse.

"Me too," the two women added in unison.

"Seriously Rigby," said Jesse, "do you think it's safe to eat? Whatever they're cooking smells terrible."

"Why would you ask such a question? Of course it's not safe to eat. No telling what, or rather who, these buggers are cooking. Dutchy, would you eat this shit?"

"I'd rather make love to one of those hippos." Dutchy pointed at some hippos waddling down the bank.

"Spooner, I told you everything on this bloody continent was trying to kill you. I can't have one of you down with dysentery. If it all goes well, you can enjoy the cuisine on our return trip. There's no quarantine on Captain Johnston's booze. Cheers."

*     *     *

Two days later, they drove up the ramp and onto the Entebbe wharf.

It was a short ride from Entebbe to Kampala. The road follows the papyrus-lined lakeshore. Bahima boys herded Ankola cows onto the road's shoulder, giving them room to pass.

Under colonial rule, Kampala was a clean and tidy city, but now it gave off the citified stink of automobile flatulence and human waste. Snowy-white cattle egrets in the city's botanical gardens were replaced by dirty-faced Marabou storks feeding on the uncollected garbage. Without stop signs and streetlights, the downtown traffic was woven as tightly as Irish linen. The noise was intolerable: A deafening blend of horn blowers and whining motorbikes.

By prior arrangement, Connelly and Laycock met Rigby at the Blue Mango restaurant in the center of the city. The parking lot was fenced in by a concrete wall topped in razor wire. The lone Land Cruiser sitting under a mango tree was too new not to be owned by a foreign government official. The two Brits were waiting at the outside bar. After introductions, Jesse and Rigby followed them to a table next to the swimming pool.

"I was wondering, didn't I see mosques on the drive in?" Jesse asked.

"Fifty percent of the population in Uganda is Muslim. It's about the same for the rest of central Africa. The number of converts is growing by leaps and bounds. In the old days, the Arabs were strict followers of the Quran. That is to say, no Muslim shall hold another Muslim in slavery. Africans became Muslims as a protection against ending up on a slave ship headed to the New World."

Laycock's answer was a little too matter-of-factly to suit Jesse. "I'm glad that part of history's behind us," said Jesse.

"Slavery's a big business in this part of Africa. Women from Somalia and Chad are purchased for Arab concubines everyday." An unnecessary smile sneaked into Laycock's expression. "Don't blame the Arabs. This is Africans selling Africans," Laycock added.

"Gentlemen," said Rigby, "I'm afraid we'll need to resume the African history lesson another time. Now, what can you tell me about my chances of getting in and out of the Sudan?"

"I'd say your odds are pretty good. You did survive Johnston's ferry. Did he tell you about the accident?"

"What accident?"

"Captain Johnston's last ferry was the *Bokoba*. Ring a bell?"

He thought for a moment and then replied. "The *Bokoba* sank six years ago. Eight hundred passengers drowned."

"That's the one. If Johnston hadn't lost his wife, he'd be up on charges. Poor bugger."

Rigby listened to the Englishman without really hearing him. In his mind, he was checking and rechecking the logistics of the rescue. The satellite telephone was essential, as was the global positioning device he would carry. When and if he found Arthur Turner, he would call in the aircraft and have Turner flown out of the country. If things got too dicey, he could get on the same plane himself. The airplane was his ace in the hole. The weak link was his age: At fifty, Rigby knew he was a step slower. One mistake, one failure to see something coming, could put the rescue at risk. The meeting ended with the usual best wishes, but Rigby sensed Connelly and Laycock were happy he was leaving Uganda.

*       *       *

The next day, they drove down a winding dirt road to the Masindi airfield. A Cessna 185 stood ready at the end of the grass runway. The pilot and two Africans waited in the shade under a wing.

"I don't know if you remember me," the pilot said, offering his hand. "I'm Otto Bern. I flew you into Mozambique during the Rhodesian War."

"Good God, Otto. It's been a long time. That operation into Moz was a pisser. Somebody on the inside gave us up. The ambush was a nightmare."

"I remember you lost a good mate. I believe his name was Willie something?"

"Willie van Piet."

"The other Selous Scout was black. Whatever became of him?"

"He was killed by a lion in Mozambique."

"Poor bugger. I guess we'll all be dead soon enough."

"I'd like my death to be from natural causes." Changing the subject, Rigby turned his attention to the task at hand. "I'll need you standing by ready to take off at a moment's notice. Getting in there as fast as possible for the extraction is important. I hope we're both on the same page."

"We're most definitely on the same page. Mr. Turner's paying me to stand by for as long as this takes." Otto stroked his airplane's propeller like it was a woman. "Look, Croxford, this plane's everything I own. I can't afford to have it blown out from under me. I'd like to keep the shooting to a minimum."

"No shooting? My God, we're fussy! Why, Otto, I think you've become a nervous Nelly in your old age."

"You're damn right, I'm nervous. Not too many of us old bush pilots left in this part of Africa."

Otto motioned for them to climb onboard and spoke to the group. "Folks, I believe my boys have got your kit loaded. If you'll kindly climb onboard, I'll have you at your hunting camp in two hours."

"Otto, are you serving tea or coffee?" asked Rigby, grinning.

"I've got water, just in case we... No need to go there." Bern had difficulty bending his prosthetic leg as he climbed into the pilot's seat. "Wish another part of my anatomy was as stiff as my buggered leg," he whispered to Rigby.

"Say, how *did* you lose the wheel?" Rigby asked.

"Stepped on a landmine at the end of the war. Bloody wogs. Better fasten your seatbelts."

# 13
# THE SUDAN

The children of the Sudan found themselves between a hammer and an anvil. The hammer was the Janjaweed who wanted to exterminate them. The anvil was the Sudanese People's Liberation Army who wanted to use them as cannon fodder.

It was a miracle that Abel Deng wasn't killed by the Arabs during the attack on the refugee camp. Shortly after his capture he managed to slip away. After wandering in the desert, he sought the help of a band of Murle tribesmen. The Murle traded him to the SPLA for four sacks of corn meal.

\*     \*     \*

Abel tried to roll over, but the shackles on his ankles prevented him from moving. He used his body as a windbreak to block the cold wind from the young Nuer girl lying next to him. The girl had been taken by a soldier into the bushes that night. When the man returned the girl, she was crying. He came for her every night. There was nothing Abel could do to stop him. When her sobbing subsided, he rolled over and pulled the girl next to him. She placed her hand on top of his.

Even though Deng was only fourteen, his medical training made him invaluable. He had dreamed about killing the man who raped the young girl sleeping next to him. He prayed the man would come to him for medical attention.

Abel woke up to the sound of a bellowing camel. A soldier rousted the children with kicks. The young girls, having fulfilled their nightly duties, were in charge of the cooking. The boys gathered up camel dung to fuel the campfires. Deng was charged with redressing the bandages of a wounded soldier. As he was cleaning the soldier's wound, he felt someone tap him on the shoulder. It was their self-appointed leader, Captain Bol.

"Medic, come with me. My brother's ill. His groaning is robbing me of my sleep."

They walked up behind a man straining to urinate. When the man turned around Abel was stunned. He was the rapist. "This medic will help you," Bol said to his brother. Abel instructed the man to peel back his foreskin and milk it. A yellow bead of pus appeared.

"The sickness can be easily cured. You need one injection now and one more tonight. By tomorrow, the symptoms will have vanished." Deng proceeded to pump a syringe of worthless saline solution into the man's buttocks.

"The Nuer whore who gave me this will die a slow death." He gasped from the needle prick.

"I doubt you contracted the sickness from a Nuer girl. Maybe you caught the disease in one of the brothels in Khartoum." The man hit Abel with the back of his hand; it knocked him to the ground. He got to his feet, but fell from the dizziness. "Do you want me to come back?" Abel asked, feeling the side of his face.

"If you don't come back, I'll kill you."

Abel turned away. "As you wish," Abel said.

That evening Abel watched the Nuer girl carry some pots down to the waterhole. He kept the tethered camels between him and the soldier on guard duty. He knelt next to the girl washing the pots and scooped up a handful of water. "Listen carefully and don't look up," he whispered, hiding his mouth with his hat. "Tonight we run. The soldier has given you a sickness. I'm going to give you the cure by injection. You cannot cry out. Do you understand me?"

"When the soldier comes for me and learns we've run away, he'll hunt us down. You go. Let me keep him occupied."

"We go together. I'm treating the soldier for the disease he's given you. I will inject him with a poison. He'll never use you again."

"My life's over. The soldier has soiled me. Give me the same poison."

"Such childish talk. Who will cook for me and wash my clothes?"

"We have no food, and you're wearing rags."

"Woman, if you don't stop talking I promise you'll have your wish. Ready yourself, the needle will sting."

*     *     *

Abel found the soldier lying on the ground with his head resting on his saddle. He had a dirty rag draped over his face.

"You," he hissed, looking up. "Your cure is worthless. I've never felt such pain. I'm thirsty, but I'm afraid to drink. Passing water will kill me."

"I've only given you half of the cure. This will bring you relief," he said, holding up the syringe to clear it of bubbles.

"If I'm not cured by tomorrow, I'll slit you open like a ripe pumpkin."

"You must lie still. Let the drug work through your veins. I'll come back in one hour."

One hour later, Abel checked on the soldier. When he removed the rag from the man's face, he was surprised to find him still breathing. The man couldn't move. He stared at Abel. His mouth was locked open. A steady stream of saliva ran down his chin.

"The Nuer girl you violated wanted me to give you this," he whispered, sticking a camel turd in the man's mouth. Abel covered the soldier's face with his hat, stood up and walked away.

*     *     *

Under the cover of darkness, they slipped into the shadows and disappeared into the night. Their pace was deliberate and steady throughout the night. Abel was surprised by the girl's stamina. She would not accept water, and when he asked her if she needed to rest, she refused. They arrived at the edge of the Kangen Marshes just as the first light of dawn peeked over the Sudd.

Abel's heart slammed against his ribs. A thin wisp of dust rose skyward on the horizon. By now, Captain Bol would have discovered his brother's body. Abel imagined the soldiers trotting beside the captain's camel following their spoor. There was only one way to lose their pursuers. They would have to use the swamp to hide their tracks.

"Woman, if we are to die together, I'd like to know your name."

"My name's Tabitha. Abel, can you swim?"

"Of course I can't swim. The Dinka are cattle herders, not lowly fishermen like your Nuer tribe."

"I'm told the Dinka burn cattle dung and mix it with urine to make tooth powder," she said, holding her nose.

"What you say is true. We use the same mixture to drive insects away. Tonight you'll wish we had some of that powder. That's if we're alive tonight."

"The Dinka have strange customs," she said, wading into the water. "Hold on to me and don't thrash about. If we don't move, the crocodiles will leave us alone."

Abel studied Tabitha from behind. She was in the full bloom of puberty. Her breasts were hard and proud and showed no evidence of sagging. Her silky brown skin beaded water like beeswax. Her ribs showed, but her buttocks were round and plump. Decorative patterns of ritual scarring adorned her back.

Instead of drifting with the current Tabitha forged against it. The channel they crossed was shallow, giving her good footing on the sandy bottom. Abel held onto her shoulders, letting his body float as the current pushed his legs out from underneath him. Without warning, he felt her body sink as the water deepened. He let his hands slide down her back until they hooked in the leather band of her apron. His concern turned into panic, but he fought off the impulse to grab her. A minute later, she regained her footing. She parted the papyrus reeds and pushed him into some bulrushes.

"The soldiers will be here in a few minutes. You need to practice what I'm about to show you." She laid her head back until just her nostrils were exposed above the water. When Abel laid his head back, his nose filled with water. He came up sputtering.

"Try again." This time, she supported the back of his neck. The third time, he was able to stay under until she pulled him to the surface.

"Stay here. I will confuse them with a false spoor." She ran back and placed her footprints on the bank. She returned as the soldiers appeared on the crest of the bank. She locked her legs around the reeds, gathered a clump of water hyacinthine and gently pulled him under.

Abel felt her glossy skin brush against him. Her powerful yet gentle arms held him like his mother used to cradle him. At that moment, he knew Tabitha was destined to be a part of his life forever. He felt a strange calmness.

Captain Bol was so piqued by the time he reached the marsh he was unable to control his rage. When his trackers seemed confused by the spoor, he fired a warning shot at one of his men. They stopped to water the camels, but abruptly raced away. One of the trackers had found Tabitha's footprint and was fooled into thinking they were headed downstream.

She raised her head until her eyes were above the water. When she was sure it was safe, she helped Abel to the surface. He pulled her shivering body against his. For a split second, they were spellbound in each other's gaze. They both sensed a flicker of affection between them, but seemed confused by the intimacy.

"Those Nuba devils won't be fooled forever. We need to put some ground between us and them," she said, helping him up.

"Yes, but when we get out of this smelly swamp, I'll be giving the orders."

Tabitha acted like she didn't hear him. She averted her eyes and smiled.

They walked all day, stopping to eat the grasshoppers and waterbugs she caught clinging to the papyrus reeds. Abel discovered a malachite kingfisher's nest. The male's wing feathers were metallic-blue colored, and his chest plumage was brilliant red. The less attractive female hovered motionlessly over a school of minnows. As Abel and Tabitha approached, both birds darted back to defend their nest but it was too late. They gobbled up the tiny eggs like ravenous mongooses.

Before dark, Abel gathered elephant droppings for a fire. Tabitha roasted a small leatherback tortoise she captured earlier that day on a sandbank. The elephant dung helped repel the insects that had tormented them earlier. After their skimpy dinner, they listened to the swamp serenade. Smaller frogs produced a continuous high-pitched whine and larger bullfrogs erupted with thunderous croaks. He teased her by saying the turtle was tough and rank as cowhide. She retaliated by telling him maybe he would have liked it better if it had been soaked in cow urine. After all, the Dinka use cattle urine for everything.

"Tell me more about the *Khawadja*. I think you love this white man more than you loved your own father. What's his Christian name?"

"His name's Arthur, Arthur Turner." She's right, I do love him, he thought. Before he could explain, he fell asleep and started to snore. She sighed and snuggled next to him.

*     *     *

Abel was awakened by something strange. An old woman had stumbled onto their hiding place. She tickled his nose with the hairy plume of a papyrus reed. When he opened his eyes and saw the woman, he jumped to his feet screaming, which startled Tabitha. The woman cackled hysterically and slapped her leg. Her bald head was crisscrossed with a network of bulging veins. She was naked except for a loose-fitting loincloth.

She tugged at a crocodile tooth on her necklace before speaking. "My children, you're lucky I'm not the Janjaweed. It would be their swords you would feel and not my reed. Restart your fire so I can roast these plump catfish. You both look like you have not eaten in weeks," she said, tossing the stringer of fish on the ground.

The old woman watched them suck the fish bones clean. She giggled and cocked her head. "I've seen you before," she said to Abel. "You work with the *Khawadja*. You were with him when he treated me at my village. The minute I saw you, I knew."

"What's happened to your family? Where are your children?" Tabitha asked.

"All killed by the Janjaweed. They stole my goats. I have nothing left, not even my clothes. Tell me, what's become of your families?"

"Our families were also murdered. When was the last time you saw the *Khawadja*?"

The old woman told them about meeting Arthur Turner at the burned out village. She also told them about the militia attack on Turner's refugee camp. When she spoke about the French nuns getting killed, Abel got up and walked away. When he returned, his face was puffy and his eyes were swollen. They both knew he had been crying.

The old woman stayed with them for four days. She showed them her boat made from a hippo's hide stretched over tree branches. She taught them how to catch catfish in woven papyrus reed traps and how to steal eggs from the crocodile nests.

*     *     *

Abel and Tabitha were sleeping soundly the night she shook them. She placed her finger to her lips and motioned for them to follow her into the blackness.

"My children, you must leave this island. The soldiers who hunt for you have camped on the far shore. The Arabs are camped on the other shore. We are in the middle of the killing ground. In the morning, the Arabs will attack. Take my boat and leave."

"You're coming with us," Abel whispered.

"We're not leaving without you," added Tabitha.

The woman placed her spider-thin fingers on Tabitha's lips to prevent her from speaking. "A thoughtful gesture, but a foolish one. My little boat won't float with three of us. Go now, before the moon escapes the clouds. And don't worry about me. Besides, why would they kill a harmless old woman?"

Abel glanced at the shore and shuttered. "If the Arabs attack, the Dinka and Nuer children will be caught in the middle. If only there was a way to warn them."

"Let me worry about warning them. Go, and when you see the *Khawadja,* tell him how I helped you."

The rounded hippo boat spun out of control in the current until Abel used his push pole to steady it. The old woman waded out and hugged them. The moonshine illuminated her for a second. She disappeared behind a black curtain. The frogs stopped croaking. Only whining mosquitoes broke the silence. The boat drifted in the sluggish current, coming within a few meters of the Arabs' camp. Sparks and voices rose from their campfires. A stallion's whinny from the Arabs' camp was answered by a mare's whicker from the Africans' camp on the other side of the river. As the river widened, the current slowed down. Fearing they would be seen, Abel poled their boat into the heavy papyrus reeds before sunrise.

*     *     *

General Mohammed Nur adjusted his binoculars until the image of an old woman came into focus. She was walking towards the camp on the shoreline.

"Sergeant, let's see if you're any good with that rifle. Take the woman."

The sound of the shot caused him to lose the image. The general's smile revealed his iron-colored teeth. "She's down. Good shooting," he said, tapping the sergeant on his shoulder.

*     *     *

The dawn was greeted by the pop and crack of gunshots. It was over in less than five minutes. The mounted Arabs raced their camels up and down the riverbank killing those who escaped the initial assault. Some smacking sounds echoed over the water; it was the noise of bullets hitting human flesh. A soldier carried the general on his back to the other shore. His men laid out the old rifles and ragged clothes they stripped off the dead and dying Africans. One of the men dragged four naked girls out of the marsh. Their hands were tied behind them. They were joined by leather neck leashes. General Nur stopped in front of one girl and pinched her tiny breast. "This one's mine. You men do what you want with the rest of them."

*     *     *

Abel and Tabitha worked their way back upstream to the scene of the attack. The smell warned them. What they found was horrifying. The crocodiles were in a feeding frenzy. A bull crocodile held a woman's torso in its massive jaws as a smaller croc spun and twisted off her head. With its scaly head thrown back, the croc gulped the head down its bulging gullet. The feeding of the crocodiles caused human arms and legs to flop in a windmill fashion, giving the appearance of animation to the dead. Hunch-backed vultures waited impatiently along the shoreline. Hyenas and jackals feasted on the bodies away from the water's edge. They buried the old woman's half-eaten body, but there were so many dead; it was impractical to bury all of them.

"I should have warned them," said Abel.

"Don't blame yourself. You're not God."

"Why would God let this happen? I curse your God and everything he stands for."

"Oh Abel, what are we to do?"

"The old woman said Arthur Turner's alive. Finding him is our only hope. It means crossing the desert. The Arabs will have no trouble seeing us, but we have no choice."

Abel saw movement out of the corner of his eye. He pushed Tabitha behind him. A man crawled out of the bulrushes. He was too weak to stand up. "Help me. In the name of Allah, I beg you," the man whimpered.

When Ali Osman was wounded in the attack he was abandoned by his fellow Arabs. Abel picked up a tree limb and walked over to the injured Arab. He raised the log to hit the man, but something stopped him. The Arab looked up at him, mumbled a passage from the Quran, and passed out.

"Bring me my knapsack." Abel examined the man's head wound and found it to be superficial. A gunshot must have knocked him unconscious, thought Abel. After he built a lean-to over the Arab, he cleaned and dressed his head wound. That night Tabitha made a thin stew from boiled crocodile eggs and a tilapia fish she caught the day before. Abel fed the man all of the stew. Osman grabbed Abel's arm and pulled him closer. "Dinka, tell me why you saved my life."

"I don't know why. I want to become a medical doctor when I'm grown."

"Grown? This life is so cruel—there is no time to be a child. I pray Allah helps you attain you dream." The Arab looked away, which ended their conversation.

Abel, Tabitha and the Arab fell asleep by the fire. Sometime during the night the Arab vanished. Later that morning, as they searched the reed beds for fresh crocodile nests, Tabitha confronted Abel. "You curse God, yet you are like God. I would have killed the Arab, but you saved his life. He never even bothered to thank you. Abel, you are a good man."

At dusk, they started walking towards the setting sun. The flat arid plain appeared endless. The ground would have been flooded in the rainy season, but now the parched land was crisscrossed by deep cracks. The darkness came as swiftly and stealthily as a lioness on a hunt. Their sightlessness made them stagger and fall repeatedly. The glowing eyes of hyenas followed their progress. At times, the predators became too aggressive and had to be chased away. The marching numbed them, but they pushed on into the night.

*     *     *

In the darkness before dawn, Tabitha and Abel stumbled upon a razed village. Exhausted, they fell asleep between the remains of two huts. They were awakened by a malicious sun and buzzing flies. At first, he thought her screaming was caused by a bad dream, but as he looked around he realized they had slept on a bed of bones. The bones could

have been from animals had it not been for the skulls. The white crani-
ums were topped in twisted patches of ratty hair. One skull was missing
front teeth. The rest of the skulls were twisted into gruesome smiles. The
bleached skeletons had been scattered by scavenging animals. Even the
victim's clothes had been stolen. There was nothing left. Nothing but
their gaping mouths defining the horror of their deaths.

# 14

# THE DARFUR REGION OF THE SUDAN

Arthur Turner stooped to see himself in the side mirror of his Land Rover. He hardly recognized his reflection. Deep parentheses outlined his mouth. The dark shadows under his eyes gave him a ghoulish appearance. The three-pill malaria cure had taken longer than normal. Dizziness made him grab the door handle to keep from falling. A tall native approached him from behind and touched him on the shoulder.

"*Khawadja*, I have been waiting to speak with you. You have been very ill. I bring you good news. Some Nuer refugees from the Sudd say they have seen Abel Deng. They say he treated one of their elders."

"When did you hear this news?"

"Three days ago."

"And you believe the news to be true?"

"Yes. The people of the Nuer tribe can be trusted."

"I knew my prayers would be answered. We'll leave at first light. We've got lots to do. What's your given name?"

"My name is Agrippa."

"Agrippa, you must cover your nakedness. It's offensive to the nurses."

"Dinka men do not cover themselves in summer. It has always been so."

"Yes, but…never mind." He felt too lightheaded to argue.

The old Dinka stood guard outside of the tent. He leaned on his walking stick and placed his foot on the knee of his other leg. His buttock was hollowed and his knees were knobby. There was pride in the way he carried himself. He looks like one of the open-billed storks I've seen in the swamps, Arthur reflected. Arthur wiped the perspiration from his forehead. A wave of disorientation clouded his thinking. He picked up a pen and started to write.

My dearest Lynn,

So much has happened since my last letter. I'm afraid the news here is not good. I thought the Janjaweed might leave us alone, but it was not to be. We lost our two French aid workers in the last attack. You may have already read about it, although I believe the news is being censored by the government in Khartoum.

Abel Deng, the young Dinka boy I wrote to you about, disappeared during the attack. I received news today that he's alive. I leave tomorrow morning to find him. I have taken the necessary steps to get him into the United States. When the time comes, I'll need you to take care of things on your end. Please order me a copy on Evan's book: Traditional Medicine in Ghana. Post it to the same address in Kampala. Sorry about the brevity of this letter, I'm a little under the weather. Make sure Ashlyn receives the enclosed sealed envelope.

All my love,

Arthur

He put his pen on the table and buried his face in his hands. Trying to rub the dryness out of his eyes didn't work. The nagging fever made him woozy. His bouts with malaria were the catalysts for nightmares. He stretched out on his cot and closed his eyes. The dreaming started with a vision of his wife, but diverted to his childhood, as it had done recently, to a place and time he wasn't sure ever existed.

*It happened on a cruise in the Bahamas. His parents weren't speaking to each other, which wasn't unusual. He watched them duel like fencers probing for each other's weaknesses. The confrontations always ended with Max beating her. It would have been a normal holiday of horrors, but something awful happened.*

*The ocean was calm. He remembered the night air was warm and friendly. Flying fish skipped away from the bow on transparent wings. Tangled beds of yellow seaweed floated by. He heard them fighting on the deck above him. He heard the smack of his father's fist. A stroke of heat lighting lit up his mother's face as she fell past the porthole in his cabin. They locked eyes and she screamed, but he couldn't hear her words. He ran up on the deck. The crew threw life rings over the side, but she was gone. He ran to his father, but Max pushed him away. He knew Max had killed her. Later on, he pretended to believe the therapists, but deep down he knew the truth.*

"*Khawadja*, you were having a bad nightmare," Agrippa yelled. He helped Arthur sit up on the edge of the cot. He took a few seconds to find his bearings.

"The malaria is giving me nightmares. I need to stay awake. Let's get the truck loaded."

Arthur and Agrippa waited for sunlight to give form to the desert. The orange rays made the sands appear almost hospitable, but as the light got harsher it made the desert look unforgiving. It was the end of the dry season. The woodland acacias could no longer afford the luxury of foliage; their branches were as emaciated as the animals that used them for shade.

Arthur's Land Rover was painted with a red cross, but so was the one that had been attacked two weeks earlier. They passed small groups of refugees walking in the opposite direction. All of them told the same story: They were heading west to escape the violence.

Arthur looked out across the vast plain and trembled. Heat waves rose from the land like gas fumes. A spinning dust devil momentarily disturbed the stillness.

"This is as far as we go on the road. We'll stop here until its dark. Better to cross the desert at night. No sense making ourselves a target."

They rested in the shade. Arthur tried to sleep, but the sweltering heat made it impossible. Agrippa's catnap was interrupted by an annoying fly. He used a cow's-tail flyswatter to shoo it away. Arthur studied the black man. The Dinka are perfectly adapted to this environment. What a pity to eradicate these wonderful people, he reflected. A people fashioned by a million years of evolution. The old man stood up and looked out at the desert. "I hear cow bells," he said, cupping his ear.

Arthur climbed up on the truck's roof. It took binoculars to see them. Tall men, like apparitions in the desert heat, walked towards him. They used their fighting sticks as canes. Their cows trudged in front of them. Agrippa picked up a water bottle and ran out to greet them. Each man took a small sip of water. They clapped their hands as a sign of gratitude.

"*Yin aca leec*," one man yelled at Arthur.

"You're welcome. Has your friend been injured?" Arthur asked pointing at a man struggling to walk. The Dinka men had smeared dung ash and cow urine on their faces to repel the insects. The urine bleached their hair orange. The dust gave them a ghostly appearance. One man retrieved some of the concoction and offered it to Arthur. Arthur wiped it on his face.

"He's lost God's gift of sight. The Arabs hide bombs under the earth. One of his favorite cows stepped on a bomb. The cow is dead and he was blinded."

"Let's have a look at him," Arthur said.

The man's face was disfigured. His eyes had turned milky. "I'm afraid there's not much I can do for you. Was your march from the Sudd difficult?"

"No more difficult than usual. God bless you for trying to ease my suffering."

"I'm looking for a young Dinka boy. His name's Abel Deng."

"Deng is a common name in the Sudan. The boy you're looking for, has he undergone the rites of passage?" one of the men asked.

"I don't know what you mean."

"Dinka boys have six of their bottom teeth removed and four deep incisions cut in their foreheads. Only then have they proven themselves worthy of taking a wife. Some say, we must discard our ancient customs. They say our ways are foolish."

"Abel has no such mutilations," Arthur explained.

"The government in Khartoum calls us savages," the man said. "The changes in this country fill me with a great sadness." The others shook their heads in agreement. "The boy you seek, does he have a scar on his chin?"

"Yes, yes, that's him. Where did you see him?"

"They camped with us two weeks ago. The boy has taken a young Nuer wife."

"Are you sure? He's only fourteen."

"Fourteen years is a lifetime in the Sudan. We asked them to join us, but they prefer marching at night. We must travel by day or the lions will eat our cows."

Emotions strangled Arthur's response. "God forgive me, I'd almost lost hope." He offered the men more water, but they refused. Water was so precious in the desert; it would have been considered improper to accept it. The men rested for a short time. There was no escape from the sun. The cows huddled together trying to steal each other's shade. They swished their tails to dislodge the flies.

A man walked over to a black-and-white spotted bull. He spoke to the bull. Instantly, the animal took up the lead. The cows fell in behind the bull. Without saying a word, the men followed their herd into the desert. The tall figures grew small from a distance. Within minutes, they disappeared into the heat waves.

*     *     *

The full moon made traveling safer, but driving with the lights turned off caused Arthur to pass unseen within a mile of Abel and Tabitha walking in the opposite direction. It was dark by the time they stopped at the same razed village Abel and Tabitha had stumbled on. Agrippa seemed agitated and refused to get out of the truck. The light of day revealed human skulls with sunken eye sockets and gapping jaws. A myriad of human bones lay scattered in the sand. There was a strange dank odor in the air. The smell of death made Arthur queasy.

"This place is giving me the willies," he said. "How far is the swamp?"

"We are close. If we were herding cattle, they would be increasing their pace. I smelled the marsh before sunrise."

Arthur slowed down. The water hyacinth and papyrus reeds expanded like a green blanket. The air was scented by swamp flowers.

"You're a gifted navigator. I can't tell you how many times I would have turned in the wrong direction," Arthur said to Agrippa. They retrieved their canteens and walked down to the water. Agrippa used his hand to swirl away the floating vegetation and started filling the containers. Arthur knelt beside him to lend a hand.

"This looks like a good spot to camp," Arthur suggested.

"When it gets dark, this place will have many mosquitoes. It would be better to camp back there," he said, pointing back at the dried plain. "We must burn elephant dung or the insects will have a great feast."

"God, I'm glad I brought you along." He touched the old man on the shoulder. Agrippa responded with a toothless grin.

*     *     *

Over the next four days, Arthur and Agrippa skirted the western edge of the Sudd. Their campfires attracted local fishermen who would appear each morning in their dugouts or hippo-hide round boats. Arthur treated them for a variety of ailments. The fisherman presented him with gifts of fish and turtles. Each day, they moved farther south.

On the morning of the fifth day, Arthur stopped to watch a pair of fish eagles soaring high above an island. Without wind to ripple its surface, the water looked like black marble. Tiny bee-eaters no larger than butterflies fluttered above the tangled mass of purple convolvuli and thick papyrus reeds. Flocks of blue teal zoomed by before flaring to land between the pods of hippos. The hippos' periscopic eyes slipped beneath the surface and then reemerged. The dominant bull hippo warned them with whiz-honking. A large crocodile waddled down the bank and slithered into the water. It submerged under some white-flowered water lilies.

As Arthur adjusted his binoculars, a narrow reed-boat rounded the bend. Two men waved and paddled towards them. The men showed no embarrassment at their nakedness. A monofilament net lay between them.

"*Habari*," one man yelled in Swahili.

Arthur answered him in his native language. "*Ichiyo nade?*"

"My morning is going well," the man replied in English.

Agrippa got a fire going. He pushed a scorched kettle into the coals. A few minutes later, he offered the fishermen tea. Unable to withstand his scratchy pants, Agrippa took them off. Arthur glared at him, but said nothing. One man crammed a clump of fatty biltong into his cheek before speaking. "The Sudd is a dangerous place. At first we thought you might be lost. You don't seem lost."

"We're not lost," Arthur answered before taking a sip of tea. "We're searching for a young Dinka boy. His name's Abel Deng. We heard he might be traveling with a young Nuer woman. He was captured by a band of Sudanese thugs. I believe their leader's name is Bol."

The fishermen looked at each other and shook their heads. When one of them spoke, there was sadness in his voice. "I'm afraid we have very bad news."

"Well, let's hear it." Arthur braced himself.

"It grieves me to tell you that Captain Bol and all of his men, including the captive children were killed by the Janjaweed."

"You're wrong! Why, only a few days ago some men told us they met Abel and the girl."

Embarrassed by Arthur's obstinacy, the fishermen stood up. "We witnessed the attack. There were no survivors. If you follow the shoreline, you will see for yourself." The men climbed into their beached reed-boat. *"Nyasaye Ogwedhi,"* one man yelled before pushing away from the shoreline.

"And may God bless you also," Arthur yelled back.

Arthur and Agrippa did follow the shoreline. Agrippa spotted a spiral of white-backed vultures corkscrewing into the sky. Marabou storks were silhouetted against the sun. They got out of the truck and wandered off. When they reunited, they were speechless. Agrippa hurled hardened pieces of dung at the hyenas and jackals, but they were so emboldened they wouldn't budge. Half-eaten bodies lay rotting in the sun. Only a greasy spot and a million flies marked the place where each person had been killed. They covered their faces with rags, but the smell overwhelmed them. Agrippa had found a blood soaked hat. Averting his eyes, he handed it to Arthur. Both knew the hat was Abel's.

They didn't wait for nightfall to leave. Arthur stared at the never-ending desert. He wiped his tears on the back of his sleeve. The waning moon made the driving difficult. To hell with the Arabs. He switched on the headlamps.

# 15

# CENTRAL AFRICAN REPUBLIC

The hunting camp was surrounded by jungle. A clay-colored runway bisected the camp. Tented chalets lay nestled under some mahogany trees. Colobus monkeys howled about prowling chimpanzees. During the day, the jungle hummed with the songs of exotic birds. The nights were silent except for the occasional trumpeting of a forest elephant.

Otto Bern flew to Uganda once a week to bring back supplies. Rigby and Dutchy pretended to hunt with their rich American client, Jesse Spooner. Everyday they drove illegally across the border into the Sudan. The Darfur region was so vast they seldom encountered people. When they did run into refugees, none of them had information about Arthur Turner. It was evident they needed to cover more territory, and that meant using Bern's Cessna.

A scowl crept onto Otto's face as he listened to Rigby. "My arrangement with Mr. Turner was to make one flight into the Darfur. Now you're asking me to fly reconnaissance flights over hostile territory. In the past five years, I bet I've patched a dozen bullet holes in my old bird. I'm not proud of the cargo I hauled, but I needed the money. These Sudanese are better shots than the Africans we faced in our war. I told you, this airplane's everything I own."

"Otto, you're a worry-wart. Let's say they do shoot us down and we survive the crash. You know the bloody savages will kill us. You won't need your airplane if you're dead, old boy." Rigby was grinning.

"Now isn't that a lovely argument. All right, I'll do it."

"Attaboy, Otto, I knew you'd come around. It's gonna be just like the old days in Rhodesia."

"That's what I'm afraid of. If you remember, we lost that war."

"Yes, but think of all the fun we had."

*     *     *

Africans refer to gossip as bush-news. It travels without the aid of telephones. When word got out about Helen being a doctor, she was inundated with a never-ending stream of patients. They emerged unannounced from the jungle every morning. Some of them had diseases that had been cured fifty years ago. They brought her gifts of bananas, yams, unidentified fruits and herbal weeds. They also gave her two gray parrots; one parrot spoke French and the other cursed in Swahili. She received six green parakeets and three orphaned monkeys. The monkeys had a preference for crapping on the mess table. Lynn was pressed into service as a wildlife caretaker. The camp was starting to smell like a zoo.

Rigby and Otto started making daily flights into the Darfur. Each morning, Otto marked a new section on his map. The first areas they explored were in the north near Chad. Otto circled every tented refugee camp. If the ground was flat enough, he would land.

As their excursions reached into the interior, they saw hundreds of burned villages. The chaos was abstract from a thousand meters, but from a hundred the reality was heart-wrenching.

Both men were frustrated. It all changed the day they made the emergency landing. It happened fifteen minutes into the flight. Rigby pulled the headset mouthpiece to his lips. "Why are you landing? There's nothing here."

"I'm landing because the bloody engine just quit, unless of course you have a better suggestion. Better cinch your seatbelt. This might be unpleasant."

He setup the landing at two hundred meters. Some flat-topped acacias blocked the end of the only clear piece of ground. Otto jammed the left rudder pedal to the floor and rolled in right aileron. The old Cessna shuddered from the slip, but she fell sideways three hundred feet. He jerked her hard around and pulled in full flaps. A second after he touched down, the plane was vaulted into the air by a termite mound. He jerked back on the yoke, causing the plane to stall. They hit with a thud and he locked the brakes. The Cessna started to go over on her nose, but stopped just short of vertical and fell backwards. They sat frozen, looking straight ahead without uttering a word. The propeller had stopped two meters from an acacia tree.

"I must say Otto—your landing was brilliant. I'm curious—how far is it to the border?"

"Well, let's see. We were traveling at one hundred and sixty kilometers per hour and we were airborne for about fifteen minutes. I'd say we're about forty kilometers from the camp. I hate to remind you, but I only have one fucking leg."

"I know you have one leg. Let's not get huffy. Maybe we can fix the problem."

"We've just crash-landed in a country that forbids over flights. A country where killing people is a sport. And you tell me not to get huffy."

"Look at the bright side. You did park in the shade."

*     *     *

Helen received the call from Rigby about their emergency landing on her satellite telephone. Otto and her husband were working on the plane. If they didn't make the repair quickly, they would have to spend the night in the desert. The instructions were clear: Stay by the telephone and do nothing. If they were unsuccessful in repairing the plane, Jesse and Dutchy would have to drive into the Darfur to rescue them. They had the approximate bearing from the camp, but locating them would be like finding a needle in a haystack.

*     *     *

Otto stuck his head out from underneath his airplane's instrument panel. The desert heat had caused him to strip down to his underpants. His face was covered in black grease. "I found the problem. The throttle cable's buggered. I've got a spare cable, but its back at the camp. Bloody bad luck."

Rigby walked over and started to inspect Otto's man-made leg.

"We're not dismantling my leg. Do you have any idea how much one of these legs cost?"

Rigby slung his rifle over his shoulder and picked up a water bottle. "Give me five days. If I'm not back, you'll figure something out."

"That's it? You're gonna leave me?"

"There's no sense in us both dying. Goodbye, Otto."

Otto extracted a small piece of stainless steel cable from the joint mechanism. He spliced the throttle cable in one hour, but the light was fading fast. Finding the camp in the dark would be difficult—landing at night would be suicidal. They decided to spend the night in the desert. Both the sun and the temperature fell quickly in the desert. Rigby and Otto huddled next to their campfire. The darkness gave birth to night sounds. The giggling of hyenas was momentarily quieted by the roars of a desert lion.

"I'd trade my own leg for some whiskey," said Rigby.

"There's a bottle under the rear passenger seat."

"I knew it. You forgot the throttle cable, but you remembered the booze. Bern, you're the best."

Otto elevated his stump before speaking. "You better hope I can fly without my leg."

They drank whiskey and reminisced about Rhodesia. "Otto, did I tell you I ran into Ian Rhodes? He tried to arrest Spooner on some cocked-up charge. You know, I always suspected Rhodes was a spy."

"I never told this to anybody, but Rhodes was snooping around when we did the incursion into Mozambique. He wanted to know the exact coordinates of the drop zone."

"Christ, Otto, you should have told someone. Willie Piet was killed."

"Rhodes was my superior officer. One week later, I stepped on a landmine. For me, the war was over."

"Willie had a wife and two kids. Someday, I'll set it straight with Rhodes," said Rigby, yawning.

"How long has Mugabe got?" When Otto didn't get an answer, he realized Rigby had passed out. He used his good leg to push a log into the fire and pulled the blanket up under his chin.

*     *     *

Rigby was jolted out of a deep sleep by something jabbing him in the ribs. He grabbed the butt end of a fighting stick and sat up. "Wake up, sleeping beauty, we've got company."

Four naked Dinka men stood over them. One was holding Rigby's rifle.

"I didn't think this was supposed to happen to a Selous Scout. I mean, getting your weapon pinched."

"Shut up, Otto." Rigby directed his question to the man holding his rifle. "*Utenpenda kunywas nini?*"

"What did you say?"

"I asked him if he wanted something to drink."

"But we don't have anything to drink."

"It's the first thing that popped into my head."

Otto did the same thing he did every morning; he reached for his artificial leg. When he pulled the plastic leg out from underneath the blanket, the Dinka men jumped back. They looked afraid. The man with Rigby's rifle put it on the ground and stepped back.

"It's nothing to be frightened of," Otto snickered. He hopped towards them on his good leg. After retreating, one man stepped forward and reluctantly touched the plastic limb. He turned and said something to the other men. Otto strapped on his prosthetic leg with the intention of giving them a demonstration, but without the cable, the foot swung around causing him to lose his balance and fall. He cursed the leg and realigned the foot. After a few steps he fell again. "Well anyway, you get the idea." He tossed the broken leg into the backseat of his airplane.

One man pointed to the airplane and said something to the others. All four of them laughed.

"What was that all about?" asked Otto.

"I suspect he said something about your buggered leg and your airplane being made by the same company. Anyway, whatever he said, they seem amused, which is promising."

The men offered them curdled milk, a Dinka delicacy. They accepted it without reservation. It proved to be a fine remedy for their hangovers. After the men helped them turn the airplane around, Rigby asked one of them if he had heard of a white man living with the Dinkas. He said he knew of only one white man. He was living in a refugee camp not far from there.

"We've been looking to hell and gone, and he's been right here under our noses. I'd like to land and see if it's Turner."

"Oh no, you don't. I'm flying nonstop back to our camp. Why, you'd have to be an imbecile to land a tail-dragger with one leg. I'm not sure the splice will hold. No sir, you're not talking me into this, so you can forget it."

*     *     *

"I can't believe I'm doing this," Otto yelled, preparing to land. Even without his leg, the landing was silky smooth. He spun the Cessna around and back-taxied up to the tents. Rigby uncoupled his seatbelt and leaned over to make sure Otto could hear him over the engine noise. "Better keep the engine running until I find out what's going on." Otto gave him a thumbs-up response.

Dozens of naked children ran out to meet Rigby as he exited the aircraft. He gave Otto the cut throat signal to shutdown the engine.

The tents were filled with sick and wounded Africans. The sound was a depressing cacophony of children moaning and hacking. The Italian nurse explained that the camp had been attacked twice by Arab militias in the last three weeks. The relief pilots were refusing to fly in supplies for fear they would be shot down. She was forced to reduce the daily food rations. When Rigby mentioned Arthur Turner, her eyes lit up. She told them Turner had gone off on a rescue mission to save a Dinka boy. As recently as one week ago, refugees coming from the east had crossed paths with Arthur.

Croxford stuck his head under a tent flap. There was a small girl lying naked on a blanket. She was frail and lifeless. The sound of her breathing was shallow and uneven. Flies had collected in the child's eyes and around her mouth. The air in the tent was fouled by the smell of human waste. The girl stared up at Rigby, but she was too weak to speak.

"Why is this little girl alone?" Rigby asked the nurse.

"She's dying. We isolate them when they're near death."

"What's wrong with her?" Otto asked.

"Sleeping sickness. I injected her with the drug we normally use, but she had an allergic reaction. Don't look so shocked. We see children die everyday."

"What's the name of the drug you gave her?" Rigby asked, dragging the nurse outside to get better reception on his satellite telephone.

"Suramin. Why do you ask?"

"My wife's a doctor." It seemed like an eternity before he heard Helen's voice. She had another drug used to treat sleeping sickness. He wrapped the girl up in the blanket and ran to the airplane. Otto hobbled after him. Within minutes, they were flying back to the hunting camp.

*     *     *

As soon as the propeller stopped, the camp workers rushed out and carried the little girl into a tent. Helen hooked her up to an intravenous dip laced with Eflorithine. When she finished examining the girl, she pulled her husband aside. "You missed it last night—all hell broke loose. Apparently, Lynn and Jesse haven't been straight with us. Even now, I'm not sure I know the whole truth. At this point, they're not speaking to each other. Let's take a walk." She stuck her arm through his elbow and guided him behind one of the tents. Helen told him about Jesse Spooner making secretive satellite telephone calls to the States. Lynn had listened in on one of his conversations. According to Lynn, Jesse's purpose from day one was to arrest Arthur Turner for illegal arms trafficking. The story about using Arthur as a witness against Nelson Chang was a fabrication. When Lynn accused Jesse of using her, things got ugly.

"What about the girl?" Rigby asked, changing the subject.

"It'll take twenty-four hours to see if she responds to the drug. Rigby, I think we should go back to Zimbabwe."

"Maybe you're right. Let's see if we can get some answers."

Helen rounded up Lynn and Jesse. Rigby stood next to the plane watching them walk towards him. When the silence didn't incite a response, he squinted at Jesse through a cloud of cigarette smoke for a few more seconds before speaking. "Before I get myself killed, I thought it might be nice if you two would kindly tell me what's going on. Let's start with you, Spooner."

"You already know I'm an ATF agent. Lynn thinks I'm here to arrest Arthur Turner, and she's right. Arthur Turner's involved with his father in illegal arms trafficking. If he decides to cooperate, I might be able to help him. We know he's received large sums of money in Uganda. That money's coming from selling weapons."

"You don't know what you're talking about. I told you, the money has nothing to do with arms trafficking," said Lynn.

"Okay, Lynn. Why don't you tell them where he got the money?" said Jesse.

"I sent him the money. I've lost track of just how much money, but it has to be around ten million dollars. I transferred most of it through Barclays. I glued thousands in cash between the pages of the medical books I mailed to an address in Kampala. He needed the cash for bribes. It was the easiest way to get money to him."

Jesse continued to press her. "Where would you get ten million?"

"We've been blackmailing Max. It was Arthur's idea. I got involved as a money courier. Max has been pretending his money's going to Sudanese criminals. He says its ransom money to keep his son alive. By now, I'm sure Max knows everything." Lynn shivered when she realized what she'd just told them.

"You're on a roll—keep talking," said Helen.

"Arthur witnessed his mother's murder. It happened on their family yacht—Max threw his wife overboard. He hired therapists to convince Arthur what he'd seen wasn't real. He's kept his mother's death hidden. The Ugandan massacre triggered flashbacks. Arthur's used every dime of that money to help the Sudanese people. Jesse, do you still want to arrest him?"

"I got news for you," said Rigby. "Nobody's going to arrest anyone unless I go in there and bring him out. That's assuming he wants to get out."

"You have to get Arthur out before—."

"Before what?"

"Max hasn't hired you to rescue Arthur. He's hired you to help him kill his son."

\*     \*     \*

Rigby leaned against a tent pole smoking a cigarette. He had been watching Otto and Dutchy struggle to replace the throttle cable. The sounds of the tropical forest were blotted out by the hum of the camp's generator. Helen walked up behind him and put her arms around his waist. "Penny for your thoughts," she said.

"Sometimes I think you might have been happier married to someone else. Africa's such a mess. The only thing you've seen is misery."

"My, aren't we gloomy."

"I keep hoping it'll get better. Deep down, I know I won't live long enough to see it. I'm sorry Helen, you deserved better."

"Do you really think I'd be content living in Connecticut? I wouldn't have missed this for all the tea in China. After thirty years, you still don't know me, do you?" Instead of answering, he kissed her on the cheek.

"How's our little girl doing?"

"She's better. It's too early to tell, but it looks like she'll make it."

"That's great." He picked at a scab on his shin.

"Stop picking at it," Helen said.

He rubbed the wound as if he didn't hear her. "You said you thought we should go back home to Zimbabwe. Do you still feel that way?"

"Don't try to pin this on me. We both know you've already decided to see this thing through."

He put his arm around her and grinned. "I'm the one who married the wrong person. A man should never marry a woman smarter than himself."

Spooner stooped to duck into the tent. Helen bristled and pulled away from Rigby. "Helen, could I speak to your husband?"

"Not before I say my piece. I can forgive you for lying to us, but you've been a real shit to Lynn, pardon my French. Men have taken advantage of Lynn her whole life, but you've taken abuse to a new level."

Jesse glanced at Croxford, hoping for support, but Rigby stayed out of it. Helen waited for his rebuttal. When he didn't offer one, she got up to leave. "That's all I have to say." She walked past him, refusing to make eye contact.

Jesse looked sheepish. He waited for Helen to leave before speaking. "Rigby, do you still need me for the rescue?"

"I'd like to do this alone. It's wrong to take Dutchy. He's got a wife and kids, but he'll raise three kinds of hell if I leave him. I need Otto standing by with the airplane. If I need backup, I can get you on the satellite telephone."

"I can help you with these people," Jesse argued.

"Don't think that because your skin's a little darker, these people are going to greet you as their long lost brother. I've got news for you, my friend, I was born in Africa. I'm more like these people than you are. Maybe you don't know that, but they do."

"Look, you're taking this the wrong way. I just thought you could use some help. If you don't need me, I think I'll catch a ride with Otto to Kampala." Jesse's tone of voice exposed his annoyance.

"Under the circumstances, I think it might be better."

Jesse walked away, and then turned back around and stuck his head under the tent flap. "For the record, I've loved two women in my life. One's my mother and the other's Lynn Allison."

"Why haven't you told her?"

"C'mon, Croxford, you of all people should know better. What kind of a life would she have married to me? She deserves better."

# 16
# KHARTOUM

The Arabic word Khartoum mean's elephant trunk. An outline of the city resembles the appendage. It's an ancient capital of clay-colored buildings located on the western bank of the Blue Nile. The metropolis forms a triangle with the Great Mosque at its center. Zealots have fought over Khartoum for centuries.

Nelson Chang pulled the curtain back and mentally recited the slogan written on a billboard across the street from the Chinese Embassy. It was a picture of smiling Chinese workers with the words: Your Close Friend and Faithful Partner inscribed at the bottom.

"The book you're reading about Khartoum's history, what have you learned?" Chang asked, turning to his personal assistant.

"Christians and Jews were not allowed within the city limits until 1881. The only Africans allowed in the city were slaves. The Mahdi laid siege to Khartoum in 1885. His dervishes killed the British General, Charles Gordon, and all of the British and Egyptian soldiers under his command. It was a lesson the British couldn't forget. In 1898, they sent Lord Kitchener to avenge the defeat. Khartoum fell to the British."

"But hadn't the Mahdi already died?"

"Yes, they say he died from consumption. Historians say Scottish troops blew up the sacred tomb and played soccer with his head. Later, Kitchener had an inkwell made from the Mahdi's skull."

"That's enough history for today. The British are even more savage than these Africans," Chang uttered. He moved in front of a mirror and straightened his necktie. "What time does the press conference start?"

"In thirty minutes."

* * *

Reporters milled around the embassy's conference room. Nelson Chang entered the room through a private door and found a seat in the back. A spokesman thumped the microphone to start the news conference. The Chinese ambassador sat to the right of the moderator. The Sudanese minister of information sat on the left.

The spokesman asked for the first question. A woman approached the microphone. "Mr. Ambassador, the United Nations Security Council recently passed resolution 1564, which threatens Sudan with oil sanctions unless the Sudanese government curbs the violence in the Darfur. As a member of the Security Council, China has vetoed that resolution. Has China become Sudan's chief international protector for selfish reasons? Is it because of Sudan's vast oil reserves?"

"As a member of the world community," said the ambassador, "of course China deplores the violence in Darfur. But it makes no sense to punish the Sudanese people for the actions of a few misguided criminals."

"Sir, as many as four hundred thousand Africans may have been slaughtered. Somehow, calling it 'the action of a few misguided criminals' seems understated."

The Sudanese spokesman grabbed the microphone. "That number has been grossly exaggerated by known enemies of the Sudanese people. It's true that unfortunately, some people have been killed. I can assure you, my government is doing everything in its power to address this problem. Next question, please."

"Mr. Ambassador, China has invested fifteen billion dollars in Sudan's petroleum infrastructure. This includes an eleven-hundred-kilometer pipeline linking the Heglig oilfield in the Kordofan province with Port Sudan on the coast. My question is, has the Chinese National Petroleum Corporation made any geological surveys in the Darfur region? Simply put, what is their estimate of the oil reserves in the Darfur? As a part of that question, how many Chinese troops are currently deployed in the Sudan?"

"No comment. Next question please," said the Sudanese minister.

A reporter in the back of room yelled, "You have committed terrible crimes against humanity." Sudanese policemen grabbed the reporter and escorted him through a side door.

Chang touched his assistant on the shoulder and nodded at the exit. Book-ended by two armed bodyguards, Chang was whisked down the stairs leading to the parking garage. The Land Cruiser waiting for him was wedged in between two Sudanese police Jeeps.

Chang covered his nose with a linen handkerchief as they drove past the camel market. The road was devoid of trucks and cars. An old man wearing a white robe and turban led a camel in the opposite direction.

The Chinese military garrison was located on the outskirts of Khartoum. It was large enough to house the four thousand Chinese soldiers who lived there. The perimeter barricade encircling the compound was a solid fence topped by razor-wire. Nelson Chang presented his credentials at the guardhouse. Two armed guards framed the walkway to a building in the middle of the compound. Chang and his two bodyguards were greeted by a uniformed soldier wearing white gloves. They were ushered into a room where General Muhammad Nur and two Chinese military officers had been waiting.

The Chinese officers jumped to their feet and bowed politely, but the general remained seated. Chang said something in Mandarin to the general. The officers looked mortified, but Chang's bodyguards smiled. The Sudanese general looked inconvenienced by the meeting. He picked his nose and wiped the contents on his robe.

"The general's interpreter asked, "Have you enjoyed your stay in Khartoum?" General Nur offered to shake hands, but Chang refused. Instead, he placed a cardboard box wrapped in brown paper in the general's lap. "Tell him to open it." Chang said to the interpreter.

The general had been the recipient of countless bribes from the Chinese. He was too impatient to wait for a paperknife. Instead he used his teeth to tear the paper. There was a manila envelope inside. Disappointed, he turned the carton upside down and shook it. A puzzled smile crossed his lips. "The general says he's confused."

"Perhaps, I should tell him what the correspondence says. The letter is from President Omar al-Bashir. It places the general under my direct authority. It states that if he fails to obey me or if he demands a bribe, I am duty-bound to inform his Majesty. He has assured me that he will have the general executed at my convenience. To protect him, I neglected to say that I've already given him a fifty thousand dollar bribe."

The general bypassed his interpreter and gushed, "In the name of the

Compassionate One, I am your trusted servant. Tell me what you wish me to do."

"I want you to finish the job I gave you. It's the American living with the Dinka. This man has been blackmailing his own father."

Chang got up and walked over to a serving table underneath the office window. He filled a tumbler with water. Instead of drinking the water, he handed the glass to the general. "There's an agent of the American government trying to do great harm to me. I have reason to believe this man is in the Sudan. Here's his photograph." Chang handed Nur a picture of Jesse Spooner.

"As Allah is my witness, I will do as you wish. This time it will be different."

"I know it will be different. This time, I'm going with you to make sure you keep your promise."

"Ah, Mr. Chang, you will love the desert. It's truly a magical place."

"I'll hate the desert just like I hate everything in Africa."

\*     \*     \*

# 17
# KAMPALA, UGANDA

The road from the airstrip to Kampala looped around emerald green hills ripe with unpicked coffee and tea. Women dressed in brightly colored sarongs worked the fields. Jesse stared out the window but saw nothing. His sendoff had been cordial, but reserved. He couldn't get Danny Gillespie out of his mind. The police report stated that Danny had died from an accidental gunshot wound. Six months ago it all seemed plausible, but that was before he found out about Max Turner allegedly killing his wife. He reached over the seat and tapped his driver on the shoulder. "Take me to the American Embassy."

The American ambassador kept him waiting. When he was shown into the ambassador's office, he was surprised to find another man standing next to the ambassador. After the introductions, they sat down. He's with the CIA, Jesse thought.

"Mr. Spooner, what can we do for you?"

"This is a courtesy visit. I'm not sure how much you know about my assignment."

"We have a vague idea."

"Mr. Ambassador, I wanted you to know there's an American citizen still in the Darfur."

"It's wonderful news about Arthur Turner being alive, although he's become somewhat of an embarrassment for us. There's a State Department travel restriction on entering the Darfur. As you know, all of the relief organizations have left the region. I'd like the major to bring you up to speed on the current developments in the Sudan."

The major started his dissertation with the 1973 assault on the Saudi Embassy in Khartoum. "Palestinian terrorists, members of the group,

Black September, murdered the American ambassador, who had the misfortune of attending a party thrown by the Saudis. Ten years later," he
continued, "the Sudanese government declared a jihad against the country's Christian minority. Eight years after that, Osama Bin Laden, who
was living in Khartoum, declared his infamous *fatwa* against the United
States for desecrating the holy cities of Mecca and Medina. Al-Qaeda
operatives have moved large amounts of gold into Sudan to finance all of
the major terrorist organizations. Hamas, Hezbollah and Abu Nidal all
have training camps in the Sudan. The 1995 attempt to assassinate
Egyptian President Mubarak and the bombings of our embassies in
Kenya and Tanzania were planned and financed in Sudan."

When the major paused to collect his thinking, Jesse barged in.
"Look, Major, I get it. The Sudan's a snake pit. We're letting the Sudanese
reek havoc as long as they help us gather intelligence on the terrorist
organizations you just mentioned."

"I wouldn't put it that way," noted the ambassador.

"Oh? I'm curious, what's our policy with regard to rescuing people
in the Darfur?" Jesse asked.

"We haven't had a permanent diplomatic presence in the Sudan since
Clinton's missile attack on the so-called pharmaceutical plant in 1998."

Nice evasive answer, Jesse thought, staring at the ambassador. The
ambassador retrieved a pipe from his desk and banged it on the edge of
a wastepaper basket. He refilled it with tobacco, lit it and sucked until it
made a low gurgling sound. He pointed the stem at Jesse before speaking. "I thought you'd like to know that Maxwell Turner is here in
Uganda." Jesse was so befuddled he didn't respond.

"Mr. Spooner, it's certainly been a pleasure meeting you. Both men
stood up and shook Jesse's hand. "And for God's sake, stop worrying
about your American friends. Let me worry about them. After all, that's
what I'm here for."

*         *         *

The drive to the hotel was slowed by heavy traffic. There's something
unsettling about the ambassador and the major, Jesse thought. Maybe it
was the beads of sweat on the ambassador's upper lip or his clammy
handshake. The major was calm and collected, but that was to be
expected. Spooner, you've seen too many spy movies. Well, one thing's

for sure—Lynn was probably telling me the truth about Arthur not being involved in arms trafficking. How could you be so stupid? Spooner thought, reprimanding himself.

The hotel clerk at the front desk was a light-skinned African woman. She became overly attentive when she found out Jesse was an American. When he ignored her, she became sullen and slowed his check-in to a crawl.

In his room, Jesse handed the porter a tip and collapsed on the bed before the man could close the door. Seconds later, he was snoring.

A ceiling fan sliced the light into spinning shadows. Jesse glanced at his watch from different angles trying to calculate the time, but it was too dark to see it. A soft knock on the door startled him. He noticed an envelope on the floor. He opened the door and looked up and down the hallway, but the messenger had disappeared. The note read:

> Dear Mr. Spooner:
> You and Arthur Turner have been targeted by the Sudanese government.
> Good luck,
> A friend.

*　　*　　*

# 18
# THE DARFUR

Arthur and Agrippa camouflaged their vehicle as best they could. After they burrowed out a depression under the truck, they crawled underneath. The desert heat made it difficult to breathe. They lay motionless as another helicopter flew overhead. Arthur felt the rhythmic vibrations from the rotors beating against his ribcage. They had stopped near the refugee camp. Arthur's plan was to sneak into the camp under the cover of darkness. If the camp was occupied by an Arab militia, driving in would be a fatal mistake.

Arthur wet a rag with canteen water and draped it over his forehead. He closed his eyes and revisited the Ugandan massacre. *There was no escape plan—it just happened. Arthur tackled his wife and they rolled end-over-end over a cliff and fell into the river. They surfaced gasping for air. The rebels fired shots, but the current pulled them out of range. In spite of the terror, an exhilarating release washed over him. For the first time in his life, Arthur had taken control of his own destiny. He watched a Ugandan military patrol rescue his wife. He heard her calling for him as she was led away. He wanted to yell out, but he couldn't. Arthur was saved that day in a different way.*

*A soldier from the Lord's Resistance Army found him wandering in the jungle. His body was racked with malaria and dysentery. The women who traveled with the army nursed him back to health. Arthur opened his eyes on the day his fever broke and knew his father was a murderer.*

\*     \*     \*

Abel and Tabitha walked at night. As they marched, members of the Asholi, Bari and Dinka tribes joined them. The refugees were old men and women. Spotted hyenas followed their exodus. As they moved across the desert, some people died. They buried them in shallow graves. The hyenas dug up the bodies. Jackals ate what the hyenas left.

They stopped at a dried up *wadi*, or riverbed. Abel re-excavated a borehole in the river bottom. He found percolating water, but the precious moisture seeped into the tiny hole very slowly. Abel handed up one muddy cupful at a time to Tabitha, who passed it to an old woman. The woman carefully carried it to the people hiding in the shadows. Each person sipped the water, savoring the last drop. All waited patiently for their turn to drink. Finally, it was Tabitha's turn. She started to drink but handed the cup back to Abel and ran into the bushes where she vomited. Two women ran to help her. When they reemerged, the women were smiling, but Tabitha looked heartbroken.

Abel felt her forehead. One of the women grabbed his hand and led him away. When he glanced back, he saw the other women gathered around Tabitha. "It's a gift from God. The girl is carrying your child," the woman said, smiling.

He found Tabitha squatting in the sand with her face buried in her hands. She was sobbing softly. He shooed the women away and sat down next to her. When he put his hand on her shoulder, she looked up at him. "You should have poisoned me when I asked you to. Now I have dishonored you. Abel, you're the best man I've ever known. You deserve a good wife. I wish the baby in me was yours."

"I'm the father and that's all anyone needs to know," he whispered, smiling at the others.

"But Abel, it can't——."

"Quiet woman, you're embarrassing me," he said, pulling her closer. He kissed her on the cheek and brushed away her tears. The old women showed their approval by making their traditional trilling sounds. A new life in the Sudan was a reason for celebration.

*     *     *

When Ali Osman staggered into the Janjaweed camp on the eastern edge of the Sudd, the men who had abandoned him on the battlefield were taken aback. They had witnessed his wound and the blood. No man could have survived such a horrible injury. The fact that he was spared, meant Allah must be protecting him. Ali didn't tell his fellow soldiers that Abel Deng had saved his life.

Abel used cow urine mixed with iodine to sterilize Ali's head wound, which bleached his hair orange. Having red hair is seen as mystical to the True Believers. Ali wore a *hijab* around his neck for good luck. It was a necklace composed of small leather pouches containing Quranic verses. For those soldiers who didn't wear *hijabs,* there was a mad scramble to buy them.

Ali Osman basked in his celebrity. When word of his miraculous survival reached Khartoum, General Nur ordered that he be flown by private helicopter to the new Sudanese bivouacked staging area for a meeting.

Three days later, Osman stood at attention in front of the general. Perspiration dripped from the tip of his nose, but he was afraid to wipe it away. It should have been a time of celebration, but Ali was worried. He was told that he was to receive his own command. This meant a percentage of the looted booty he could pilfer. The cattle and goats they stole were always reserved for the Janjaweed commanders. Now he could start his own herd, which he needed desperately as his wife was pregnant again.

Ali's wife was the only decent thing in his life. Taking an additional wife was encouraged under Sunni Islamic law, but the concept repulsed him. Ali had a problem. His wife was a black African and a member of the Nuer tribe. The Arabs were encouraged to rape African women, but marrying an infidel, especially a *Zurga,* or black African, was contrary to the president's strict Islamic teachings. The punishment was death by stoning.

There were rumors about the general. It was said he sometimes allowed African parents to choose between having their children shot or burned alive. Ali felt weak and dizzy from fear. He glanced indirectly at the general, who was sitting behind a desk. "So, you're Osman?"

Ali cleared his throat. "Yes, sir." His voice sounded squeaky.

"I see the savages have scarred you like they scarred me," the general said, turning his face to show him his disfigurement. "I'm looking for a special officer. The man who held the position deceived me, and that I cannot tolerate. What do you have to say for yourself?"

"Sir, I'll do my best," Ali replied, stiffening to attention.

"Are you married?"

"No, sir." Ali felt his heart pounding.

"Good. There's no room for a family in a warrior's life. In the name of Allah, we must purify this country." He unfolded a map of the Darfur on his desk. "There's an American living with the Dinka in this area," he said, pointing at a spot on the map. "There may be another American with him." The general handed Osman two photographs. "I want you to eliminate these men. There can be no connection to me. Do you understand?"

"Yes, General," Ali answered, studying the pictures of Arthur Turner and Jesse Spooner.

"I'm providing you with two assault helicopters. One helicopter is carrying two drums of paraffin. I want the bodies burned. Go now—your men are waiting for you. That will be all, Osman."

"Yes, sir." Ali saluted.

"Remember, no survivors. I'll be observing your assault from my helicopter. I pray Allah protects you."

*      *      *

Ali Osman was so excited, his body tingled. He wondered how the general would reward him. He never shared his military experiences with his wife. This time I can tell her, he thought. He tucked his black robe between his legs with one hand and held on to his Kalashnikov with the other. A soldier helped him up into the backseat of the general's private helicopter. There was a snarling lion painted on the gunship's nosecone. Blood dripped from the lion's fangs. Within minutes, he was flying back into the Darfur.

*      *      *

Abel was chosen by the refugees to lead them out of the desert. He knew they were close to the displaced persons' camp where he had last seen Arthur Turner. He could see the distant hills that marked the border. He decided the group needed to rest before making the final push. Abel had something new to fret about: Tabitha and the unborn baby she was carrying.

At dusk, he sent out small search parties to scrounge the *wadi* for anything edible. Some of the women picked through the cannonball lumps of elephant dung for undigested seeds. Others picked grasses and turned over rocks searching for insects. When a man captured a small crocodile hibernating in a sand cave the group erupted in prayer.

Abel divvied up the watery crocodile stew. The group demanded that Tabitha be given the largest portion. She accepted their generosity and then inconspicuously dumped the contents of her bowl back into the community pot. The group settled in for the night without the comfort afforded by a campfire. Abel was afraid the light might serve as a beacon for marauders.

*     *     *

Ali Osman didn't know any of the militiamen now under his command. The story of his miraculous recovery from the gunshot wound had preceded him. The Arabs believed Osman was protected by the Prophet. If they fought next to him, they should also be protected.

Ali decided to rest the camels and horses. Some of his men gathered around the campfires cleaning their weapons. Others smoked strong Turkish tobacco. A few of them knelt on rugs reciting the *Tahajjud*, or night prayers.

Osman rested his head on his saddle and looked up at the stars. The crackling campfire spawned the only light. He thought about what they might plunder from the refugees in the upcoming assault. The guttural braying of a camel alerted him. He jumped to his feet and ran to the corral where his men had tethered the animals. One of his sentries walked out of the night towards him.

"Praise Allah, I thought a lion had taken one of our camels. Why have you left your post?" Ali demanded.

"I came upon a group of *Zurgas*. They're camped along this same *wadi*."

"Did they have any weapons or livestock?"

"They're only starving beggars. They have nothing but the rags they wear. Not one of them is worthy of a bullet."

"Come, show me." The two men rode their camels into the darkness. The broad-footed animals moved quietly in the thick sand. At a short distance from the camp, the sentry indicated they should dismount. They swung down out of their saddles and walked into the middle of the sleeping Africans.

"Wake up! Get up, you filthy *abids*," the sentry shouted, kicking a man who was slow to budge. "Get up, you worthless niggers. As Allah is my witness, I'll kill all of you."

The women screamed and the men cried out for mercy. They surrounded Abel and Tabitha knowing the Janjaweed seldom kill old people. It was better to let them starve than waste precious ammunition.

"What are you hiding there?" the sentry demanded. He waded into the crowd, pushing people aside. When he reemerged, he was dragging Tabitha by her wrist. Ali focused his flashlight on the girl as the man ripped her ragged dress off. She cried out and tried to cover her nakedness with her hands.

"This one's a fine *Zurga*. She has a plump ass for fucking," the sentry yelled, grabbing a handful of Tabitha's buttocks.

"Don't take too long. I haven't been with a woman in weeks," the sentry said to Ali, assuming Ali would take her first. The light illuminated the sentry's eyes. His decaying teeth were reduced to blackened stumps.

The Arabic name for the Dinka is *Tagbondo*, or stick people. Dinka boys are trained to fight with parrying sticks. The sticks are cut from the rock-hard ebony trees. Like all Dinkas, Abel was never without his fighting stick.

The sentry's last conscious thought was, "What's that swishing sound?" He turned his head to investigate the noise, giving Abel a perfect target. The boy swung his long stick with the velocity of a bolt of lighting. It crashed into the Arab's face, driving his nasal bones deep into his brain. The sentry would have fallen no faster had he suffered a fatal rifle shot to the head. The refugees gasped as Osman cocked his AK-47 and stuck the barrel into Abel's belly.

"Get down on your knees, Dinka." Abel fell to his knees, waiting for the bullet to end his life. Tabitha knelt in the sand next to him and put her arms around him. They waited, but nothing happened. Abel looked into the light, but was night blinded. His eyes were transfixed by the nearness of his own death.

"On your feet, Dinka. I want to see your face before I kill you. Is the black whore your sister?"

"She's my wife."

Osman shined the light in Abel's face. He stared at him, and scratched his chin. "Dinka, tonight Allah will spare your life. Surely, you haven't forgotten me?" he asked, shining the flashlight on his own face and pointing to the scar on his forehead.

Both Tabitha and Abel nodded affirmatively, but were unable to utter a word. Osman led them back to where he had tied the camels. He handed them a goat-skinned water-bag and sat down in the sand. He placed his gun across his knees and motioned for them to sit down in front of him.

"So, Dinka, Allah has brought us together again." He picked up his gun and accidentally pointed it at Tabitha causing her to flinch. He reached forward to reassure her, but she flinched again.

"Why are you frightened of me? I am also married to a Nuer woman," he whispered, nodding at Abel. He glanced nervously over his shoulder as if he was embarrassed.

"Dinka, why aren't you speaking?"

"Can I give this water to the others?" Abel asked.

"Why would you waste water on those old people? Better to give it to the camels." Osman got up and walked over to his camel.

Abel glanced at the rifle, but the Arab was too close. Ali walked back carrying three water-bags and dropped them in the sand at Abel's feet. "Dinka, your people are ignorant savages, but you're different. Give them this water. Tell them it's a gift from Allah."

Abel slung the water-bags over his shoulder and headed back to the others. Ali waited until Abel was out of earshot before turning to Tabitha. "I think maybe we could become friends, I mean, the Dinka and me. What can you tell me about him?"

"When I first met him, I thought he was just a skinny boy, but I was wrong. He's the wisest, most decent man I've ever known."

"The man he just killed might have a different opinion of him."

"Can I ask you a question?" When Ali nodded yes, she continued. "Why do you hate us?"

"I don't hate you," he answered.

"Then why do you rape our mothers and kill our children?"

"My people have lived in the Sudan for thousands of years. The great Nubian pyramids in the north prove that I am telling you the truth. Your people have invaded us from the west. Some of the tribes look like pre-historic monkeys. Their customs makes us look foolish to the rest of the world. It's my duty as a devout Muslim to purify this land."

"When you say purify, you mean kill. Is this a gift from Allah? Do you discuss these things with your Nuer wife?"

Osman raised his hand to strike Tabitha, but something stopped him. He looked at her for a few seconds before speaking. "Tell the Dinka to take you south. In two days, I will lead a glorious attack on a camp not far from here. I give you this fine camel as a gift. One more thing—tell him he saved my life and I spared his. Now we are even. If he should appear in my rifle sights again, I will not hesitate to kill him." Ali Osman stood up and walked into the night.

Tabitha led the camel back to where the others were camped. Abel looked over her shoulder expecting to see the Arab following her. She told him of the warning.

"We must leave at once." Abel stared into the night and shivered. There's nothing in that camp but old people. Why would they attack it?" he asked himself.

*   *   *

Rigby listened to the dispossessed natives pouring out of the Darfur. It was obvious the Sudanese government had ordered a massive genocidal sweep. Helen and Lynn treated as many of the sick as possible, but the sheer number of patients was overwhelming. Otto Bern's Cessna was pressed into service as an ambulance plane. He flew out the injured and brought back medical supplies. The hunting camp was turned into a field hospital.

Getting Arthur Turner out of the Darfur was put on the backburner. That was until Otto relayed the message that Max Turner had chartered a helicopter and would be arriving at the hunting camp the next morning.

Rigby knew the rescue wouldn't be easy. With tension on the Chadian border escalating, it became evident the Darfur was becoming more dangerous. Arthur may not have known it, but he needed to get out of harm's way.

Rigby and Dutchy set aside the humanitarian work and refocused on the rescue. They reassembled the two Barrett fifty-caliber rifles. Dutchy tried mounting one of the weapon's tripods on the back of the truck, but the vibration from the engine made sighting of the rifle impossible. The men were discussing what to do with the weapons when Otto Bern buzzed the camp in his Cessna. Otto made another low pass, circled and landed in the opposite direction. He taxied up and parked under a large mahogany tree. The cloud of orange dust kicked up by the Cessna engulfed Dutchy and Rigby.

"Well now, look what the cat dragged in," said Rigby as Jesse crawled out of the copilot's seat. "What do we owe for the honor of this visit?" He slapped his hat against his thigh to knock off the dust.

"Croxford, Dutchy," Jesse said, shaking each man's hand. "Where's Lynn?"

"She's with my wife tending to sick Africans," Rigby answered.

"The Sudan's becoming very unstable," stated Jesse.

"Did you hear that, Dutchy? I buy him a book and he chews on the cover. Spooner, what other tidbits of top-secret intelligence have you uncovered?" Rigby's smirk infuriated Spooner.

"Look, I admit I'm no expert on this fucked-up continent. Just hear me out."

"Please continue, President Mandela, we're all ears."

Croxford pretended to pay attention, but his thoughts were elsewhere. He was consumed by the nauseating prospect of meeting Max Turner. When Jesse mentioned that he had talked Otto into making a reconnaissance flight over the refugee camp, Rigby's interest was renewed.

"You say you saw militia encampments just east of the refugee camp?"

"We counted three. Take a look at this note. Someone slid this under my door at the hotel in Kampala."

As Rigby read the note he scratched his stubble. "Who do you think wrote this?" he asked, handing Dutchy the note.

"My hunch is that it was written by a man I met at the American Embassy."

Rigby put his hand on Dutchy's shoulder and smiled. "I guess we should have snatched Arthur Turner before he got so bloody popular. We may have to give these Arabs a chance to meet those seventy-two vestal virgins—or is it two seventy-year-old virgins?" Rigby laughed at his own joke.

"I can't believe you find humor in this," said Jesse.

"It's like the Zulu warriors taunting the British soldiers before the battle of Isandlwana."

"Did the Zulus win?" Jesse asked. Secretly, he was hoping for a Zulu victory.

Rigby ignored Jesse's question. He blew a smoke ring in the still air and raked his fingers through his hair before speaking. "My friend, you should go find Lynn and get Otto to fly you both back to Kampala. I'd have you take my wife, but I know she'll tell us both to go to hell."

Spooner walked over to the truck and examined one of the Barrett fifties. "Have you ever fired one of these M-82s?" he asked.

"No."

"It's not as easy as you might think."

"And I suppose you've fired a fifty-caliber sniper rifle?"

"I'm an ATF agent. That's Alcohol, Tobacco and *Firearms*. I've fired every weapon manufactured in the United States. I went to a training school on this baby," he said, stroking the barrel. "Somali snipers were firing at American soldiers and then ducking behind concrete walls. A sniper, using a Barrett can fire three feet right or left from the last muzzle flash. Bang, right through the wall—one very dead sniper."

"You're so full of shit."

"All right, what's this called?" Jesse asked. He touched something that looked like a microprocessor.

"I haven't the foggiest," admitted Rigby.

"It's called a Barrett Optical Ranging System, or BORS. It measures air temperature, barometric pressure and bore line angle. In other words, it takes the mystery out of bullet drop." Rigby stooped to inspect the mechanism. He rolled his eyes and shook his head. "Oh no, you don't. I know where this is going. There's no way you're going with us."

"Why not?"

"Why? You've lied to me so many times, I've lost track. And you'll shit in your pants if there's any real shooting. You see, I went to school too. It wasn't some technical weapons class. It taught me to kill real people with real bullets. It was called a war."

Dutchy put his hand on Jesse's shoulder. He spoke softly. "What about the buffalo hunt? You said he saved your life."

"That buffalo just happened to get in the way of Jesse's bullet."

"I shot that buffalo in the leg because that's where I was aiming," Jesse said.

"Now that is bullshit, and you know it."

"Croxford, I've seen you shoot. I could outshoot you blindfolded. I don't give a shit what you did in your war. That's ancient history."

"Dutchy, I believe I've been challenged. Pity dueling's been out-lawed."

"If I win—you take me with you," said Jesse.

"Done."

Jesse let Rigby pick the weapon and the target for their shoot-off. Croxford opted for his namesake rifle, his old bolt-action .416 Rigby. Jesse fired three practice rounds to get the feel of the gun. The target was a whiskey bottle hung from a tree at two hundred meters. Both men would shoot from a standing position without the aid of a brace.

Helen and Lynn suspended their medical duties to join the spectators.

Jesse motioned for Rigby to step forward. "You go first."

Rigby set his rifle in the crease of his shoulder and placed his face against its walnut stock. He had already calculated the bullet drop, which made a leaf on the tree above the bottle a perfect target. Exhaling, he put the crosshairs on the leaf and began to squeeze the trigger. The earsplit-ting crack sent a cloud of fruit bats into flight. Monkeys screeched and baboons barked. The whiskey bottle moved from the bullet's air-stream, but didn't break. He frowned and handed his rifle to Jesse. "Whatever you do, don't hit Otto's airplane."

Jesse waited for the mayhem to settle before squinting through the scope. He held the gun rock-solid against his chin. The sound of the shot echoed through the jungle. The bottle disintegrated. When Jesse heard Lynn cheering, he turned, but she stopped her applause and looked down.

"You beat me fair and square. That was a damn fine shot. Now, I want you to tell me the truth. Where were you trying to hit that buffalo?"

"What buffalo? I was so scared I don't remember pulling the trigger."

"The truth becomes you, Spooner. Why don't you take care of the real reason you came back?" Rigby nodded at Lynn.

Jesse walked over to Lynn. They talked briefly before moving to one of the tents. Helen put her arm around her husband's neck and pulled him down to whisper in his ear. "You haven't changed one iota in thirty years. You've never lost a shooting contest in your life. You missed that bottle on purpose, didn't you?"

"You know it and I know it, but let's keep it between us girls," he confessed. "Helen, I couldn't find a better man to cover my backside."

*     *     *

Lynn studied Jesse's face. He sat down and propped his elbows on his knees. She got down on the floor in front of him and crisscrossed her legs. "What made you come back?" she asked.

Jesse stood up and looked out at the setting sun flirting with the top of the jungle canopy. With his back to her he answered. "I've been thinking about us, you know, about what we talked about. Lynn, it won't be easy. People will stare. They'll whisper behind our backs. If we do have kids, they'll get teased."

"I've seen mixed couples make it. Besides, I'm a Louisiana coon-ass. I'll bet my great grandfather was blacker than yours." She moved next to him and rested her head on his shoulder. He put his arm around her waist. They stood together watching the orange equatorial sun slip behind the trees. There was no need to speak.

*    *    *

The men drove out of the hunting camp two hours before sunrise. Rigby wanted to avoid seeing Max Turner. He had no illusions about Turner. Max was despicable, but Rigby didn't buy Lynn's chilling account of Max's intentions. How could a father kill his own son?

After four grueling hours of driving, they hid the truck in some acacias. It gave them time to rest, and it gave Spooner a chance to teach them how to aim and fire the fifty-calibers.

As they got ready to leave, Rigby described what they might face. He remembered large sand-dunes at the south end of the refugee camp. Rigby would walk into the camp alone, in case the camp was controlled by the Janjaweed. Dutchy and Jesse could use a dune as an observation point. If something went wrong, they would have to leave him.

Jesse made a weak argument that he should be the one to walk into the camp, but Rigby's exasperated expression dissuaded him. "If you stripped naked and we had time to burn those tribal markings into your face, you might pass for a Dinka. Of course, you'd need to shed thirty kilos."

"It was a stupid idea. Let's forget I mentioned it."

"Well, it was a lovely gesture. Don't you agree, Dutchy?"

"Jesse looks more like a Zulu," the Dutchman bellowed.

"We could use some Zulu warriors, right about now," said Rigby.

*    *    *

The landscape turned crueler as they drove eastward. They had been driving for ten hours when Dutchy noticed the feathery wisps of campfire smoke on the horizon. Rigby turned to a more southerly heading. A short time later, he spotted the sand dunes that overlooked the camp.

He stopped at the base of the dunes. "All right boys, this is as far as we go. Let's climb so we can get a look-see."

They waded up in the heavy sand and crawled the last few feet on all fours. The men slithered up to the edge and looked down at the camp. Rigby used his binoculars to scan the area. He whispered to Spooner. "It looks harmless enough. Keep an eye on me. If I drop my weapon and hold up my hands, you'll know it's not going well. Wish me luck," he said. He stopped and turned to face them. "Jesse, remember our agreement. Make sure the girls get back to Zimbabwe. Dutchy that goes for you too." He took a deep breath and rolled over the edge.

Spooner refocused the binoculars on Rigby as he watched him struggle down the slope. He scanned the tents and tarpaulin-covered lean-tos. The area was teeming with hundreds of Africans. Many of them huddled around the cooking fires. A few boys played soccer. Older boys tended a small herd of goats and some hollow-rumped cows.

The children saw Rigby first. They ran away screaming. Tall African men poured out of the tents and started to climb up to meet him. Two of the men were carrying old rifles. Everyone in the camp was pointing and yelling. Spooner handed the binos to Dutchy and picked up his rifle. He zeroed in on the man closest to Rigby. He pushed the safety off and set the crosshairs on the man's head.

"Whatdayathink, shall I drop him?" Before Dutchy could answer, Rigby turned around and waved. Jesse let out a sigh. "That was close."

It took thirty minutes to drive around the dunes. By the time they arrived at the camp's barbed-wire gate, it was almost dark. Cheering children and old women gathered around them as they climbed out of the truck. Rigby stood between a white man and a young African couple. He was not smiling.

"Jesse Spooner, Dutchy Bosshart, this is the elusive Mr. Arthur Turner. And these are his friends, Abel and Tabitha Deng." Both men stepped forward and shook hands with Arthur and Deng.

Arthur Turner was distinguished-looking with affable blue eyes. There was an aura of serenity about Turner that Jesse found puzzling given the chaos of his surroundings. When Jesse noticed Rigby's dire expression, he realized something was wrong.

Rigby put his hand on Arthur's shoulder before speaking. "Mr. Turner has just informed me that he has no intention of leaving the Darfur. As a matter of fact, he says he's prepared to die here. And if the information I just received from the young Mr. Deng here is correct, he may get his wish in short order."

Turner motioned for them to step into his tent. "I'd like to offer you a drink, but the best I can do is warm water."

A young girl ran out of the crowd and latched on to Rigby's leg. He reached down and picked her up. She was the girl his wife had treated for sleeping sickness. He handed the girl back to her mother. The woman pressed a gift in Rigby's hand.

Once they were inside, Turner continued. "There's no need to upset these people. They've suffered enough. At this point, I'm not sure much can be done for them. We've survived attacks in the past, but we hear this one will be brutal. Gentlemen, these people think you're here to save them."

"What's he talking about?" Spooner asked.

Rigby outlined what Abel and Tabitha had told him. The Janjaweed was planning a massive attack on the refugee camp. In twenty-four hours, three groups of armed militiamen would sweep into the defenseless camp from three directions. They would charge their war camels and decorated horses into the tented city, killing as many Africans as possible. To make it even more horrifying, the Sudanese military had provided three Chinese attack helicopters.

Jesse glanced at the crowd gathered outside. All of them were dressed in rags. Many of them leaned on walking sticks. Their lives were so bleak, yet they appeared hopeful.

When Turner spoke, his words were strangled with emotion. His beleaguered expression was illuminated by a campfire. "Mr. Croxford, you need to take your friends and leave. The Arabs usually attack in the afternoon. Just be sure to tell the rest of the world what they're doing to us."

When Croxford spoke, it was as if Turner's warning hadn't registered. "So Deng, how many Arabs were in the group you encountered?"

"About fifty," he answered, glancing at Tabitha for confirmation. She agreed.

"So that's one hundred and fifty Arabs, plus the three helicopters. Boys, I guess the odds could be worse, although I don't see how. Jesse, at first light you get in the Rover and hightail it out of here. This is more than you bargained for. I won't think any less of you."

"Does that mean you're staying?" asked Turner. Jesse stepped forward before Rigby could open his mouth. "Mr. Turner, we're all staying."

Croxford shook his head and grinned at Jesse. "Just when I think I've got you figured out, you throw me a bumper. Don't look so dumbfounded, a 'bumper' is a term we use in the great game of cricket."

"I need one of your cigarettes."

"I didn't know you smoke."

"I never have, until now."

"I've got a bottle of whiskey under the front seat. Spooner, it looks like I'm gonna make a proper African out of you yet."

*     *     *

Rigby, Dutchy and Jesse marched around the camp perimeter twice before daylight. The desert morning was crisp in the predawn darkness and the sand was still dewy. As the light broke, Rigby spotted a snake eagle soaring high above the dunes searching for geckos. He started to identify the bird for Jesse, but hesitated. By the time he turned around, the bird had vanished in the smoky haze.

The men attracted a mob as they inspected the camp's defenses, or lack thereof. The refugees chattered optimistically and seemed almost giddy. Their spirits had been buoyed by the men's interest in their welfare. When they arrived back at Turner's tent, he was already busy treating sick Africans. Tabitha handed them mugs of hot tea.

"Good morning, Arthur. I trust you slept well," said Rigby.

"And you, Mr. Croxford, how did you sleep?" Turner answered, tearing a long strip of surgical tape from its roll.

"I've never had a better night in my life. I could get accustomed to living in the desert. What about you, Jesse?"

"I'm getting that queasy feeling again. Helen warned me about your exuberance."

"I have surveyed the upcoming battleground and I've found a flaw in the Arab's battle plan," Rigby said.

"How do you even know their plan?"

"The key is in the terrain. Think about it, Spooner, an army of three outnumbered by one hundred and fifty bloodthirsty, screaming Arabs. And Spooner, you will have been a part of it."

"I can hardly wait," said Jesse.

Croxford walked to a sandy spot in front of the tent and drew an outline of the camp. At one end he heaped a pile of sand to replicate the sand dunes. He pulled Dutchy forward and pointed at the sand map. "Dutchy, assume you were a Janjaweed commander. From what direction would you attack?" The Dutchman looked down at the map and scratched his head. "I would come from this direction and trap the Africans against the dunes."

"Don't you see? They're the ones who'll be trapped."

"I'm sorry," said Jesse, "I don't get it."

"Don't worry, it'll all come together. Gentlemen, let's get to work."

*     *     *

Abel called for the Dinka men who owned firearms to assemble. A dozen tribesmen came forward with five antique rifles and seven shotguns. The women, children and elderly who were physically able to run would gather at the base of the sand dunes at the first sign of the Arabs. Tabitha took charge of those too weak to walk, directing them to hollow out shallow bunkers under their tents. Arthur Turner suspended his medical duties to lead a work detail digging trenches at the foot of the dunes. Spooner and Croxford climbed to the crest and dug two foxholes twenty meters apart, connected by a ditch.

As Jesse watched the preparations unfold, he realized Rigby's strategy was brilliant. If the Arabs took the bait and attempted to trap the Africans against the sand dunes, they would find themselves targets in a perfect field of fire. The militiamen used the weapon of choice for most Third World countries, the AK-47. It was an ideal weapon for close combat, but no match for the long range of the M-24 rifles. They would also be disadvantaged by trying to shoot uphill from galloping camels and horses. Rigby had carefully estimated the height of the dunes and found the distance to be beyond the accurate range of the Kalashnikovs. If things went according to plan, the defenders would wreak havoc on the Arabs with total immunity. There was only one stumbling block: the attack helicopters.

It was no secret, that the success or failure of the plan lay squarely on Spooner and Dutchy. They would be firing the fifties, and would have to disable the helicopters. If they could shoot one down, the remaining helicopters might turn and run.

Jesse practiced aiming the Barrett at one of the tents below. Thinking about the imminent violence made him feel weak. He distracted himself by thinking about Lynn.

*    *    *

### The Hunting Camp

When Lynn heard the thumping of a helicopter, her heart-rate quickened. She watched the helicopter turn back up into the wind, hover and then momentarily disappear in a dust cloud before touching down. Max and two people exited the Jet Ranger before its rotor stopped. Otto hobbled down the makeshift runway to meet Max and the woman with him. A second man lagged behind, struggling with some duffel bags.

As soon as they were clear of the rotor, the pilot increased the throttle. The helicopter lifted off, dipped its nose and headed back in the direction of Uganda. It took them a few minutes to walk from the far end of the dirt airstrip to the tents. Helen whispered, using her hand to block the sound. "Lynn, he's got your sister with him. God, I wish my husband was here."

"Good morning, Dr. Croxford," said Max, looking over the top of his sunglasses. "Sorry to pop in on you like this, but I've been worried sick. Otto tells me your husband isn't here."

Helen's response was interrupted by Lynn, who ran forward to embrace her sister. Max glared at the two women as they walked hand in hand behind the tents.

"Mr. Turner, I'm expecting my husband anytime now. Hopefully, he'll have your son with him."

"Otto says the refugee camp is a short flight from here. You wouldn't object if we fly out and make sure everything's running smoothly. I've endured this nightmare for so long, I'd like to be reassured. I'm sure you understand." Max appeared distracted and moved away from Helen to look over her shoulder at the sisters. He studied them for a few seconds before speaking. "Oh Dr. Croxford, I almost forgot, I don't know if you remember Bob."

Reluctantly, Helen accepted his handshake. "I think you met my husband in the Bahamas." Bob's grin disappeared.

"My husband gave explicit instructions. He wanted Otto to stand by in case there's an emergency."

"Nonsense. You can use my satellite telephone to contact your husband," he said, nodding at Bob, who showed her the phone.

Max put his arm around Helen and started her in the direction of the plane. "Well now, I guess we've fixed that little bump in the road. Otto, get the plane ready. Bob, if you'll get the girls, we can be on our way. Please, after you," Max said to Helen, picking up her medical bag.

*       *       *

General Nur pointed at a herd of elephants browsing on an island in the Sudd. The dominant bull whirled around to challenge the strange noise. He shook his ears and trunk like a dog shaking off water. The rest of the herd encircled him. In Arabic, Nur instructed his helicopter pilot to make a low pass. Chang gave him a thumbs-up response, but showed little enthusiasm. He reclined his head and closed his eyes. One hour later, the pilot flared to land in the middle of an Arab militia camp.

Ali Osman stooped to avoid the whirling rotor blades and helped General Nur and Nelson Chang exit the helicopter. The men came forward and gathered around them. Nur waited for the whining turbine to wind-down before speaking. "In the name of Allah, today you will destroy the black seed that has soiled our beloved country. You are doing God's work by exterminating the defilers. Feel no remorse in killing the infidels. Spare no woman or child, as their offspring will continue to plague this land.

"This man is a friend of the Sudanese people," he continued, introducing Nelson Chang. "We will pay each of you twenty thousand dinars for the work you will do today, and we will pay the additional sum of two hundred thousand dinars to any man who brings us proof that he has killed one of these two Americans." He passed out pictures of Arthur Turner and Jesse Spooner. "The Americans are sworn enemies of Islam."

The assembled Arabs fired their weapons in the air and gave a trilling ovation.

Osman dispersed his men and turned to Nur. "A scout has informed me the American known as the *Khawadja* is with the savages. The camp is undefended. The Prophet himself could not have designed a better place to trap the *Zurgas*. In the name of Allah, I pledge my life. My men will corner them like rats and cut them to pieces. If it pleases the general, I would like to postpone the attack until tomorrow morning."

"Why not attack now?"

"Our camels and horses will have better footing in the wet morning sand. And the rising sun will be at our backs. They will be expecting an afternoon raid. Better to surprise them."

Nur was conflicted by different motivations. The attraction of a soft bed and his mistress in Khartoum was potent. He was about to overrule Ali when he envisioned Nelson Chang spending the night in the desert. He could almost hear him complaining. Witnessing Chang suffer was too good to pass up.

Nur's disfigured face twisted badly as he addressed Ali. "Osman, I may have underestimated your abilities. Your plan is excellent. I couldn't have designed it better myself. When this is finished, you should consider a career in the Sudanese Army. I have a place for a man with your talents."

"I will order some of my men to construct a place for your sleeping," Osman offered.

"Nonsense, we shall sleep under the stars with the rest of the men." The general laughed inwardly at the thought of Nelson Chang sleeping in the open.

"Sir, I hope I can live up to your expectations."

"Let's pray your raid is successful. Your life depends on it." Nur smiled at Osman stroking his sidearm.

\*     \*     \*

Croxford and Spooner inspected the camp from the highest sand dune. Jesse pointed at Dutchy, who was leading a native towards them. There was a rope tied around the man's neck. They were followed by a dozen Dinka tribesmen. The camp women were yelling insults and making obscene gestures at the man. The native who was the object of their taunting was a toad of a man with bowed legs. Clearly, he had suffered a beating. The Dinka men appeared ready to kill him.

"What's this about?" inquired Rigby.

"This man's a Murle," the big Dutchman said, jerking on the man's leash. "Someone caught him making love to a goat."

"What? You must be kidding." With that, Spooner and Croxford burst out laughing. Tears ran down their cheeks. Dutchy and Rigby hunched over, holding their sides. The Dinka men were not amused. They failed to find humor in this vilest of human indecencies.

"What in God's name do they want me to do?" Rigby asked, trying to act serious.

"I'm not sure," said Dutchy. "I guess perform a marriage." His remark triggered another bout of uncontrollable laughter. The frowning tribesmen tightened their circle. The commotion attracted more curious onlookers. Upon learning of the man's sin, they also became enflamed. Rigby realized the offender's predicament was grave.

"Will the owner of the violated goat please come forward?" Rigby yelled. He looked away trying to regain his composure. The owner of the goat was pushed to the front of the crowd. He appeared saddened, but seemed to relish his role as the injured party.

"Since you're the plaintiff in this felonious enterprise, it's only fitting that you should pass sentence on this man," he declared, giving the goat rapist's leash a jerk. "Speak up. What do you want us to do with him?" Rigby had to bite his lower lip to keep from laughing. He glanced at the perpetrator. The accused looked pitiful but, oddly, not overly embarrassed by his deviant behavior.

The goat owner shrugged his shoulders in resignation. Someone in the back of the crowd shouted, "As the father of the goat, you should demand a dowry." The man's comment caused an eruption of laughter among the Africans. The giggling started slowly, but escalated into hysteria. The people weakened by malnutrition laughed until they were exhausted. Satisfied, the villagers staggered back down the dune. Rigby released the goat violator, banishing him from the camp. The refugees had been sitting on pins and needles. They needed something to defuse the tension, and it had happened.

The dunes merged into the shadows as the sun began to set.

\*     \*     \*

Rigby watched Otto's Cessna zoom overhead. As the airplane circled to land, he ran down to find Spooner and Dutchy. The Italian nurse and hundreds of camp children rushed out to meet the plane as it shut down on the far end of the airstrip. Rigby lagged back until he saw his wife and Max Turner emerge from the crush of the crowd.

Otto shrugged his shoulders at Rigby. "Don't look at me like that. I didn't have a say in this."

"I'll deal with you later. How much time do we have before it's too late to take off?"

Otto glanced at the sun and said, "thirty minutes at best."

"Otto, did you see the Arab encampments?"

"It looks like they're getting ready to move at first light."

"If I were leading the raid, that's the way I'd do it," Rigby stated.

Rigby moved to the head of the crowd and whistled to focus their attention. "All right, listen up. Max, you and your daughter-in-law step into that tent. Your son's waiting for you. Helen, you and Lynn come with me and Jesse. Otto, get your plane turned around and ready to fly the hell out of here. Dutchy, your job is to keep an eye on him," he said, nodding at Max's bodyguard, Bob.

"I'm giving the orders here," said Max. "Maybe you've forgotten who's footing the bill for this operation."

"I could forgive you for showing up unannounced, but putting my wife and Lynn in danger is unforgivable. I'm gonna say this one time, and one time only. You will do as I say or I'll deal with you in ways—Max, it won't be pretty."

Max Turner mumbled and looked to his bodyguard for support. Bob raced forward to defend his boss, but Dutchy stepped in front of him. When Bob stepped to the side, Dutchy also moved. He wagged his finger in Bob's face like he was reprimanding a child. "Do you want me to break his neck?" he asked, grinning.

"We need him for tomorrow."

"Tomorrow? What's so special about tomorrow?" Helen asked.

"Not now, Helen. We're running out of time."

The ensuing quarrel between Rigby and his wife was like a new song scored to old music. She went through the halfhearted motions of trying to convince him to abandon the refugee camp, but deep down she knew he wouldn't leave the Africans. His final words to her were "Besides you, Africa's the only thing I ever loved. You know I can't leave these people. If I did run, you'd end up not liking what I would become. I know I wouldn't."

Helen tried to persuade Rigby to let her stay with him, but that also failed. She kissed him and ran to the idling airplane.

Lynn tried the "this-isn't-your-fight routine" on Jesse, but she also realized it wouldn't work. He told her he was staying and ended the discussion. He walked her out to the airstrip. Otto motioned impatiently for Jesse to bring his last passenger. The window for his takeoff was closing.

Arthur Turner waited for his father. He clasped his hands together to stop the trembling. He heard his pulse throbbing in his ears. He had dreamed about confronting his father, and now that the time had arrived, he felt sickened. Max entered the tent with his son's wife, Ashlyn, in tow. He hugged his son, but there was an antiseptic stiffness to the embrace. Ashlyn hung back in the shadows.

They stood frozen, sizing each other up. Each one was reluctant to speak first. Arthur thought time hadn't changed his father's looks, only deepened his wrinkles. Max sensed his son seemed more self-assured; it annoyed him, and, as much as he tried to hide his annoyance, he couldn't.

Max's voice sounded cool and impersonal. "How're you feeling, son? I know you've been through a lot, but you have no idea what this has done to me. I've got the best psychiatrists in the world standing by to treat you. They believe someone has been manipulating you. Call it brainwashing, whatever you want. You were always a sickly child. I'm here to protect you like I've always done."

Arthur held up his hand to stop his father. "What are you really doing here?"

"I've come to take you home, son. Tell me you're ready to end this madness?"

"Do you really think I'd risk becoming a despicable bastard like you?"

"You mean a despicable bastard who spent millions keeping you alive?"

"No, I mean someone who stole millions from his clients. Someone who'd do anything to avoid giving his wife, my mother, a decent settlement. My God, you've got no idea how long I've waited to say those words."

"You're delusional. Your ordeal has driven you to the brink of insanity."

"Can't we end this charade? Ask her if I'm crazy." Arthur glanced at his wife.

Ashlyn walked away from Max and put her hand on Arthur's shoulder. He put his hand on top of hers. There was no need for her to answer. Max squirmed under her glare. He shook his head in disgust. "Arthur, there are things about her you need to know, sordid things about her background. I've got it all documented. I tried to protect you from the truth. Did you know she's been blackmailing me? You heard me. I could have had her arrested, but I didn't want anything to get in the way of your rescue. It's all in these," he said, holding up some letters. "Here, read them if you don't believe me." There was desperation creeping into his voice.

"You can save the divide-and-conquer crap. It's demeaning, even for you. The letters were my idea."

"Just as I suspected, you're all plotting against me. I've got news for you. I'm smarter than all of you combined."

"You're so smart you threw my mother overboard like a bag of garbage. You killed her over money."

"I never touched your mother, although I had every right to. She was nothing more than a lowlife blackmailer. For someone who has such disdain for money, you weren't above taking mine."

"What drove you to become so evil? You're so twisted I'm not sure you realize what you've done. As for your precious money, you'll be happy to know I spent every dime helping these people."

"We've revisited your mother's accident a hundred times. You were just a child. You'll never believe me no matter what I say. This little charade, as you call it, has cost me millions. If you wasted my money on these wretched people, you're dumber than I thought. It could've been different. If only...."

"If only what? If I could forget what you did? Look the other way while you embezzled millions? You're contemptible. Someday, you'll hear a judge say, 'Maxwell Turner, you're guilty as charged.'"

Max pushed back the tent flap and looked out at the Africans staring back. The silence weighed heavily. He turned around and faced his son. His expression lacked conviction. White spittle balls outlined his mouth. Eyes that had been confident now looked jittery. "Why, you ungrateful little shit," he screamed, running at his son. The punch was more of a slap, but it knocked Arthur down. Max started to kick his son in the face, but stopped. "Do you really think you had a chance?" he shouted at Arthur. "It's like it says in the Gospel of Matthew: 'Brother shall deliver the brother unto death, and the father the child.'"

Arthur stood up, walked over to his cot and sat down. A steady flow of blood oozed from his nose. His wife dabbed at the blood with her sleeve. "If it'll make you feel better, hit me again. I don't need to prove which one of us is the better man. And by the way, your bible quotation isn't complete. The very next line is: 'and the children shall rise up against their parents, and cause them to be put to death.'"

Turner didn't hear his son's retort, his mind was elsewhere. "You can't win. I've got powerful friends."

"You've never had a friend, you didn't pay for."

"Not even you, Arthur?"

"After what you tried to do to my wife. How can you even go there? I suppose you think it's normal for a father to try to seduce his own daughter-in-law. It must kill you knowing there's nothing you can do to hurt me."

Before Max could stop himself, his ego got the best of him. He blurted out a bit of damning information. "Who do you think is behind these attacks? These criminals were holding you hostage and I made them pay."

"What are you talking about?"

Although Max's confession about ordering the Arab attack was accurate, he never admitted intent to harm his son. If he had, his story would have been more believable.

"Let me get this straight. You want me to believe you were trying to frighten these people into releasing me."

"I can see you don't believe me, Arthur. Luckily, I've stopped the attack on this camp. I'm the only thing between you and these barbarians. And this is the thanks I get."

"Well, I'll say one thing. It'll be ironic if you had anything to do with the attack that's coming tomorrow. Yes, it's tomorrow. Haven't you heard? The Janjaweed is attacking in the morning, and there's nothing you can do to stop it. You're about to witness cruelty the likes of which even you can't imagine.

"Think about your epitaph: 'Here lies Maxwell Turner. He's passed on to his just reward.' Know the only thing wrong?" He waited for his father's response. When he didn't get one, he continued. "Nobody gets buried over here. Everything that dies ends up in a hyena's belly."

Turner didn't walk out of the tent, he bolted. He ran through the camp until he found Rigby. When he spoke, his voice trembled. "I have to get on that plane."

Rigby turned and pointed at Otto's Cessna as it lifted off. "Your place is here with your son." It took an instant for Rigby's words to sink in.

"Then you need to get someone to drive me over the border."

"I can't spare the vehicle. I sure as hell can't spare a driver who can fire a weapon. Tomorrow morning, a mob of screaming Arabs will stampede into this camp. Their purpose is to massacre these helpless people. I aim to ruin their day. Now, you and your bodyguard can either fight or hide with the women. It's your call, Max."

Max's face was etched with fear. He started to protest, but had second thoughts. Wordlessly, Max walked away. His usual weightlifter's swagger was reduced to a slumping stagger. He sat down on a cot and buried his face in his hands. Bob tried to console him, but Max pushed him away.

*     *     *

That night, Rigby, Jesse and Dutchy rested on the crest of the tallest sand dune. They passed a cigarette back and forth until it was too short to hold. The night air smelled musty. Snaky streaks of lighting illuminated the horizon. The jagged flashes were followed by low rumbling thunder. Above them, the unpolluted sky was filled with stars.

Croxford glanced at Jesse before disrupting the quiet. "Thanks for not hassling Max about the illegal arms dealing."

"At this point, I'm not sure he's involved in arms trafficking."

"After this is over, do whatever you want with him."

"You mean assuming we're still alive. By the way, what are the rules of engagement?"

"Dutchy, did you hear that? Spooner wants to know about the rules of engagement." Dutchy didn't answer. His short whistle followed by a snort meant he was asleep.

Rigby digested the concept in silence before answering. "Jesse, just make sure you take out one helicopter. You let me worry about the rules."

"What about the warning I got in Kampala? It said someone has targeted Arthur Turner and me."

"What difference does it make? Anyway, I think whoever sent you that note was trying to make sure you left Africa. Looking back, it wasn't such a bad idea."

"Oh, I don't know. I might have missed meeting the goat rapist."

"Humor in the face of great peril. Jesse, you're the best."

The desert air seduced Jesse. Exhausted, he fell into a deep, dreamless sleep.

Rigby, on the other hand, was too restless to sleep. His dream was a war flashback. It started with a meeting in the colonel's office. *Rigby glanced at Willie, and thought about how bad they both felt. They hadn't drawn a sober breath in five days. "I apologize for cutting short your leave," the colonel said. "We're having a problem with a rather disagreeable chap in one of the indigenous tribal territories. Your third man's name is Sam Mabota?"*

*We both nodded affirmatively. The sound of the colonel's voice made my head pound.*

*"And would you be disposed to call Mabota a Christian?"*

*"Well I suppose he's a Christian." I burped painfully. "Colonel, could I trouble you for a glass of water?" He smiled but ignored my request.*

*"Let me ask you both, a question. Do you believe in witchcraft?"*

*"Of course not," Willie answered without consulting me.*

*"Does Sam Mabota believe in witchery?"*

*"Probably, but there isn't an African on this continent who doesn't believe in some type of sorcery," I said.*

*"Have either of you heard the term, 'tokoloshe'?"*

*"Africans believe a* tokoloshe *is a demon. They say they're short, hairy little buggers running around impregnating married women. I might have gone to boarding school with a* tokoloshe." *When the colonel didn't smile, I apologized. "Sorry, sir, we had a long night."*

*"Some women sleep on elevated beds to prevent these mythical dwarfs from sneaking into their beds," said the colonel. "My God, it's hard to comprehend the ignorance. Why can't we have a normal war? Did you know Rhodesia has a law against using witchcraft? It's called the 'Witchcraft Suppression Act.'"*

*The colonel turned his back to us, he sighed deeply before continuing.*

*"When this war ends, I plan to return to Ireland. I've heard some say that
Africa marks the soul with unseen graffiti. I'm afraid it hasn't been that way
for me, certainly not in a good way."*

*"Sir, don't the Irish believe in leprechauns?" I asked.*

*He was red-faced when he spoke. "Mr. Croxford, leprechauns are born in
a bottle of Irish whiskey. I would expect if you continue your excessive consumption, someday soon you'll find yourself visited by lots of creepy-crawly
things, including leprechauns."*

*The colonel gave us a description of our target, which was the antiseptic
term we used to label someone marked for assassination. The tribal chief was
a self-proclaimed wizard terrifying the local population. Intelligence reported
that the man was using his influence to win support for the armed insurgents.
Those terrorists were setting explosive booby traps on the only road to
Botswana. The road was a vital link to South Africa. He was also using his
self-proclaimed supernatural powers to foretell the future. The future he saw
was one with the whites losing the war. He had preached to his followers that
the whites would eventually be forced to leave Rhodesia. He was also accused
of masterminding the poisoning of white farmers.*

*"Gentlemen, normally this would be a simple matter of one bullet, and
one very dead witchdoctor. This old boy's a special case. He has a large following, and that's precisely why an African should be involved in his death.
Show the populace he's no more of a witch than I am. That's why I asked you
about Sam Mabota. Well, there you have it."*

*"Sir, if you could possibly spare us another week of leave, we would be in
your debt." I looked over to Willie, who put on his best pathetic look.*

*"Nonsense, I've already arranged a helicopter. The flight to Bulawayo
should sober you both up. Goodbye and good hunting."*

*"Thank you, sir," we exclaimed in unison, coming to attention.*

*As soon as we were outside, Willie spoke. "That was a lousy selling job
you just did. We just came off twenty straight days on patrol. Why didn't you
mention that?"*

*       *       *

*Sam was happy to see us. He reveled at having a helicopter pick him up.
That was before we told him about our mission. Sam listened patiently and
then spoke. "This chief is a wicked sorcerer. He says that someday a terrible
disease will afflict those men and women who have sex with strangers. They*

say he's never without his pet tokoloshe *at his side. The* tokoloshe *is invisible and drinks human blood. If we kill this chief, he'll come back as a hyena to avenge his death. When he kills, he kills without mercy."*

*"Sam," said Willie, "if it makes you feel any better, I'll do the shooting."*

*It was a long flight to our victim's village. For the last ten kilometers the pilot flew at treetop level hoping to mask the sound of our helicopter. Sam was insistent about where he wanted the pilot to land. When the pilot refused, Sam pitched a fit. Willie held his rifle to the pilot's neck and demanded that he follow Sam's instructions. We didn't believe in witchcraft, at least not entirely, but we believed in Sam. He had kept us from getting killed too many times not to.*

*Willie found a perfect hide on top of a hill looking down on the village. We used the old ploy of me fronting as a captured soldier and Sam masquerading as the conquering terrorist. Reluctantly, Willie supplied me with a few facial bruises. Sam marched me into the village at gunpoint.*

*At first, the chief was friendly, but something made him suspicious. The other villagers lingered in their huts. The village dogs were hostile, and nipped at our ankles. Sam sensed it was turning against us. He took his hat off and dropped it on the ground. It was the predetermined signal for Willie to fire. It seemed like an eternity, but I heard the distant report of Willie's 206. It was a long shot, but Willie was an accomplished marksman. The high-speed bullet smashed into the chief's torso. He just stood there looking confused, gasping for air. He went to his knees first and then fell forward flat on his face.*

*It was the only time I ever saw fear in Sam's eyes. We didn't say a word to each other. We didn't need to. He untied my hands and we started to run. We didn't run around the mopani shrub, we ran through it. I heard the hiss and whistle of their bullets and felt the ricocheted sand hitting my legs. Up ahead I could hear the Bell-205 spooling up. And then something strange happened. The wind shifted one hundred and eighty degrees and started to blow. We jumped into the helicopter and lifted off in a hail of incoming small arms fire. Willie and I laughed and patted each other on the back. Sam never uttered a word during our flight back to the staging area.*

*As soon as we landed the pilot pulled me aside. "Rigby, that was close. If your man hadn't convinced me to land where he did, we'd have been finished. He had me pointed directly into the wind. If I'd been forced to turn into the wind we'd have been a sitting duck."*

*I remember Willie making fun of me. "Croxford, you've been in the bush too long. All this talk about black magic is making me thirsty. Let's have a beer."*

Two weeks later, *Willie was killed in an ambush. Sam never said I told you so.* Rigby's dream ended with an apparition of Sam standing at the base of the dune looking up at him. *"Never try to kill a charging lion with a head shot," Sam yelled. He was smiling. When I tried to speak to him, he disappeared.*

\*   \*   \*

# 19
# THE DARFUR

Ali Osman waited for his men to end their morning prayers. The men rolled up their prayer rugs and tucked them behind their saddles. Ali walked down the line of Arabs standing at attention. He stopped to examine each man's weapon. Some of them had decorated their horses' rope halters with red-and-black tassels. The horses pranced restlessly. The camel riders rubbed their animal's necks to reassure them.

The Africans called them, "the faceless devils of the night." They were dressed in dark robes. Black turbans covered their heads and faces. Their eyes remained hidden. Ammunition bandoliers crisscrossed their chests. Some of them wore long, hooked knives with ornately carved handles. Satisfied with his inspection, Ali mounted his kneeling camel. The men followed him into the desert.

*   *   *

The Sudanese helicopter pilots used flashlights to complete their pre-flight inspections. The flickering campfire illuminated the snarling lion's head on the general's command helicopter.

General Nur felt revitalized after sleeping in the desert. He could hardly contain himself as he watched Nelson Chang wading towards him in the sand. Nur had given Chang a midnight dissertation on identifying poisonous snakes and scorpions. When the general learned that Chang was up all night, he was delighted.

"I trust you rested well?" The general asked Chang who grunted, but didn't answer.

Chang asked his own question. "How long before you attack?"

"In two hours, it will all be over. The savages will scatter when the first shot is fired. They have no stomach for fighting. It might take us a few hours to round up and kill the survivors. My helicopter should have you back at your hotel in Khartoum before sundown."

"I'm only interested in the two Americans. Make sure your men bring me proof."

"Their fate has been written. If the Americans are with the *Zurgas*, they're dead men."

Chang's stomach grumbled. The general smiled as he watched Chang walk to the edge of the camp. When he heard Chang interrupt his urinating to break wind, he had to choke back a belly laugh.

\* \* \*

Arthur woke Rigby before dawn. His news caused Rigby to explode in rage. He paced back and forth like a caged leopard, chiding himself and cursing the other men. Sometime during the night, Max Turner and his bodyguard had stolen a Land Rover and sneaked out of the camp. To make things worse they stole two M-24 sniper rifles. Arthur apologized for his father's cowardice, but Rigby took the blame. The loss of the firearms had a devastating effect on the defenders' morale.

Jesse put his hand on Rigby's shoulder. "At least we still have the fifties."

Rigby lit a cigarette and offered one to Jesse, who declined it. "I dreamed of Sam last night. He was trying to tell me something, but for the life of me I can't make heads or tails out of it." He inhaled deeply then let the exhaled smoke drift to check the wind direction.

"By God, I've got it! Help me," he yelled at Dutchy, picking up one of the fifty-calibers. They scrambled down the sand dune's face. Some of the refugees met them at the bottom to help carry the ammunition cases.

"Arthur, if you were gonna hide during the attack, where's the safest place?" Rigby asked, leaning forward to hear his answer.

"Underneath one of the vehicles. The trucks are the only valuable assets. It's a big deal to capture an undamaged Land Rover."

Rigby needed to make a change in the camp's defenses. He ordered the men to park the two Land Rovers in plain view at opposite ends of the camp. He was betting the attack helicopters wouldn't fire on the trucks. The Arabs would have already inventoried the trucks and would be including them as part of their spoils. His plan was to station Jesse and

Dutchy behind the trucks in the open, armed with the Barrett fifties.

Jesse was troubled by Rigby's last minute change in his firing position. "I think the easiest shot for me would be a head on shot. Let's assume the helicopters will be flying directly at me. It would be a level shot if I stayed on top of the dune."

"You're wrong. Sam talked to me in a dream last night. It would be like trying to shoot a charging lion with a straight-on head shot. Your target size is too small. Besides, most of the armor plating is in the nose. We need to give you a broadside shot. I'm betting the helicopters will hover right about there." He simultaneously pointed out two spots, one with each hand.

"So, your plan is based on a dream?" Jesse asked Rigby.

"I'll tell you what Sam used to tell me. He used to say, 'You're not a real African. There are some things you'll never understand.' If my plan works, we'll catch them in a crossfire."

"And if it doesn't?"

"Never show indecision going into battle. It weakens the soldiers' fighting spirit."

"What soldiers?"

"What the hell happened to humor in the face of peril?"

*       *       *

Abel tapped Croxford on the shoulder. When he didn't turn around, Tabitha pushed Abel to be more insistent. "Not now, Deng. Can't you see I'm busy?"

Arthur Turner interceded on Deng's behalf. "Rigby, I think you should hear what he has to say."

Deng told him about how they found Osman dying in the Sudd. He described how they treated the Arab's head wound. He also detailed their violent encounter with him in the desert. Croxford listened politely, but showed little interest in Deng's story until he mentioned the rumor about the Arab being heralded as a religious prophet by the Janjaweed.

"You're telling me the Arabs believe this Osman is protected by Allah?" When Abel and Tabitha both nodded affirmatively, he continued. "So if we shoot the bastard, the rest of them might lose a little of their enthusiasm. Well, it's a long shot—figuratively speaking. Could either of you recognize Osman?"

"I could," Tabitha snapped, stepping forward. "He rides a light-colored war camel. His yellow saddle blanket is decorated with red ribbons."

"We need an edge. This just might turn the fight in our favor. I want both of you to stay close to me. Your job will be to identify Osman. Oh, there's one more thing we need to discuss. Arthur, we could damn sure use your help."

"Just tell me what to do."

\*       \*       \*

As the grayish dawn shrugged off the night, Abel pointed at a tiny speck wavering on the horizon. As it came within binocular range, they recognized it as a green Islamic pennant carried by a camel rider. A Dinka tribesman blew a bull's horn to alert the camp. The deep, reverberating sound had a chilling effect on the refugees. They looked like a nest of disturbed fire ants as they ran to take up their assigned positions. Two attack helicopters popped up over a sand dune. A third helicopter hovered slightly higher in the middle. Their spewing exhaust fumes mildly distorted the image, but the three wingless machines resembled angry wasps.

As the Janjaweed got closer, they fanned out into a broad battlefront line with the slower camels in the middle and the swifter horses on the flanks. Their pace was a slow, plodding walk. Osman was careful not to expend the animals' energy too early, knowing the footing would be difficult in the desert sand. The attack helicopters flew zigzag patterns over the outer reaches of the camp to discourage any refugees from fleeing. At first, the general's command helicopter stayed behind the advancing raiders. But his pent-up lust for bloodshed caused the general to order his pilot to fly nearer to the action. When he noticed Nelson Chang squirming in the backseat, he ordered his pilot to fly even closer.

The Arabs stopped on a rise. Osman and the two militia commanders rode up and down the battle line exhorting their men. One helicopter made an initial strafing run down the first line of resistance. The machine-gun bullets kicked up sand before striking two tribesmen. Armed refugees fired their rifles, but the helicopter was flying too fast. Rigby grimaced watching them waste ammunition.

The Arabs raised their rifles and kicked their animals into a slow trot that quickly converted into a gallop. They used trilling war cries to petrify the Africans. Usually their screaming would scatter their victims, but not this time.

When Rigby sensed his men's resolve weakening, he climbed out of the ditch and screamed back at the Arabs. He raced up and down the ditch, inciting his men to taunt the attackers. His belligerence was contagious. Some men hooted and hollered insults. A couple of them pulled up their robes and bared their asses at their adversaries. The rest of the refugees got caught up in the show of defiance. Their rumbling roar startled the Arabs, causing them to slow their charge back to a trot.

Rigby jumped down into the ditch. The closest attacker was the man carrying the green Islamic flag. The bullet hit the man high on the shoulder knocking him out of his saddle. The startled camel bucked and kicked in protest. The shock of seeing their flag bearer go down slowed their charge to a walk. The leaders began threatening their men, pressing them forward. The Janjaweed had blinked. The hesitation caused the lead helicopter to overrun the militiamen.

Dutchy swung his Barrett fifty like a fly swatter, but he made the error of zeroing in on a target too close. The nearness of the helicopter made its image unfocused. He fired aimlessly without success. Jesse, more familiar with the weapon, opted to forgo firing at the helicopter flying directly overhead and concentrated on the same one Dutchy was trying to hit.

C'mon Spooner, you can do this, he thought. He kept the optical range finder locked on the helicopter's turbine engine. He was careful not to flinch from the anticipated kick of the big gun. He squeezed the trigger with increasing pressure. The muzzle flash obscured his target. "How could you miss?" he yelled at himself.

But he didn't miss. White smoke trailed the helicopter as the Chinese pilot fought to regain directional control. It yawed slightly before narrowly missing a sand dune. The pilot noticed a drop in the rotor thrust. He scanned the gauges before instinctively pulling the collective pitch lever up and pushing the nose over to land. The helicopter slammed into the desert floor. The crash wasn't violent enough to produce an explosion. From a distance, the landing appeared normal and didn't discourage the Arabs.

Rigby fired his sniper rifle. He knocked three Arabs out of their saddles so fast they almost hit the ground at the same time. Abel and Tabitha reloaded his weapon as fast as they could and handed it back to him. He fired six more times before he missed. The miss made him curse himself. He was accurate again, hitting three more attackers.

When Osman realized the shots were coming from the top of the sand dunes, he ordered fire on Rigby's position. The incoming rounds kicked up sand.

The raiders were beginning to overwhelm the defenders. The Arabs breached the first line of defense and rode into the center of the camp firing at the fleeing refugees. Men from both sides went down.

Dutchy grabbed his .570 nitro express and ran straight at the attackers. His discharge scattered the Arabs, but as the smoke cleared they encircled him.

Smoke from the burning tents blanketed the camp. Rigby used his scope to scan for targets. He saw Arthur kneeling over a wounded man with Dutchy standing next to him. Through the smoke, he saw a man riding a camel towards Turner. Tabitha grabbed his elbow causing him to lose the image. "That's him!" she screamed pointing at Osman. She stood up to point, but Abel pulled her down.

When Rigby refocused, he realized Dutchy was trying to reload. In the same view, he saw Osman kick his camel into a trot. Osman raised his AK-47 to fire point blank into Arthur's back, but Dutchy used his rifle as a club and smacked him in the face. He slumped over in his saddle for a second, then fell, unconscious, at Turner's feet. Rigby dropped two more Arabs trying to sneak in behind Arthur. Dutchy turned and fired at an onrushing Arab without bringing his weapon to his shoulder. The blast lifted the man up into a cloud of white smoke.

Having seen one of his helicopters crash, General Nur pressed his own pilot into the fight. The helicopter zoomed in over the camp. The pilot turned up into the wind and hovered at the exact spot Rigby had predicted. He banked as he prepared to launch his missiles into the refugees cowering at the base of the sand dunes. Rigby was so close he could see Nur and Nelson Chang glaring at him. He fired his rifle, but the small caliber rounds ricocheted off the armored fuselage. "Come on, Jesse!" he screamed.

It was a perfect shot for Jesse. He used the snarling lion's shoulder as his target. When the incendiary round exploded, it blew shrapnel into the pilot. A muscle contraction made him yank back on the control stick, putting the helicopter into a spinning vertical climb. Billowing black smoke poured out of the windows. Both Nur and Chang wrestled to take control away from the pilot, but his death grip was iron tight. The helicopter floated momentarily, rolled over on its back, then death-spiraled to the ground. It exploded in an orange fireball.

Fascination with the crash caused a lull in the shooting. Sporadic shots were followed by an eerie calm. With their leader down, the Arabs lost their will to fight. Those who could ride away did so. A few injured raiders were left behind to fend for themselves.

No cheering erupted from the camp. What had happened was too horrific. Spooner and Dutchy helped Arthur set up a triage tent for the wounded.

At the end of the day, Rigby radioed Otto, who was already flying back to the camp with Helen, Lynn and the Italian nurse. He landed two hours later. The three women went to work, treating the injured.

*     *     *

Just before sundown, Rigby and Dutchy found Jesse sitting in the sand against the side of a truck. Rigby kneeled down on one knee and offered him a cigarette. Jesse took it, but his hands were shaking so badly he had trouble holding the match. Rigby steadied his hands. "How're you feeling?" He reached down and picked up the fifty-caliber rifle. He checked to make sure it wasn't loaded and carefully placed it in the back of the truck. "Jesse, you did good today."

"I guess you saw the lion on the helicopter?" Jesse asked.

"I saw it."

"It's not like it is in movies, is it, Rigby?"

"No, it isn't." He handed Jesse his bottle of whiskey. "Have a swig. It'll settle the old nerves." Without hesitating, Jesse took a long swallow. He gagged, but forced it down.

"Do you think the Sudanese Army will retaliate?" he asked.

"No, I reckon they've blown their cover. For years, the Sudanese have insisted the Janjaweed was acting alone. I've got pictures of the downed helicopters. We need to get these photos to the American Embassy in Kampala," he said, holding up a camera. "This implicates the Sudanese government. In a few days, these pictures will be shown all over the world."

Rigby and Dutchy sat down in the sand. He took another pull of whiskey before handing the bottle back to Jesse. "I told the American ambassador I was confused about my purpose here in Africa. I was duped."

"Jesse, you're a bloody cynic. The Sudanese government has got to stop the killing. That's gotta be satisfying."

"Look at Arthur Turner," Jesse said, pointing. "He's treating the wounded Arabs and the refugees like they were his children. Meeting Turner makes you proud to be a part of the human race." Jesse shaded his eyes and looked out at the desert. "Wonder what'll become of Max."

Rigby spit in the dirt. "I have a feeling it won't be good."

"I think maybe he ends up in a hyena's belly," Dutchy said.

"In the end, all living things are consumed by blowflies, including hyenas." Rigby squinted at the horizon. He sighed and whispered, "Max, too bad you didn't stick around. Sam and I had plans for you."

*　　*　　*

Max Turner and his bodyguard had trouble following the desert trail. As they got closer to the Ugandan border, the first seasonal rains caught them. The rain washed away the road. By the second day, they were lost. By the third day, they ran out of fuel. Max sent Bob to find help. When he didn't return the next day, Max panicked and set out on his own. The first rains to reach the Darfur were light. The parched sand absorbed the moisture like a sponge causing the desert to return to its harshness. The land showed no signs of life. Without water, Max started hallucinating. Too exhausted to walk, he passed out under a desert acacia.

At first he thought he was paralyzed, but then he realized he had been tied to a tree. His neck was secured so tightly he couldn't turn his head. His hands had been lashed behind him and his ankles were bound. He could see a smoldering campfire with two men dressed in black robes sitting with their backs to him. Beyond the campfire, there was a camel.

"Help me!" he screamed. His voice was feeble.

His captors stood over him speaking to each other. One man pulled Max's toupee off and handed it to his friend. The man stuck the hairpiece on his head and danced around the fire. Both men slapped their thighs and laughed.

"Let me go and I'll make you both rich," Max pleaded. They answered him in a language he didn't understand.

The larger man squatted in front of Max. He pulled back his sleeve showing he was wearing Max's Rolex watch. He reached over and pulled up his friend's robe. Max recognized his bodyguard, Bob's hiking boots. This time, his voice was shriller. "Untie me, you fucking savages."

One of them dumped a powdery substance into a cup of water. The Arab smiled as he kneeled in front of Max. He encouraged him to drink by holding the dented cup to his lips. Turner was so thirsty, he greedily gulped it down. The man wearing the toupee stuffed a gag between Max's teeth.

One man came forward with something he had taken from his saddlebag. It was a faded photograph of an Arab boy. Max had no way of knowing it was the man's son and that the boy had been killed during the attack. When the Arabs found Max and his bodyguard, both were carrying M-24 sniper rifles. The men were sure Max and Bob were responsible for the boy's death.

Max felt lightheaded. He couldn't stop staring at the camel chewing its cud. The animal's lower jaw moved sideways and independently from its upper teeth. The man with the picture smiled as he pulled a short, sickle-shaped knife from its sheath. He held it up, letting the hooked blade glimmer in the campfire light. He licked the blade and shaved the hair on his arm. Max squirmed against his bindings as the man reached down and slowly unbuttoned Max's pants.

"Don't touch me. Don't do this." He cringed and fainted when the man laid the cold knife blade on his penis. With the dexterity of a surgeon, the man opened a small incision just above Max's pubic hair. He stuck his finger into Max's abdomen and pulled out a small section of his entrails. His friend handed him a stick, which he placed behind the protruding intestine to prevent it from reentering the stomach wall. Satisfied with their surgery, the Arabs kicked sand on the fire and led their camel into the night.

*    *    *

Max was awakened by a noise. The hair on his neck bristled. He heard giggling. The moonshine illuminated sets of glowing eyes bobbing and weaving. There were shadowy figures moving around him. He smelled something rotten. An animal was breathing in his face. The stench was so hot and putrid it made him dry heave.

Lightning snapped and crackled across the sky. In a flash, he saw death. The hyena's snout was a few centimeters from Max's face. Long stringy ropes of drool hung from her massive jaws as she sniffed him. He kicked at her, but his feet were tied. He screamed, but his shrieking was soundless. His eyes were wild with terror. Hunger drove the hyenas into a tighter circle. The big female's belly rumbled as she licked Max's open wound. She nipped at the fleshy bulge protruding from his stomach. Getting no response, she clamped down and raced away, dragging Max's intestines behind her. Other members of the pack latched on, starting a game of tug of war.

Max felt no pain, only an emptying sensation. He was sure he wasn't meant to die. As he slipped into shock, he saw a black man beckoning him.

The hyenas devoured Max's body. A small male rolled on the greasy spot where Max had been consumed and another gnawed on his skull-cap.

The alpha female loped along the edge of a dried riverbed. With her belly extended, her gait was troubled. She was heading to her den where she would regurgitate pieces of Max Turner for her hungry pups.

# EPILOGUE

## Rigby & Co.

"The defenders," as they were named by the press, stayed in the Darfur for another week. News of the refugees' ordeal eventually leaked out of the Sudan. International condemnation was followed by an appeal of neighboring African countries to the United Nations to send peacekeepers into the region. In a matter of days, the furor over what had happened died down. The Darfur returned to an uneasy truce between the Janjaweed and the indigenous Africans.

A Sudanese army patrol stopped and interrogated the two Arabs who killed Max Turner and his bodyguard. One of them was wearing Max's watch. They denied any wrongdoing even after they were tortured. The soldiers finally accepted their account of discovering the victims' skeletal remains. Without sufficient evidence, the authorities released the suspects.

\*   \*   \*

There were lots of tears when it came time to leave. It wasn't a surprise when Arthur and Ashlyn Turner announced they were staying in the Darfur. Their commitment to the refugees had become their calling. They promised to fly home in six months, but it was an acceptable lie to end the awkwardness. Helen agreed to return the following year to volunteer her medical services. Lynn made a pact with her sister to return as well.

The refugees gathered around them as they were leaving. The children sang songs. The women handed out homemade gifts. It was an emotional farewell. The little girl the Croxfords had saved clung to Rigby. She had to be consoled by her mother as Rigby waved goodbye.

Otto did a low flyby over the camp before turning on course. Early rains had spotted the land with patches of grass. The cloudless sky was azure blue. The land passing beneath them looked impersonal, but all of them had memories to the contrary.

As soon as they landed in Kampala, the American ambassador and his staff quietly whisked them away to an undisclosed location. Embassy staffers had already moved Croxford's vehicles in an effort to avoid the press.

The Croxfords and Dutchy had just enough time to catch the Lake Victoria ferry. It would be the first leg of their journey back to Zimbabwe. Helen hugged Lynn and said goodbye. The men gathered for one last smoke.

"Spooner, I'm gonna miss you," Rigby said, shaking hands.

"If you're gonna miss me so much, why not come back to the States with us?"

"You still don't get it. I love Africa. I could never leave here."

Croxford grabbed Jesse in a bear hug. The honest affection was embarrassing for both men. Rigby stepped back and smiled. "You'll be back. Don't look at me like that. Hey, it wasn't all bad."

"Maybe we'll come back on our honeymoon," Jesse said, glancing at Lynn.

Rigby's face twisted around his cigarette into a roguish grin. "Better give me a year. It'll take me that much time to stir up another war."

# AFTERWORD

During the mad scramble for Africa, which started in the 1880s, Europeans colonized parts of the continent without considering the repercussions from mixing peoples with vast cultural differences. Their miscalculations have caused genocides and civil wars.

Three great deserts—the Sahara, the Kalahari and the Namib—make up over one third of the African land mass. The Sahara alone is approximately the size of the United States. Much of the land is unfit for human habitation; as a result overpopulation continues to plague Africa. In some areas, a ten percent crop failure can produce a famine.

After the industrialized countries squander their own natural resources they will look to Africa. What will happen to the Africans?

CPSIA information can be obtained at www.ICGtesting.com
Printed in the USA
LVOW041539250712

291532LV00002B/157/P